Also by Adi Alsaid

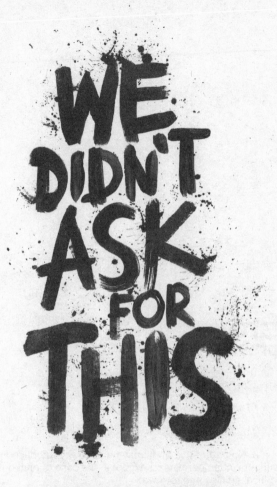

WE DIDN'T ASK FOR THIS

Author of *Let's Get Lost*

ADI ALSAID

inkyard press

Recycling programs
for this product may
not exist in your area.

ISBN-13: 978-1-335-14676-2

We Didn't Ask for This

This is a work of fiction. Names, characters, places and incidents are either the
product of the author's imagination or are used fictitiously. Any resemblance to
actual persons, living or dead, businesses, companies, events or locales is entirely
coincidental.

This edition published by arrangement with Harlequin Books S.A.

For questions and comments about the quality of this book, please contact us at
CustomerService@Harlequin.com.

Inkyard Press
22 Adelaide St. West, 40th Floor
Toronto, Ontario M5H 4E3, Canada
www.InkyardPress.com

Printed in U.S.A.

To the Greta Thunbergs, Isra Hirsis, Xiuhtezcatl Martinezes and Autumn Peltiers of the world.

PART I

LOCK-IN NIGHT

1

7:35PM

The lock-in was going fairly well until Marisa unleashed her cronies and chained herself to the main entrance.

No one really noticed right away, busy as they were taking part in a number of lock-in-related activities: laser tag in the parking garage, a sanctioned food fight in the cafeteria, a photo shoot tutorial with a renowned YouTube influencer.

Once a year, in April, the doors at Central International School's K–12 campus closed—though they didn't *literally* lock—to allow the high school students to roam free for the whole night. Having the next day off school was nowhere near the best part. Nor, strictly speaking, were the activities themselves, though they were extravagant and wonderful and distracted everyone from what Marisa was doing.

People fell in love on lock-in night. They stumbled upon new passions that would shape the rest of their lives, discovered friendships they could not imagine living without, before or after. Traumas were resolved on lock-in night, anxieties disappeared, never to return, not even after the buses arrived in the morning to take the students back home.

This was well known to the few students who had been lucky enough to have attended before, or who had siblings who had attended in years prior. At Central International School, the student body ebbed and flowed, changing drastically from year to year, and often even more frequently. It was common to have different classmates every semester, and sometimes students would find the person who sat next to them in class—the alluring redhead who scribbled song lyrics on the margins of their textbooks, who one time turned and asked to borrow a pen they never returned, though they had offered a smile that carried with it joy beyond a simple gesture; the redhead who might have one day soon become more than just a classmate—was simply gone from one day to the next.

Even by international school standards, the turnover rate of both students and faculty had always been high, though it had a great academic reputation, and the city in which it sat was a diverse and world-class cosmopolis. Yet people never seemed to stick around for long, as if families were carried in by the seaside breeze, and carried away by the same. Most students had multiple passports, and their parents were multinational, or transient because they were diplomats, or titans of industry, or missionaries, or digital nomads, or teachers within the international school world. They had roots in many places, thought of no one place as home—or rather, thought of everywhere they'd been as home.

So it was rare for a student to be around for several lock-in nights. Even the locals, who made up a mere fifteen percent of the school's population, often temporarily relocated during their high school years—a boarding school exchange in Switzerland, a South American road trip in a van with their family, a missionary excursion in Central America.

Despite all this, the lore surrounding lock-in night was always momentous, starting as an excited murmur the first day of school and building to a frenzy by the night before the event itself a month or so before the end of the year. Students wondered how, exactly, their life would be improved by the evening. There was no question it would—they could feel it on their skin, their heartbeats thudded with the knowledge that things were about to change, they had absorbed the gossip, not just a rumor or two, but dozens and dozens of first-hand accounts or verifiable secondhand stories, so many of them that it did not feel like hearsay but like fact—it was the *how* that was exciting. Would the redheaded classmate return to slip a hand into theirs during the movie marathon on the roof garden? Would their fear of heights be cured by the trapeze the school had set up on the football field? Or would it simply be a night of such fun that the joy would sink into their bones and change them into happier people?

Lock-in night, simply put, was magic. Even all those who had never experienced it knew it to be true.

Which, of course, was why Marisa planned her protest

11

for that well-loved night. To make people pay attention, disrupt what brings them joy.

The mad desire to act had existed long before her plan did.

Marisa loved the water as a baby. Her parents told the stories to anyone who would listen. She always feigned embarrassment at their anecdotes about her hour-long baths and surprising performance in toddler swimming classes, her dark, curly hair unfurling in the water behind her like a mermaid, her brown eyes huge within the goggles she always carried around. But the truth was that she loved the stories. They confirmed this was not a passing fad, not a childhood obsession that would lose its significance over time, not a baby blanket carried around charmingly until age ten, when it was shoved into a box and donated.

When she discovered snorkeling and, later, diving, that love blew wide open. *This?* This had been possible this whole time?

Though Marisa was only seventeen, her parents' constant relocations for work meant she'd seen a hefty percentage of the world's waters. She'd snorkeled in Mexico, Fiji, the Philippines, the Great Barrier Reef, Belize. And the more she did it, the more her heart broke. Human beings had found a way to kill water.

The places famed for their snorkeling were heartwrenching. The destroyed beige reefs littered the oceans like ornate gravestones. They should have been resplendent with color. Books and scientists told her as much, and other divers did, too. Of course, though, they weren't. Not anymore. The world had ruined that particular beauty before Marisa had ever had a chance to see it, killing the corals with spilled chemicals, suffocating the oceans with heat. Every time she surfaced, she would dive into the internet, trying to find a way to help. Changing her sunscreen to the reef-safe kind, cleaning up plastic on the beach, asking her parents to donate yet again; nothing felt big enough.

Then came the three-day weekend at the start of the school year that changed it all. She had convinced her parents to take the family to the beach, and the Cuevases, who knew their frequent moves could be hard on the children, relented despite the fact that neither of them felt settled in at work yet, and they would have really liked to stay in the city and run errands.

Marisa had heard amazing things about the snorkeling in the region surrounding the beach. She was always skeptical when she heard anything like that; she'd been disappointed enough. She was fine just swimming among whatever fish remained in the area and pretending this was what it had always been like, this was the wondrous alien world other divers described. After their most recent move, she'd done her usual research and found on the most trustworthy sources that an untouched blip still existed, not too far from her new school.

She convinced her parents, who knew it was better to indulge Marisa than fight her, to take a boat to an island, then another, smaller boat to another, smaller island. Arriving at the clear, turquoise waters, which were peppered with butterflies from who knows where fluttering across the surface, whole waves of them outnumbering the tourists she had seen even on the mainland, Marisa allowed herself to hope. Well before her family was ready, Marisa was in her flippers and mask, and she sat on the edge of the boat and let herself fall backward into the warm waters. At first, her heart had soared: greens! Purples! Oranges! Bright colors in the reefs, finally. The schools of fish were more like armies, numbered not in dozens but in hundreds, maybe even thousands, various species all swimming in their separate schools, like great big flags unfurling mightily in the water.

Marisa followed them, kicking delightedly, her heart flooding with joy. Then she turned a corner around some rocks and her breath caught, as if someone had reached inside her chest and closed a massive fist around her lungs. Even here, she found murk and drudgery, the reef not on display so much as its dying was.

She emerged from the water and took off her mask, tears mixing with the waves. People and the trash with which they suffocated the world. She looked around, shading her eyes from the shimmering sunlight with her free hand. Maybe it was time to accept the world as it was.

As she turned to swim back to shore, she caught sight of something on the far end of the island. A construction site. Large, acres and acres of it, from what Marisa could tell, and a handful of bulldozers. She swam closer and saw the sign announcing the coming resort. Nearby, a trickle of brown-gray water weaved its way from below the makeshift wall around the site and dribbled onto the sand.

Yes, it was a travesty, an outrage that the world had been ruined before her arrival. But that trickle hadn't reached all the way to the shore, not yet.

As soon as she and her family made it back to their eco-hotel that day, Marisa decided she had to stop that waste from reaching the ocean. Whatever she could do for the reefs, she was going to do it. If it was just shutting down that one construction site, or if it was something much bigger, she had to try. What else was there but to try?

Months of stewing later, of planning, of seeing the ruined remains of the ocean floors every time she closed her eyes, of thinking of a way to make everyone else see what she saw. It all led up to this moment, when Marisa hoisted a chain from the duffel bag she'd hidden on campus a few days ago. She weaved it through the handles on the double doors that led into the main school building, then she wrapped it three times around her own body, uncomfortably tight, so bolt cutters could not break through the metal without snagging on her skin. When she was satisfied, she grabbed three giant padlocks from the bag and locked herself in, meaning to stay.

She set the keys in the middle of her palm, rubbing them each in a pad of butter procured earlier from the cafeteria, and which had warmed nicely in her pocket throughout the afternoon. Then Marisa, rehearsing her speech in her mind one last time, looked up. She expected to see a sizable crowd already gathering. What she saw instead was a lanky blond sophomore leaving the bathroom across the open expanse of the building's foyer. The boy was checking to see if he'd remembered to zip up. He had not.

When his eyes met Marisa's, he could tell she had seen him checking, and he stepped quickly away from her line of sight, failing to notice the heavy metal chain wrapped around her torso.

★ ★ ★

This boy was on his way to the gymnasium, where Amira Wahid was waiting for the whistle that would signify the start of the CIS Intrasport Decathlon. The year before, arriving from a school in Colombia only weeks prior to the lock-in, Amira had won the girls' category, which annoyingly came with the qualifier of best *female* athlete. This year, Amira had enrolled in the boys' decathlon, not bothering to check if it was allowed, wanting it to be known that she was, at least in this one aspect (or rather, these ten aspects), better than all. Basketball, running, rock climbing, it didn't matter. She could beat anyone. For once, she did not want her gender to qualify her.

There was some resistance, but in the end the parents and board members at CIS were a little more liberal than not, and the fight was dropped. Already inspired by Amira, several girls crossed the gender distinction, and some boys, in what they believed was a show of solidarity, signed up for the girls' competition. In the end the lists were too hard to distinguish, and the gendered distinctions were dropped altogether.

Amira for her part didn't pay much attention to the "controversies" or general conversation. She was too busy training, sweating, repeating the same motions over and over again until they became as ingrained and natural and unconscious as breathing. Some of her exercises, Amira came to believe, even took on the rhythm of her heart: the jab-hook combo against the punching bag, thunk thunk; the two dribbles she needed on a basketball court to take the ball from the top of the three-point line to the rim, thunk thunk; her feet on the track, on asphalt, on grass, thunk thunk.

She loved how the world felt while she trained, loved that it all seemed designed for her enjoyment, the air and the sun and the ground beneath her feet. She loved the strain of her body, how she could feel it getting stronger, more limber, how she could get better at controlling its movement day by day by day.

More than anything, Amira loved to surprise people, to anger them, confound them with the things she could do with her body. The look on boys' faces when she was stronger, faster, better. The look on those boys' dads' faces, the look on her coaches' faces, when she outshone them all.

Amira's mother was not aware of any of this. Not the training, not the decathlon and certainly not the anger. Amira was a different girl in front of her mother—at home in general—than she was at CIS.

This wasn't out of necessity—at least Amira didn't think so. Her mother was strong-willed, sure, but Amira had never tested that will. If she pushed back against her mother's beliefs about what Amira could not or should not do, about what girls could not or should not do, her mother might very well respect her wishes. Her dad, certainly, was less of a traditionalist than many Malaysian men of his generation.

Amira became someone else at school merely out of opportunity. At home there were expectations pressing down on her—not forcefully, but they weighed heavily just the same. Expectations of what a girl should do and be, expectations of religion, expectations of family, expectations of sexuality, expectations that she did not feel equipped to go against. And though she did not hold herself to many of these expectations, her parents did, and that wasn't something she could ignore.

Amira did not know how her parents would react if she outwardly bucked any of these expectations, and so she tried as best as she could to fit within them. She was never forced to act a certain way; the expectations were so heavy that she didn't dare subvert them.

At school, though, the expectations felt easily shed. They were not religious or familial, they weren't ingrained into the history of who she was. The expectations outside of her home felt, at worst, superficial. Society and its expectations, albeit plentiful and obsequious, were not tethered to Amira's soul. So she could leave them behind, chasing the thunk thunk of her heart instead.

Most people expected Amira to win, though a handful of others believed Omar Ng's strength and speed were superior simply because of his masculinity. Omar, for his part, standing on the opposite side of the gymnasium from Amira, likewise awaiting the first event (a one-on-one basketball tournament), wished Amira the best, and at least partially hoped she would beat him. He wanted only to do his best, or whatever amount of athleticism might impress Peejay Singh.

Omar eyed the bleachers, looking for Peejay's magnificent face in the stands. Those dark eyes of his, that unblemished brown skin, the softness of which would be apparent even from across the gym. There were plenty of people, many holding up poster board signs in support of Amira and a handful for Omar, with a few more scattered signs for other competitors unlikely to succeed against the two front-runners. Others had signs advertising their team or club's event or booth at the lock-in. Some held signs simply in support of lock-in night itself. Omar couldn't see Peejay there, but right before the whistle sounded he thought he saw his younger sister, Joy, fiddling near the exit to the gymnasium, holding something shiny.

While her brother checked the ball to his opponent, Joy Ng tried to remember Marisa's exact instructions. Loop twice, then over and through, or over and through, then loop twice? She'd lost the notebook paper where she'd written it down. Joy didn't want to disappoint Marisa by messing up the chains and not having everyone properly locked in.

She pushed her glasses farther up the bridge of her nose and fixed her hair back up into its usual messy bun, figuring it would be enough to simply make the metallic knot as convoluted as possible. The steel clinked satisfyingly in her hands, and she smiled as the gym burst into cheers around her (Amira had scored her first basket of the tournament, a beautiful pull-up jumper from the elbow). Joy felt like she was making Marisa proud, but right at the moment she clicked the locks into place, she realized she had forgotten to use the bathroom. Longingly, she looked across the gym, where at that moment Celeste Rollins emerged from one of the two unisex toilets.

Unlike most everyone else, Celeste was not enjoying lock-in night.

A new student at CIS, Celeste had never lived outside of the US before, and had struggled to make friends. *Struggled* is too generous a word. Celeste had failed to make friends for the past eight months. No one was mean to her, nor did they hold her Americanness against her. But no one made a space for her, either.

She could at least partially understand. It was what she came to think of as her unfortunate singlehood—single passport, single language, single previous home. All these other kids knew the world up close, knew its histories and beautiful nooks, knew the nuances between regional versions of Spanish, could name the king of Thailand. Celeste had not known Thailand was a kingdom. She had seen the world only in textbooks and on TV, in news segments that whittled down foreign countries to the dangers they presented.

Even the other American kids at CIS were more worldly than Celeste. They had bounced from embassy to embassy, continent to continent, as their parents were transferred or sought to be missionaries or chased their whims. And while these kids wore American sports jerseys to school and hung around together, speaking only in English, they knew how to wield the local slang, how to maneuver the metro system, where to go on weekends, how to live abroad. They didn't remember what life in the States was like, if they had ever been there at all. They lived in walled-off country clubs or came to school in a van straight from the Mormon church. Even the two other black American kids—Casey and Jay Robinson, originally from New York—offered no easy welcome, though they were instinctively the first people she would have sought out, had they not been elementary students.

Whenever Celeste had tried to squeeze herself into a group of Americans—at lunch while they sat by the soccer field bleachers, in the chatty minutes before their remedial classes meant to teach them the local language (though many of these students followed their parents' leads and barely bothered to attempt learning)—there had seemed to be no room for her. They were drawn to each other's Americanness, not hers. Whether it was racism or a lack of shared experiences in upbringing, it did not ease the pain of loneliness.

Celeste loved people. She loved their company, at least when she'd had it in Glen Ellyn. She loved their mannerisms, loved their voices and their laughs, loved when her former babysitter, Erin, came by unannounced just to see her, or when her friend Jamie texted every morning, even though they always met in front of the park district pool—where almost everyone they knew, including the two of them, had spent at least one summer lifeguarding or working the snack bar—to walk to school together. And she loved, more than anything, her place among all these people. With the younger kids from the suburban neighborhood, she was the girl with the trampoline whose parents let them come by whenever they wanted to. In swim class, she was not the fastest or the slowest, but the one who knew everyone's name and stayed up late with her mom the night before meets baking cookies. She was the Colsons' babysitter, Jamie's best friend, Mrs. Silver's newest (and briefest) employee at the kitchen supply store on Main Street. She was Celeste Rollins of Forest Street in Glen Ellyn, Illinois, a student of Glenbard West High School (Go, Hilltoppers!). She was one of the few black students there, yes, and that had come with its share of microaggressions and difficulties. But it had been home.

Glen Ellyn was all Celeste had ever known, but when her parents decided to leave the US, she had allowed herself to grieve only until the flight to her new home. Yes, she would

21

miss all these people—the way they fit into her life in the most comfortable of ways, like a play she knew by heart. Not just her lines, but everyone else's, too. But there would be a new play for her to step into, a new, rich cast of characters, and she would learn her lines quickly. She was sure of it.

That wasn't how it had happened.

Celeste thought she'd been prepared for the language barrier, but she definitely had not. After six months her brain was still struggling to retain words, because her mouth had not yet managed to grasp on to the different sounds it had to make, sounds it had never attempted before. Vowels! Who knew they could elude her? An *i* was not an *i* here.

That wasn't all. The toilets were different, the times people ate. Celeste had no idea these things could vary among nations. Noon was lunchtime. She thought that had been universal.

Still, she had been hopeful that when she met the kids of CIS, she would find her place among them. Her first day of school she woke up well before her alarm rang. She texted Jamie for support, but across the world, Jamie was at after-school soccer practice. Or was she sleeping? It was hard to do the math of time zones. Celeste practiced what she would say while she showered, while she brushed her teeth, while she had her usual Glen Ellyn breakfast of oatmeal and a banana (the oatmeal would have to be rationed out; her favorite brand was nowhere to be found). She did her hair up into a pineapple pony, and it had cooperated beautifully, the curls in her bangs perfectly springy. And when the nice, air-conditioned city bus that served as a school bus came to pick her up, she put on a smile and tried to make eye contact with the people already seated.

They had earphones in, or were dozing with their heads against the glass. Two black girls sat and spoke with each other, their hair in admirable, intricate braids that gave her an in to comment on. But they did not look up when Celeste approached. Toward the back there was a tall, curly-haired boy in a hoodie reading a book. Celeste smiled at him and he looked away immediately, shy and skittish. She thought, *Ah, I know my lines here.*

Repeating her practiced lines under her breath one last time, she stood just in front of the boy and waited for him to look back up. Then the bus jolted forward and caused her to stumble into an empty seat behind him. After that it felt too awkward to move back to him. She waited for someone to take a seat next to her, but apparently she was one of the last stops and the seat remained empty.

When she finally tried the local language on someone outside of her homeroom class, they laughed and said, "Dude, we all speak English here."

At lunch that day she finally found a group of Americans to sit with, but they didn't speak about the same things she would've spoken about with anyone in Glen Ellyn. A summer of partying on boats off the Croatian coast, of family yoga retreats in Bali, of junior internships with leading tech companies in San Francisco; instead of a summer of biking the streets, of boredom and pools and barbecues, of road trips to Wisconsin. Her lines did not fit into this play.

The misfires continued, and with each one, a terrifying realization dawned on Celeste: she was not at home anymore.

★ ★ ★

So of course Celeste had looked forward to the lock-in night. When the posters started coming up, she saw an opportunity. She'd signed up for everything that had a sign-up sheet (the ceramics club workshop, the game of tag to raise awareness about housing inequality, the Hot Sauce Club's Spice Scream Social). But for the first two hours of the lock-in, her aspirations of meeting someone to connect with, of finding even a glimpse of a home at CIS, had not come to fruition. She had sampled three hot sauces before leaving that particular room, finding it hard to interrupt the little groups of threes and fours. She had participated in the Lock-In Night Escape Room— the students who'd organized it were thrilled to hear, once the news broke, what Marisa had done—but since she hadn't arrived with a group, she had been assigned to a quartet of resentful seniors. They'd barely looked at her the entire time, speaking in a mix of languages Celeste couldn't even identify.

Now she stood outside the bathroom in the gym wondering where to go next, feeling the enormous weight of unmet expectations pressing down on her diaphragm. Everywhere, people walked and gathered and laughed in groups. Celeste felt as if there were a spotlight on every single one of them, and only she remained in the shadows.

Then she noticed another poster. More of a paper, really, obviously ripped from a notebook not long before and taped up on this spot last-minute, the font unimpressive and sloppy, unlike the majority of lock-in posters.

Wanna laugh? Improv! Funny! FUN. 8 pm, the room behind the theater.

An arrow pointed the way, so Celeste, encouraged by its goofiness, having been raised in a family that constantly poked fun at each other, headed toward Kenji Pierce, looking for the comforts of a laugh.

Kenji Pierce was at that moment standing outside the room trying to coax various passersby to come in and watch his improv team perform. Not many had heeded his call, save for a group of impressionable freshmen who had heard Ludovico Rigo was on the team and were happy to have the opportunity to watch him do anything for fifteen straight minutes. To watch him and giggle and to be expected to do nothing else. A luxury, a dream come true. Lock-in night truly was sublime.

Among all the students at CIS looking forward to the lock-in, everyone who had lain awake at night picturing the fun that was to be had, everyone who drifted off in class daydreaming, the excitement they felt deep down in their bellies as soon as they learned of the night and which had been rising to the surface as the date inched closer, none were happier right at that moment than tall, lanky, bespectacled Kenji Pierce, whose hair was eternally cowlicked, and his smile, it seemed, smeared across his face just as consistently.

Kenji, a freshman who had been at CIS a remarkable three years, and had been looking forward to his first year of high school so he could finally take part in the lock-in, had admittedly not done much in the way of activities so far. He'd half listened to the welcoming ceremony, which had featured a celebrity alum Kenji did not recognize, choosing instead to spend that time cracking jokes with his best friend, Lindsay.

As soon as they were dismissed and the fun began, Kenji and Lindsay ran off toward the food trucks parked by the soccer field. He'd ordered a trio of Southeast Asian tacos, to go. Had he known how long it would be before he was allowed outside again, he might still have chosen to do what he did next. Which was to run across the field toward the back staircase and go immediately to sit in the green room.

The green room was the classroom behind the theater, used normally for drama and cinematography classes, as well as the occasional spillover English class. There was no need for Kenji and Lindsay to be there that early. The improv showcase wasn't set to start for another two hours and all the other members of their team were playing laser tag in the parking garage. But Kenji was ready for improv, and he was happy to wait with Lindsay and ignore all other activities until it came. They sat and joked and played some warm-up games, and when Lindsay said she wanted to go check out the food fight for a minute, Kenji stood in the hallway trying to get people to fill the theater.

It would fill up. Every event at lock-in night seemed to get a far better turnout than even the most hopeful organizers had wished for. There were dozens of events going on at the same time, and a limited number of people with which to fill those activities, but no club was ever disappointed.

Kenji cared little for the crowd size. He just cared that he could play improv in front of others, that he could profess his love for it, that he could do it free of judgment. He spent all his time with improv, made any homework assignment he could about the subject, no matter how tangentially, and the people at school would ask only, "Yes, and...?" His classmates seemed to inherently understand that central tenet of improv: to accept the terms presented to you and build upon them.

His father, on the other hand, would say it was impractical to build something without first tearing down what was there before. Arthur Pierce worked in construction, and he was constantly making comments like that, which didn't entirely make sense, but rather seemed aimed to prove that Kenji was wrong.

At home, Kenji had heard "no" a lot from his father. No, a Pierce could not "opt out" of a sport. No, a Pierce could not play pranks on the whole family. No, a Pierce could not play pranks on just the British side, nor on just the Japanese side, nor on just the Spanish cousin who had married in last summer. No, a shadow puppet show wasn't an appropriate post-dinner activity at the restaurant. No, they couldn't listen to a podcast in the car. No, humor wasn't particularly important, was not to be given the weight of responsibilities, of school courses, of ambition, of concrete. No, humor could not be, in itself, an ambition.

But this place had so few restrictions, so few parameters built around what a person could be. The audience saw a Japanese boy with a British accent and a goofy sense of humor and thought, as if they had each been trained in the art of improv, "Yes, and…?" They saw someone like Omar Ng, a valedictorian and a star athlete all while being shy and awkward and they thought, "Yes, and…?" For his classmates and teachers, a person's characteristics were not boxes (or rather, buildings) to place them into; they were colors with which to paint a whole, unique picture.

Now, with the minutes until the showcase ticking away,

Kenji watched his fellow CISers (Go, Sea Cucumbers!) and felt a deep appreciation for every single one of them. The ones who hadn't heard him as they passed and the ones who absolutely had heard him but didn't pay attention alike. Those few who trickled in with full intent to watch the showcase as well as those who passed by in groups, who heard Kenji enthusiastically beckoning them inside, looked at one another with a shrug, then went to take a seat. Kenji loved every single one of them.

Here was Ludovico, fellow improv lover, who walked through the hallways not as if he had hordes of underclassmen gawking at him, but as if he was still exploring the tiny Sumatran island he'd spent six years growing up on. Ludo moved barefoot through the school, a beatific smile always on his face, like a handsome blond yogi blessing everyone in his path.

And here was Peejay Singh, speed-walking through the hallway past Kenji, headed toward the back staircase near the green room. His friend Diego Cuevas had just texted saying the door was locked, which it definitely should not have been. The back staircase was one of the keys to Peejay's whole plan. It, along with the basement, was the entryway for the booze, the hundreds of earphones, the DJ equipment, the DJ himself.

For decades, the CIS lock-in night had traditionally come with a clandestine party organized by a single student. Each year, the previous year's Partyer in Chief would pick out the one person they believed could best carry on the tradition with both secrecy and flair. If the transient nature of CIS's student body proved this impossible, it was put to a school-wide vote. That had been the case this year, and Peejay Singh had won overwhelmingly versus fellow senior Jordi Marcos.

Every student knew about the party, and everyone was invited, though many chose not to go, either because they were busy or too frightened of the possibility of getting caught. This despite the fact that no lock-in party had ever been discovered, and no single student had ever faced consequences or questioning related to their nefarious absence. Oh, the faculty had heard rumblings, of course. And each year the teachers bet money on whether the party would be discovered, and by whom, and in which room (like a CIS-specific game of Clue). Usually, the gambling ring itself would be discovered, and the organizing staff member was always the only one to face ramifications. Higher-ups in the administration didn't condone the partying, and wanted teacher efforts to focus on keeping the students from harming themselves and the school's reputation, not on profiting off illicit activities.

Regardless, Peejay didn't want to risk being the first host to get caught. Though he did want to be remembered. In fact, Peejay wanted to throw a party so great that every single CISer attended. He wanted even the teachers to attend, without them knowing it. He wanted the party to set the standard for future hosts, wanted it to be all people could talk about once the night was done.

He looked forward to the winks and high fives he would get at 6:00 a.m. when the doors opened and the buses and parents arrived to take the kids back home for the day. He fantasized about the text messages that would flood his phone throughout the weekend, if not the rest of the year. (Maybe the rest of his life? Peejay sometimes let these fantasies get carried away, imagining a time twenty years or so from the night when he would be contacted by people like Zaira Jacobson or Omar Ng, people who would clearly go on to live not just good lives but impressive ones, remarkable lives full of remarkable parties. "My partying days are coming to an end, and yours topped them all," they would say, and Peejay would look back on his days of partying and be hard-pressed to find a night that compared to this one.)

Peejay had been waiting three years for his opportunity to host, ever since he was a freshman and his brother, Hamish, had been the Partier in Chief. That year, Hamish had somehow managed to throw the party underwater.

He never revealed how he did it, not even to Peejay, but by the day of the party, a secret room had appeared beneath the koi pond at the campus's main entrance. It must have been under cover of night and involved some hefty bribes to the school's security guards, with dozens of workers needed to finish it all up from one school day to the next.

The large rocks beside the pond had been replaced with fake ones that could be easily moved, and which served to hide the trapdoor, which led into the room that allowed about twenty students at a time to party, and which those who knew about it still occasionally used to skip class and smoke cigarettes. The ceiling of the room, somehow, was the glass bottom of the pond itself, and the night of that party the moon had been full and the light refracted through the water, making the room softly shimmer, like something out of a dream.

Peejay had already been in awe of his brother, and he had ignored all other lock-in activities to stay at Hamish's side all night. He hadn't known someone could be so universally adored.

The joy that had lit up people's faces when they came down the stairs and found the secret room, the booze and the music and the couch behind a curtain for couples to make out on. It had been a masterful party, no doubt, but by nature of the room's size too exclusive. Hamish had said so himself, regretting the fact that no one wanted to leave the secret room to make space for others to experience the party, and because of that, not everyone had been able to attend.

Peejay had been dreaming of his chance to host well before Hamish's accident a week earlier, which had turned Peejay's brother into a rag doll lying in a hospital bed, his nights accompanied by the fitful snoring of people who loved him sleeping uncomfortably at his side, by the gentle whir of machinery keeping him alive, the occasional squeak of a nurse's comfortable white sneakers going past in the hall, the rhythmic beeps of monitors.

Peejay had considered skipping the party and staying at his brother's side. But it had been four straight days of just that, and Peejay's parents insisted that he take a break, distract himself. Hamish, too, likely would have agreed. And after all of the planning he'd done, much of it with Hamish in mind, it would've been a waste not to attend the lock-in. This way, he'd be able to give Hamish a story when he woke up.

A locked door would not come between Peejay and this dream to throw a party that would honor what Hamish had done three years ago, and maybe even rise above it. A party Hamish would be proud of.

He expected this door thing to be no big deal. Diego, bless

his pretty little heart, was a kind and beautiful boy who often had problems with doors. It's not that Peejay thought Diego was dumb. Diego was Marisa Cuevas's brother, so on genes alone it was unlikely that he'd come out completely inept. But Diego's intelligence was not rooted in mechanical things.

However, what Peejay found was no small mechanical issue.

It was sophomore Malik Harris, who played on the school's rugby team and was not small at all.

Malik, for some reason, had a heavy steel chain wrapped around his torso and through the double doors leading out to Peejay's staircase. Three large padlocks hung off the chains, and though Peejay (rightly) guessed two of them were purely ornamental, it still gave the impression that Malik meant to stay put for a long while. Even more troublesome: next to Malik was a five-liter jug of water, something wrapped in tinfoil (presumably a sandwich), two books, assorted snacks, an electronic tablet, a phone charger and a bucket. Surrounding Malik and staring down at him were a gaggle of freshmen, that American girl from Peejay's art class, Ludovico Rigo (swoon) and the improv team's mentor and notoriously lenient English teacher, Mr. Gigs.

There were many questions swimming around in Peejay's mind, and he didn't know why, out of all the things he wanted to ask, he chose the one question he already knew the answer to. "Malik, what is that bucket for?"

2
7:55PM

The crowds finally gathered at four of the five main exits of the school building. It was not so much that they had noticed the people chained to the doors, or had a sense that they meant to disrupt the evening, but rather that they had places they wanted to go to, activities to participate in, friends to meet.

Marisa watched their faces as they approached, watched as they suddenly understood their joy was facing an obstacle.

Good, she thought.

When she felt the tug behind her of someone trying to make their way in, she knew it was time. She reached into her duffel bag and pulled out the megaphone.

Most people in the crowd assumed it was a shtick. Performance art of some sort. It wasn't unusual for one of the artsy kids to stage their magnum opus this way. The teachers, especially, assumed it was just One of Those Lock-In Night Things. Marisa fired off a quick text to her cronies. Deliver the speech.

She turned on the megaphone, a sharp whine of feedback making everyone cringe. Marisa cleared her throat. "Attention students and faculty of CIS."

"Go, Sea Cucumbers!" someone shouted from the back. The people who couldn't yet tell this was going to ruin their night laughed.

Marisa continued. "We are all murderers, or at the very least accomplices to the atrocities committed to our oceans and our reefs." Someone groaned. The faculty gave each other looks, trying to suss out what exactly was happening, and what their responsibilities were. At three of the four other exits, Marisa's cronies read the same speech she had memorized.

"Until this school and its community members commit to take the following steps toward rescuing the reefs from the brink of extinction, especially the ones in our backyard, everyone within this building will remain inside."

Now that it had been spelled out for them, a murmur started growing in the foyer of the high school building. Marisa continued to enumerate her thirty demands. Single-use plastic was to be immediately banned at CIS. Everyone present would sign a petition to ban it worldwide, and all CIS family members would be encouraged to sign, as well. All diesel boats were to switch to biodiesel. A radius of fifty meters around any coral reef was to be designated a Marine

Protected Area. Construction of the planned resort on Lo-koloko Island was to be canceled.

"I'm sorry, did you just say diesel boats?" Peejay Singh asked Malik, who had just reached that part of the speech on the electronic tablet from which he was reading.

"Um," Malik said. Marisa had told them to ignore any hecklers or interruptions, but she had never said anything about how to handle Peejay. And here was Peejay Singh, asking Malik a direct question about the list of demands. "Um," Malik said again, and his eyes flicked back down to the screen, trying to find his place.

But Peejay snapped his fingers and said, "Don't keep reading. Are you holding this door hostage over diesel goddamn boats?"

Malik started to say no, then explained that it was much more than just boats, and on that note, it wasn't just this door. It was every way in and out of the main building. He explained that they were following Marisa Cuevas's lead in order to enact real change.

"Every way in and out?" Peejay barked, an unpleasant thought forming in his mind, the mild beginnings of anxiety.

Malik nodded.

"Name them," Peejay said, certain that Marisa—albeit better at doors than her brother was—had overlooked something. Instead, frazzled by nerves, wanting this part to be over so he could relax against the door and read, Malik started naming his co-conspirators, figuring it wasn't snitching when getting discovered was part of the point.

"No, sweetie, name the doors."

Well, there was the gym.

★ ★ ★

Joy had gotten further along in her speech than Malik, since there were few people paying enough attention to interrupt her. Omar and Amira were easily dispatching their opponents in the basketball tournament, setting up what everyone watching was hoping to see, ten times if possible: a head-to-head encounter. Whoops and cheers emanated from the stands, drowning out Joy's reading, so the three people actually gathered around her, interested in her whole situation, could no longer hear the demands.

Upstairs, Eli Mbele was feeling lucky to have been assigned the roof garden's exit to the back staircase. Not only was it a beautiful night with stars overhead and just enough of a breeze coming through the vents high up in the glass enclosure, but it was also the location of the movie marathon. All over the tennis courts and picnic tables, people huddled together, requesting more popcorn from the teachers who were fulfilling their roles as servers in good spirits. The movie currently playing was *About Time*, one of Eli's favorites, so he tried to read the speech in a considerate, quiet voice. Still, he was being shushed, and though he hated being shushed, and hated disrupting movies, too, he believed in the cause and read on.

Downstairs, chained to the secret basement entrance Peejay was hoping had been forgotten, since it was supposed to be unknown to students (everyone knew about it), Lolo Dufry was taking a nap. She figured that people would be down there soon enough. They would open the unassuming, unmarked door by the library, thinking Marisa had forgotten about the exit, and they would rush down the steps two at a time, believing they were about to escape. But Marisa was smarter than everyone at school, and Lolo was sure that if Marisa's life had turned out differently and she decided to hold hostages at gunpoint rather than at chainpoint, she would actually get the money, the plane to freedom, whatever she desired.

In Lolo's lap, the three keys that corresponded to the padlocks hanging off her like menacing Christmas ornaments rested in a pool of melting butter. Soon, the butter would attract some nearby ants (here was one now, already sniffing out the golden ambrosia and ready to report back to the colony) and Lolo would wish she had skipped the theatrics and just completed that step of the process, crowd or not.

Back in the green room, Peejay had granted Malik permission to finish reading. He was just about to reach the speech's climactic (and climatic) conclusion. Malik removed the keys from the tin foil envelope at his side, each dripping with butter. His mouth went dry. He had hated this part of the plan all along, and had tried to talk Marisa out of it. "People don't understand anything but melodrama," she'd said. "We need to put on a show."

"Dear God, please tell me you're not about to do that," Peejay said.

Malik swallowed hard. If Peejay directed the word *don't* at Malik, he might have to listen. This was Peejay Singh, this year's host, Partyer in Chief, the guy who basically ran the school with charm. Earlier that semester, Peejay had come to the play Malik had acted in, and personally delivered congratulatory flowers to every member in the cast.

"I have to," Malik said. Then there was enough of a pause to serve as Malik's window. He examined the keys: small, sure, barely an inch long and thin—but still, in the end, keys. Peejay said nothing. Mr. Gigs gasped. The freshmen cried out in delight and disgust. Malik swallowed all three at once. Someone thought they had seen him chew, which for some reason felt particularly brutal.

Eli took the keys one at a time, imagining they were popcorn kernels. Moments later, he realized he could ask for some actual popcorn from Master Declan, the head of the school, who was just now noticing Eli and his chains and furrowing his brow. Eli waved him over.

Joy took hers with chugs of water, coughing them up several times before she finally felt their bumpy surface work their way down her throat. Marisa's words ran through her mind about melodrama, and Joy played up the cough to the best of her ability. People in her vicinity winced, then craned their necks so they wouldn't miss too much of the action happening on the court.

Marisa, who had the largest crowd by far, held her keys up in the air for effect. Butter glinted in the white light shining over her head. She looked out at her audience. All these people who contributed to the sad state of coral reefs around the world, whether knowingly or not. Whose home, however temporary it may be, was being destroyed by the gray-brown water of construction runoff. One of the last remaining spots where underwater beauty could be found was about to be wiped away, and none of them cared, none of them even knew.

She made eye contact with every single person in front of her, not blinking the whole time, so they would know just how serious she was. In that prolonged eye contact alone, she won over at least three of her fellow students, who had barely ever thought about reefs before, much less cared whether or not they had deteriorated. They, plus two teachers who would silently root for Marisa throughout the whole ordeal, though their positions prevented them from cheering on her malfeasance, suddenly found themselves thinking, *I'm on her side.* The sheer determination on her face won them over, and they each took an unconscious step toward her, as if wanting her to see their gesture of allegiance. This, in addition to the handful of others who were convinced by her words alone.

Two more teachers, Ms. Duli (AP History) and Mr. Sanchez (Spanish, French, Postmodern Lit) took a step forward, too, but they were thinking they would stop her. They, more than anyone else (save for Marisa herself), were getting a sense of where this was all headed, the headaches, inconveniences and scandals to come.

Two other students stepped forward, as well, both of them, Maya Klutzheisen and Michael Obonte, meaning to profess their sudden love for Marisa. They hadn't known until that moment when she held the keys up to the light that they loved her, but now it was so obvious to them it felt ridiculous to think of a time when they had not loved her. This, they knew, was how love worked. It came with no warning, sometimes because of someone's appearance, but more mean-ingfully because of someone's actions, because someone's soul was bared, revealed to be stunningly beautiful.

Then Marisa recited the final line of her speech. "CIS, until further notice, consider yourselves locked in," and she swallowed the keys.

3
8:03PM

Kenji heard two simultaneous commotions. One was coming from downstairs, so he peeked over the banister to his left to look down at the foyer, but all he could see was a crowd near the main entrance. The other commotion was to his right, clearly emanating from the green room down the hallway. The one downstairs was louder, and possibly more exciting. But the one in the green room might concern the showcase, so he waved a flyer at a couple of cute sophomores who were trying to get a glimpse of the foyer, too, before he headed down the hallway.

When he walked into the green room, his first thought was

that they'd started the showcase early. He stepped forward, a smile plastered on his face, trying to figure out the specifics of the scene. How fun that everyone had joined in, even audience members. Come to think of it, it was mostly audience members, as most of his team members hadn't come back from laser tag yet.

Then he saw that Mr. Gigs wasn't faking a phone call, but seemed to be really talking into his phone. And the new-this-year-but-not-all-that-new American girl who'd walked by with the slightest of smiles was standing there with her arms crossed over her chest, watching with her eyebrows up and not saying anything, so it didn't seem like she was part of the scene. Kenji examined what he was seeing again.

Huh. Chain props. He didn't remember ever coming across those, though what with the budget those drama kids garnered, he wouldn't be particularly surprised. True to his nature, he decided to just go with it, saying, "Yes, and…" to the scene, whether it was improv or not. He stood near Celeste and watched.

Peejay, deep in the heart of the scene, was yelling at Malik. He knew this would do no good. This hulking, dear lump of a boy had swallowed the keys already and the decision had been made. Whether it was for diesel boats or any other more sensible reason (good God, diesel boats—any other reason would have been more sensible), the boy had screwed with Peejay's plans. Even now, the DJ equipment, the DJ himself, the booze, the last of the earphones, were waiting on the other side of the door, stacked conspicuously atop each other in a tower. They were in Diego's sweet but incapable hands, and who knew how long he could hold on to them.

As he unloaded his tirade, Peejay knew he should be yelling at Malik's organizer. Or not yelling at all, if he were to follow in Hamish's footsteps. Hamish didn't yell at people to get his way. Malik was just an underling, and whatever salvaging could be done would have to be negotiated through Marisa. For that reason, though, it was best to yell at this boy instead and have a cool head when convincing the "mastermind" (dear God, boats!) that her cause was worthy and all, but there was no sense in interrupting the lock-in party.

Deep down, Peejay had faith it would all work out. People would stop paying attention to the stunt, and the perpetrators would get bored and cut themselves free to resume the lock-in activities they were missing out on. The lock-in party had always happened, for as long as lock-in night had happened, and Peejay wasn't going to be the one at the helm when that tradition ended. Quite the opposite; he would ensure it continued to be the most anticipated night of the year. Hamish would wake up to stories of the party, not of its failure.

Still, the yelling needed to happen.

Once all his steam had billowed out, Peejay looked around the room. Most people avoided his gaze. Mr. Gigs spoke on the phone, scratching his beard and looking like he wanted to do almost anything else. Perhaps the administrators Mr. Gigs was speaking to would solve this problem before it grew. A lanky Japanese boy—these freshmen were blessed little cherubs, weren't they, so much younger-looking than the rest; it was a wonder they weren't still playing with blocks and taking naps—was smiling wildly.

Celeste Rollins was the only one looking at him with raised eyebrows. Peejay knew this girl; he'd been part of her welcoming committee, and had noticed her around school all year long, carrying herself as if she assumed others were judging her constantly. Despite his current concerns, despite knowing very little about this girl, he tried to assure her somehow with a single smile, amid all this. The way Hamish would.

At first, Celeste returned the smile. However, a smile between basically strangers was difficult to interpret, even if its intended purpose was mere reassurance. After a moment, it made Celeste wonder if she was misunderstanding, being weird in some other way. Was Peejay setting his sights on her next? Had she done something wrong? She averted her eyes, hugging her arms closer to her.

Peejay sighed, then knelt down to face Malik. "Where is your leader?" he asked in a calm voice, then laughed at his phrasing. "Marisa, was it?"

"Marisa." He was already forgetting Peejay yelling at him. This was the longest he'd spent in Peejay's presence, and he understood now why Peejay never seemed to be alone, why his parties were always crowded, why it seemed like whenever he entered a room people turned toward him. Some people were simply magnetic. If he weren't chained to the door, Malik might follow him out when he left.

"She's downstairs in the main entrance."

"She'll be the one in the chains, I assume?"

Malik beamed at the fact that Peejay was joking around with him. He nodded. Then, as if absolving Malik, Peejay touched him on the shoulder and left the room.

"Scene!" Kenji called out.

The keys had tasted, mysteriously, like salt water, like the accidental splashes that worked their way into your mouth when you surfaced to clean your mask. Marisa was glad for it, glad for the reminder of what had moved her to do this.

There was a moment of pause, an uncertainty to the air, people unsure of how they were expected to react. Then a murmur began, which quickly turned into a roar. Marisa had anticipated what happened next. She braced herself with a deep breath, tensing her muscles to resist getting turned into a rag doll beaten down by their frustration. People swarmed around her, trying to open the doors. It was exactly like she imagined it would be, but a part of her was still scared. Not for her safety, but for the chains. Would they hold? Would they keep her plan intact, in the face of all these desperate students?

They had so much they wanted to do on the other side. And even if all they wanted was inside the building, even if they had already feasted on food truck offerings, they were curious if Marisa was for real. The doors jolted back and forth from behind her, too. Most of the people on the other side hadn't heard her speech and were simply confused about the lack of flow in and out of the building. Lock-in night had never been about constriction before. Quite the opposite.

Junior Dov Nudel grabbed at Marisa's chains and gave them a few yanks. Though it pinched her skin and ground against her hip bones, nothing came loose and the doors didn't budge. Marisa smiled at Dov, who muttered something in Hebrew, then stalked away to do something useful with his time while someone else dealt with this.

Then Jordi Marcos, loser of the Partyer in Chief elections, stood in front of the doors with his brow furrowed. He looked at Marisa, surrounded by his peers, and the first thing he felt was…what? He couldn't tell. Curiosity? Sympathy? Maybe, bubbling under the surface. But then he remembered his dad watching news footage of protestors in France linking arms across a highway. He couldn't remember what their cause had been, what their demands were, just what his dad had said into the darkened living room. "If I were there, I'd drive right through them." And that, to Jordi, felt like it applied here. He pushed his way through the crowd until he was right in front of Marisa, and he attempted to break his way through.

One after another, students came by to try another place to yank, to unravel the chains in some way Marisa had not foreseen, each of them failing to so much as add an inch of slack to the chains. Some ran off looking for tools, though Marisa was not worried about them finding any. Faculty wanted to try, too, but they resisted, each looking toward their department chairs, if they were present (not all the staff attended, though there was certainly room for more chaperones. Each year an unlucky handful were called away on other adult responsibilities—childcare, a significant other arguing to take advantage of the three-day weekend in order to travel, a poorly timed visitor—all proof that adulthood was a constant double-edged sword), who looked toward the vice principal, who looked for Master Declan, who was currently awaiting his turn in the karaoke room.

Finally, Ms. Duli stepped up to Marisa. "You're not going to back down, are you?"

Marisa shook her head. Despite herself, she looked for a sign of approval on Ms. Duli's face. From the start of the year's AP European History class, they'd butted heads many times, the way people who are strong in the same way are wont to do.

Ms. Duli sighed deeply, the exasperated breath of a teacher who knew she'd have to stay at school longer than she had planned. "Okay," she said simply. "I'll go find the boss."

She walked away, and Marisa found herself wishing for… what, exactly? She wasn't certain. Approval, sure. She was only human. Or perhaps she just wanted feedback. For obvious reasons, Marisa had not shown her speech or list of demands to anyone but her cronies. Eli helped with some of the phrasing, and Malik shared some good insight about plastic straws being valuable for people with disabilities, but other than these small (and important, sure) details, Marisa's plan had not yet been assessed. Not by anyone other than herself, and though she'd complained often about Ms. Duli's hard-ass grading ideals, she found herself wanting to know Ms. Duli's thoughts. She wanted someone to scream their approval, even though she assured herself that she did not need it.

But her teacher was now crossing the foyer toward the stairs, looking down at her cell phone as she marched.

Moments later, Peejay Singh appeared in front of Marisa. The crowd had parted to let him through. She hadn't had much direct interaction with Peejay before, hadn't had a class with him, or sat next to him in the cafeteria or anything. She knew the school revolved around him and, despite herself, felt pulled in his direction, too. By his charisma, sure, but how he wielded it, too: benevolently. She'd been slightly sad to know she'd be denying herself his party.

Now he eyed her intensely, hands at his hips. She'd left her arms free, so she mimicked his pose and tilted her chin upward.

"What do you think you're doing?" he asked, not raising his voice at all, but definitely giving it an edge.

Marisa exhaled. "I knew I should have plugged into the PA system. Hold on." She reached into her duffel bag and unfurled a poster where she'd written her list of thirty demands and a brief mission statement for exactly this reason. Then she pulled out a roll of Scotch tape and started to maneuver herself around the chain as best as she could to tape the poster to the door behind her. She put it up close to the hinges, which, like with every door at CIS, faced the inside of the school so they could not be tampered with from the outside.

Peejay saw the title on the poster, *Instructions to Exit*, and rolled his eyes. He tapped Marisa on the forearm so she would stop fiddling with the tape. "I heard the spiel from your—" Peejay stopped, searching for an appropriate term "—adorable, subservient lunk."

"Malik's big, not a lunk," Marisa cut in.

"So you knew who I meant," he shot back. When Marisa started to protest, he waved her off. "Fine, then, adorable, subservient hunk. Whatever. Point is, I got the spiel. You're fighting for something you believe in—go, Mother Earth, I'm with you." For this next part he leaned in, aware that people were paying attention to them, having momentarily forgotten all about the joys of lock-in night. (Although most of them, still, were thinking this was part of the joy of it all. Drama and intrigue and excitement. What if their lock-in night extended far beyond regular hours? What luck! The longest lock-in night ever.) Among the eavesdroppers, Peejay knew, would be teachers, and discovery was not in his plans.

48

"You know this kind of interferes with my—" he leaned in closer still "—party."

"I know," Marisa replied. She resisted the urge to add that she was sorry.

"I need a way to get a few boxes and a person inside. If that happens, you can count on me to rally people for your cause." Peejay resisted the urge to say please.

The windows should have been an easy solution. In most buildings they would be. Open a window or break it if you had to, and taste freedom. But Marisa, like Peejay—like everyone in the high school after their first sweltering day when the sun shone in through the windows and heated the classrooms in a surprisingly efficient way the eco-friendly fans could do nothing about—knew the windows didn't open.

Out of paranoia, perhaps, the school board had made sure they never did. They were afraid of kids climbing out from the top floors and falling, they were afraid of letting the air-conditioning out, they were afraid of paper airplanes being flown all day. Who knew why the board did the things they did.

The only openings in the windows were these slats, three inches long and one inch wide, near the top. They allowed only the hottest of the air to come out, and kept the class-rooms about as ventilated as a coffin. Peejay would check to see how much could fit in through them, though he wasn't about to hold his breath. God, he wished he could talk to Hamish.

Peejay's offer was a tempting one for Marisa. When Peejay spoke, people listened. He had a strange pull on CIS. Like a charming hypnotist, Peejay would say, "Raise your hands up," with a smile and CIS would reach for the sky. But he'd shown his cards too early: he needed the doors to open. She couldn't have that.

"The doors are locked," she said. She looked deep into Peejay's dark brown eyes to show him his hypnosis would have no effect on her. They were beautiful eyes, and that wasn't the only reason Marisa wondered if she was right to turn him down.

"Think about what you're doing," Peejay said, still whispering, less out of a desire to not be heard, more because he didn't have the oxygen to growl. Hamish had gone through obstacles in throwing his party, but never sabotage. By a fellow student no less. Peejay felt betrayed, appalled.

If only he knew how long she had spent thinking of this, how thoroughly. Lately, it felt as if Marisa could think of nothing else, as if the lock-in was her mind's natural resting place, and any moment when she wasn't actively thinking of something else, it instinctively veered itself back home. A chuckle escaped her.

Shocked, Peejay took a step back. He wondered if she would react differently if she knew about Hamish, if he told her what, exactly, was at stake. But it felt wrong to dangle him as a bargaining chip, to use his bedridden state to inspire pity. So he kept quiet, not knowing what bargaining chips he held anymore.

The rest of the audience held their breaths, and one by one the realization dawned on them. Lock-in night no longer belonged to them. The chains, maybe, should have said that. But this was the moment they knew it wasn't all some hoax, some performance piece. This was not a performance of a protest. This was the protest itself.

Clearly, the night belonged to this girl who could look Peejay Singh in the eyes and tell him no. Even if they couldn't hear what had been said, they understood that much. And then when Peejay asked again, the girl had the stomach to laugh at him. If she could do that, what else did she have the stomach for? They didn't want to find out.

Elsewhere, another audience held its breath for an entirely different reason. Omar Ng had advanced to the finals, and Amira Wahid was only one point away from finishing off her opponent. Normally, this would have elicited cheers. But they held their breaths because Amira was about to score that last basket.

She was in the air, clearly on her way to dunk.

Her defender, a member of the boys' team named Ping Xe, still had his feet planted firmly on the ground. He wasn't even looking up at Amira, but rather at the space Amira had occupied a moment before. She'd planted her left foot down and lifted off so quickly that for weeks later Ping would look at video footage taken from the crowds to make sure she hadn't merely disappeared from sight and reappeared on the rim.

No one knew Amira could dunk. That was by her design, though she'd meant to show off the skill earlier in the competition. She wanted this exact breathlessness from the very start, just hadn't found the opportunity. Forget building up to a climax; Amira wanted it known as soon as possible, long before the final whistle of the decathlon, she was the superior athlete.

The most popular sports at CIS were soccer and rugby, so they garnered the attention of the best athletes. Basketball was a distant third, so few of the players in CIS history had ever been capable of dunking. Basketball wasn't a very popular sport locally, either, and the competition was likewise mediocre. Few dunks had ever been witnessed in that decades-old gymnasium. Certainly, no one had heard of a female dunker.

Which, of course, Amira knew. She knew the psychological impact that would ripple through her opponents as soon as she slammed the ball through. As momentous as it was for everyone else, it was now routine for Amira; it had been months since the act had lost its sheen of newness.

It was within her body's capabilities, and since her body was entirely in her command, it now felt second nature to her. What she was still getting used to, though, were the angry images that flashed through her mind when she dunked.

Mostly, the thoughts were of her mother. It was as if every dunk represented an opportunity to scream at her mom. To yell, "Yes, girls can," since Rifta Wahid was the person who most often told Amira they couldn't. Not even that girls should not be athletic, muscular, competitive, but that by sheer fact of their chromosomes the ability was beyond their efforts. Her mother never yelled it, but the repetition was loud enough.

It was only at her father's gentle insistence that Amira was allowed to join the track and field team at school, thus giving her the excuse to sneak away to train for everything else. But her mother had been skeptical of Amira's interest in sport, saying it was unbecoming for a girl, and she kept a close eye to make sure it did not distract from more important things.

Amira dunked with one hand. Not her nicest, flashiest dunk ever. She didn't even hang on. But it was unequivocally a dunk, her hand pulling down on the rim just long enough for it to snap viciously back to place, the sound like a bone breaking, like jaws dropping to the floor. It was deeply satisfying, and her desire to have her mom witness what she was capable of was matched only by a deep gratitude that her mother was not in the audience.

Amira's sneakers squeaked slightly when she landed, and that was the only sound in the gym. She didn't even look at the crowd, who, despite their posters cheering her on, despite the sheer noise they were prepared to make on her behalf, despite their adjusted expectations for what she could do, could not believe what she had just done.

Amira walked over to Ping and grabbed his limp-wristed hand to shake "good game."

Before the crowd could erupt into the cheers building up within them through the shock, three teachers (Mr. Jankowski, Mrs. Wu, Mr. Sanchez) jogged across the court. Their dress shoes clacked on the hardwood, a jarring contrast to the heavy silence. It was rare enough to see anyone but the PE teachers jogging, unless it was for some special student-teacher match, or in the wee hours of the morning, when the fanatics came in to exercise before their classes. These teachers, though, clearly had not expected to jog tonight. They were headed toward the exit, paying so little attention to the matter at hand that some in the audience were insulted on Amira's behalf. Others felt a jolt of fear, sensing that something was wrong. Some just laughed at the clumsy way people in dress shoes ran.

Then the teachers stopped. A few students started to clap for Amira, feeling like much too long had passed in silence, and she was due her ovation. The rest of the spectators, though, seemed to finally notice Joy Ng and her chains. Like elsewhere in school, a murmur began to grow. Amira noticed Joy, too, but figured it was none of her business and walked to center court to await her coin flip with Omar in order to decide who would have possession first. She would have to wait a long time.

The now-anxious crowd watched as Mrs. Wu pulled out her phone and dialed frantically. The little applause that had started died out. Amira's dunk was, for the time being, forgotten. She hoped this was at least partially due to shock. She hoped everyone had noticed. She hoped no one had.

Everyone could see Mrs. Wu talking, a hand raised to her hair as if tugging a wig into place. Then she hung up, and the school-wide PA system came to life with the sound of Master Declan's always jolly but now rattled voice. "All students and faculty, please report to the auditorium at once."

The crowd's rumbling grew louder, wondering who it could possibly be meant for, given that it was lock-in night and everyone had somewhere to be.

"All lock-in events are temporarily suspended," Master Declan's voice rang out.

Now, finally, the gym erupted in mayhem.

4
8:39PM

The foyer in front of Marisa was empty. The hallways, too. She could see into some of the classrooms, which were empty as well, abandoned midactivity as if in an earthquake drill. There were still noises coming from outside, the people there unable, for obvious reasons, to attend the assembly Master Declan had called.

In the basement, Lolo Dufry still napped, having slept through the announcement, as well as the few knocks Diego had attempted before he reported back to Peejay that the door was, indeed, shut just like all the others. Joy Ng felt a chill in the empty gym, which still reverberated with the sound of

Amira's dunk. Joy desperately needed to pee now, and sure, she had a bucket and there was no one else around, but it felt like at any moment someone could appear while she was midsquat. Then what?

Malik, happy to have been left alone in the green room, read happily, though the noise from the auditorium next door kept breaking his concentration. He shifted against his chains, trying to get comfortable. On the roof garden, Eli munched slowly on popcorn, rationing it out since he was pretty sure no one would grant him a refill now. Blessedly, someone had forgotten to pause the movie.

In the auditorium, Kenji and Celeste sat together, watching the teachers and administrators confer off-mic. Compared to the other students, the pair was quiet. Kenji kept checking the time, hoping this would be over and done with very, very shortly. Impossibly shortly. His silence came from knowing it wouldn't happen. It came from the fact that Lindsay and several other players were not in the auditorium, not in the building at all.

What's happening? Lindsay texted him.

Not totally sure, he responded. He would usually have a joke by now. His silence came from her absence, from how much of a "no" this felt like, when the "Yes, and…"s should have been flying around.

Celeste's silence came from where it had these past few months: the fact that she was observing interactions instead of having her own. She saw how Kenji kept texting someone named Lindsay. She saw the way a group of three blond kids a few rows ahead positioned themselves in the chairs so the two sitting at either end could face each other as well as the one in the middle. It struck her as such a beautiful gesture of inclusion, of intimacy. Three people could sit side by side and still feel like a group, but for them that wasn't enough. They wanted more of each other.

She craned her neck and saw a girl in fluorescent leggings propped up on her knees, her arms folded over her chair's backrest. She chatted excitedly with two boys who had matching tousled haircuts, sitting a row back. Too influenced by romantic comedies, Celeste wondered which of the two boys the girl would fall in love with. What was the girl's place among them? And were they maybe looking for new friends?

These scenes notwithstanding, the mood in the theater was tense. Most students felt the way Kenji did, watching the clock approach the scheduled time for their most anticipated event, while this friend or that remained on the other side. Some shut their eyes tightly and tried to slow the clock's progress with their minds, knowing it was silly and futile, but wanting to try all the same.

Finally, Master Declan stepped up to the podium (whose job had it been, Celeste wondered, to find a podium and set up a mic in the middle of all this?) and cleared his throat. He flashed his signature smile, all warmth and cheeks. "Good evening, Sea Cucumbers," he said for the second time that day, the exact same way he'd welcomed them to the lock-in night hours earlier. He rubbed his hands together as if trying to wring out the bad news. "I'm sure you are all happy to see me again so soon."

He waited for the joke to land. It did not.

"Right." He looked down at his notes scrawled on his left palm, smudged already by his hand-wringing. Someone coughed. "First of all, let me assure you that we have the situation under control. Myself and the rest of the staff are handling the, um..." He gestured vaguely with his hand out toward the audience, revealing the blotted blue bullet points. He wanted to say "protestors" but somehow felt like that might make him sound like a bit of an autocrat. Master Declan had come from a place with a history of autocrats, men who spat the word *protestor* and used it as an excuse to squash down others. When he unexpectedly began moving up the administrative ranks, he swore to himself he would never approach autocratic behavior. Granted, saying the word alone didn't quite qualify, but he saw it as a slippery slope. He reached for another, friendlier word. "The children currently chained to the doors." He cleared his throat again, the sound lonely in the tense auditorium.

"We would like you to know we are doing everything we can to resume lock-in activities as soon as possible. Until that time, please remain here." He stopped and smiled again, then realized he'd arrived at the end of his speech. Usually, he'd wait for the scattered applause, then dismiss the assembled. But the board, which had yet to comment on any of Marisa's demands, had decreed it'd be best to keep all the students in one place while the situation was sorted out. With no other ideas, and nowhere to dismiss his audience to, Master Declan took a step backward.

He only managed a quarter turn back to the wings flanking the stage when someone shouted out, "Just give her what she wants!"

The theater came alive. Some agreed with whoever had shouted. Some mutterings, it seemed, dissented.

Offstage, Ms. Duli widened her eyes at Master Declan. She mouthed, *Don't engage*, at him, but he couldn't understand what she was trying to communicate, so he stepped back to the microphone to field questions, which he thought was only fair. It was, after all, lock-in night.

"We are considering all options right now, and are closely reading the list of demands."

"How long is that going to take?"

Now it was Peejay raising his voice. Some who knew his role for the evening could sense the ulterior motive in his question. Others, like Celeste, took the question at face value, and did what came naturally whenever Peejay spoke: they listened.

"Well, Vice Principal Martinez is on the line with the board as we speak. I imagine it shouldn't be long." Unfortunately, everyone knew Master Declan lacked an imagination. At the holiday bake sales, he always brought sugar cookies. Just a few weeks ago at the Sea Cukelele Festival and Talent Show, he played *Somewhere Over the Rainbow*, like he did every year. The third graders played that song every year, too. What he could imagine was of little comfort to the students in the audience.

Now Ms. Duli approached the podium, putting her hand over the microphone while she whispered something in Master Declan's ear.

This whispering among adults didn't sit well with the student body, not tonight. They still had so much to do. The party hadn't even started.

★ ★ ★

Peejay eyed the clock. Traditionally, the lock-in party began at midnight. There were two ways this could go: they could tear the chains off those well-meaning rabble-rousers, or they could give the girl what she wanted. The list had been long, around thirty items, more than one having to do with boats. No way would those be done by midnight.

But the way those kids were tied up, it didn't seem like someone could just waltz in with bolt cutters. For one, the chains and locks looked like they'd been picked out specifically to resist bolt cutters. Not to mention that there was nothing keeping Marisa and the others from placing their hands in the way and forcing CIS to chop off a finger or two to gain the others' freedom. CIS was far from perfect, but the administration did tend to avoid physical altercations with the students, especially involving tools and lost fingers. So neither option particularly called out to Peejay as the most favorable for his personal interests. Did CIS even have bolt cutters?

As the hubbub in the auditorium started to build, Peejay thought about what would happen if the school started sending locksmiths around the campus to find a way in. They'd discover the booze and the earphones, and sweet little Diego twiddling his sweet little thumbs. He sent a text telling Diego to scope out a hiding spot for the contraband while all this boiled over.

So, if neither option was ideal, what was Peejay to do? It came down, as always, to Hamish.

In the future (perhaps even in the morning? Hamish's recovery occurring midparty), when he told Hamish about the night, when he came bragging to his brother about a lock-in party that included everyone, even the teachers, he wouldn't want to have to admit he had a role in helping the administration sweep these protestors under the rug. The party notwithstanding, he knew his brother would not approve of squashing down those fighting for what was right. Hamish had a righteous streak, and Peejay knew exactly what option his brother would opt for.

If there was a kind or decent bone in Peejay's body, it had been placed there by Hamish. The way he saw it, Peejay wasn't born as anything special. He was special now, but he was made that way by association. In his eyes, Hamish was the reincarnation of the Buddha, the Christ, Vishnu, whatever standard for goodness there existed. Hamish was what humanity should aspire to.

When Peejay came out to his family, his parents might have only smiled and said, "Okay," then tried to never bring up the matter again. That is, if it weren't for the way Hamish embraced his brother and showered love on him, telling Peejay that who he was and who he loved would never cause him to lose his family's love, not a single ounce of happiness they could bestow upon him.

With Hamish's words out there, his parents became believers, too, not just abiding by Hamish's proclamations but truly embracing them. Peejay had seen it in their faces, the initial discomfort (not hatred, never that, but not acceptance, either) giving way to joy. There had been negative reactions, of course, especially among less understanding relatives and neighbors. Even the Scottish side of his family, less religious, and supposedly more welcoming, had stiffened when they heard the news, and seemingly had no idea how to speak to Peejay at the last family reunion a year prior.

Or maybe it hadn't been that easy at all. Maybe there had been more hatred than Peejay would have been able to stand, more discomfort in his parents' eyes than he could bear to admit. Maybe it was just Hamish shielding him, the brightness of his brother's love making the shadows feel less dark. After all, Peejay hadn't seen his favorite uncle on his father's side since he came out—hadn't even received a birthday visit, as was the custom in their family.

Still, the experience had been better than Peejay had expected, and he attributed it to Hamish. His brother's love had the ability to change people. That love had certainly left its mark on Peejay—he firmly believed that a lifetime of sheer proximity to Hamish was the only reason Peejay enjoyed the status he had at school. And if it wasn't by mere proxy, but by his own actions—confronting bullies in the hallway, attending less popular athletic events such as the badminton junior varsity games, to cheer on those who rarely had an audience (Go, Sea Cucumbers!)—well, those actions had been learned from Hamish, too.

In the days since Hamish had his accident at his construction job and fell, quite literally, into his coma, Peejay had felt himself growing more selfish, more greedy, less compassionate. Something in him turned darker.

So no, Hamish couldn't tell Peejay exactly how he felt about this whole situation. But Peejay wasn't quite good enough at manipulating feelings to be able to lie to himself about the fact that he knew how Hamish would try to guide him toward doing the right thing here.

"We don't care about the board—we just want our night back. Give her what she wants," Peejay said, now raising his voice, knowing it would rile up the crowd. The school could use a little pressure. Indeed, others joined in with shouts of "Yeah!" And "He's right!"

Ms. Duli stopped her whispering to face the audience. She glanced at Master Declan to see what the man would do, but he seemed to be buckling beneath the pressure already. She knew very well the power this Peejay kid could yield. If they weren't careful, he could easily bring a riot upon them.

And that could have been true any other day. It may well have been true still. But some of the kids in the auditorium had seen the way Marisa laughed at Peejay, and it weakened his spell on them. Not fully, but enough that they didn't all blindly follow him, enough that before Ms. Duli could step to the mic to quell any uprisings, someone else stood up.

It was Jordi Marcos, who many knew hadn't wanted to earn Peejay's host status for the party so much as he had wanted to rip it away. Jordi thought of Peejay as his nemesis, though (or maybe because) Peejay never gave him much thought. They'd both been at CIS from first grade, and Jordi, for years, had thought that meant something. They'd both, time and again, lived through the experience of those international school goodbyes—the friends they'd tried for months to get close to, finally succeeding shortly after winter break, suddenly going away, the dreadful, harrowing prospect of having to start over when the school year started up again. Every first day, Jordi would come up to Peejay and try to talk to him about it, try to bond with his charismatic peer. Every year, Peejay hardly gave him the time of day.

By middle school, Jordi had come to an important realization: only he had trouble starting the cycle again. Only he felt the absence of a hard-earned friendship. For Peejay, everything came easily, goodbyes and hellos included, the position of Partyer in Chief. And now that Peejay had said that Marisa deserved to be rewarded for her disruptive actions, Jordi felt his conviction against the protestors grow stronger. He tried to tap into the anger his dad showed, wondered if he had the capacity for the same kind of fire.

"Cut the chains off her! Or take the doors off their hinges." Jordi was full-on shouting at Master Declan and Ms. Duli. "She has no right to mess this up for us."

Something about the way he said that made Celeste sit up a little straighter in her seat, gripping the armrests. "I disagree," she said, but it came out as a whisper only Kenji heard.

Jordi continued, emboldened by the voices who muttered or cheered their approval. "This is between the school and that..." Like Master Declan, he reached for a word. But unlike the headmaster, Jordi purposely sought out one he found distasteful. "That protestor." He tried to say it the way he'd heard his dad and uncles say it whenever it came up on television, like he could spit it out, like it wasn't worthy of his lips.

Jordi hadn't paid much attention to Marisa's list of demands when he tried to jostle her chains loose. He and his friends had been on the way up to the spray paint tutorial when they'd been distracted by the crowd and stopped to be a part of it. As far as he was concerned, her demands were beside the point. He should know how to wield a spray paint can by now, and the fact that he didn't was her fault, as well as the school's. It was Peejay's fault, too, somehow. For winning the election, for siding with her.

"Go get some bolt cutters and let's get it over with. Hell, I'd be happy to do it." The scattering of applause he'd received before now became a bona fide round of applause, louder than what Amira had received for her dunk. Celeste shook her head in the darkness. Peejay, still standing, cursed under his breath.

For years Jordi Marcos, one of the only other old-timers (students who'd been at CIS since elementary school), had followed Peejay around like a kitten, constantly pawing at him, nipping at his ankles for attention, occasionally purring at his side. Peejay had not paid him much attention because, frankly, he disliked cats.

Jordi had taken all this personally and, now that he had grown, liked to bare his teeth and extract his claws, hissing in Peejay's direction, as if that would suddenly change Peejay's stance on cats. He and Jordi wanted the same thing here, the same thing everyone wanted—to have lock-in night back in their hands again. But Jordi's stupid contrarian ways were going to create factions, Peejay could tell, pitting people against each other. This would delay everything, perhaps irrevocably.

On the stage, Master Declan smiled beatifically, hiding the heartburn rising up from his stomach by stepping into Ms. Duli's shadow. Ms. Duli, knowing this had gone on long enough, stepped up to the mic.

"Either of those options could lead to the rest of the night's cancellation." A whole room's worth of hearts skipped beats.

In the back row, Amira looked up from her trimmed nails. Thinking of the possibility that the decathlon would never happen, that she wouldn't even get the chance to earn the title she wanted so badly, made her nearly chew through her lip. At the same time, she wondered if it was a sign of some sort. She had secretly let go of the idea of God a few years ago, though she still pretended for her parents' sake, for the sake of keeping things at home as they were.

Now the notion came back that something larger than herself could pass messages down to her through others' actions, through fate's twists and turns. She felt a fleeting sense of relief thinking about the decathlon being put on hold.

She stood up and squeezed past the three people sitting between her and the aisle (they barely noticed her passing by, thought maybe it was just a bout of darkness crossing their eyes signaling that they were about to faint). Amira muttered something about the bathroom to the teacher standing by the door who had not yet thought of the possibility that someone might want to sneak out. In the hallway, Amira sprinted.

Ms. Duli relished that she'd only been teaching for six years but could already bring a room this size and this restless to complete silence with a single sentence. "You two are welcome to scream and shout to get people to agree with you," she continued, "but the fact of the matter is we are at the board's beck and call. If we do anything without their approval—whether that's accepting a slew of policy changes or taking bolt cutters anywhere near a student—they're likely to send us all home. As soon as they're able to, anyway."

"They can't do that," Jordi yelled back, but his voice was

unconvincing as a meow. When no one backed him up with a yell or two, busy as they all were waiting for their hearts to retake their rhythms, Jordi slunk back into his seat.

"Believe me," Ms. Duli said, "I understand your frustration. But it's a Thursday evening. The board members have to be pulled away from family dinners, from trafficky commutes back home, from early bedtimes. They are being gathered, and we will have a decision soon. Activities are to remain suspended at the board's request, and there is nothing we can do about that. Until then, your patience is appreciated." She looked straight at Peejay when she said this.

5
8:55PM

Marisa poured more sawdust into her bucket, covered it with its snap-on lid and moved it aside. She was glad for the quiet, glad she'd had the opportunity to pee away from prying eyes.

She reached down into her duffel bag and grabbed the foldable stool she'd packed to make the ordeal easier on her body (she'd bought matching stools for all her cronies).

She couldn't help but wonder how many more times she would have to use the bucket before the demands started to fall. Her plan called for…well, that was math she didn't like to think about anymore. She'd double-checked it plenty of times already, and now the sawdust and the bucket would last as long as they would.

She reached over near the door, where years ago the school had installed an antibacterial hand sanitizer dispenser, yielding to the pressures of some parent or the other to keep up with hygiene standards. It was this dispenser that had given Marisa the idea to stage her *protest* at CIS (she did not find the word distasteful in the least; on the contrary, when she realized that's what she had to do, her heart latched on to the word like a life raft, like a kite soaring in beautiful azure skies, latched on to the word in the way it had been used by the righteous so many times before, those on the right side of history).

CIS was the perfect setting to draw attention to Lokoloko Island. Powerful businessmen sent their children to this school, as did three ambassadors. The twin children of an Oscar-winning Hollywood director attended the school. Not to mention the countless connections all the other parents of current and past students held. Ministry heads in the local country, newspaper publishers in the US, a former Mexican president. All had attended CIS, or sent their kids there, or their nephews. They had donated large sums of money, or were in some other way affiliated with the larger CIS community (Go, Sea Cucumbers!).

All this, whatever Marisa hadn't been able to discover in class with a little prying, was easy to find online. Much of it she had discovered accidentally, by overhearing her peers' conversations before class.

The only part she'd had trouble finding was who she could get to suspend the construction on Lokoloko Island. The hotel company opening up the resort was an international conglomerate, but the construction company was based locally. Their website was frustrating to navigate, and Marisa hadn't been able to find the name of a CEO, but she was willing to bet someone at the company sent their kids to CIS.

When Marisa had started planning, the construction site on Lokoloko Island was her only focus. Then she realized if she was going to chain herself and make demands, she should ask for more than just one place to shut its doors.

The problem, after all, wasn't just this one construction site. It was the increased human activity once the resort was built, the boat traffic, the people slathering on their sunscreen every two hours, rinsing it off into the water, those tiny particles of titanium dioxide bleeding out, further harming the reefs.

It was all the construction sites on all the coasts of the world. It was emissions warming the air and acidifying the water, killing off the reefs that were the breeding grounds for so much of the ocean's biodiversity. Some of which humans depended on for food, too. Whole communities relied on the ecosystem of the reefs. Not to mention the protection those reefs provided from storm surges. Human beings, the only animal stupid enough to believe that destroying their way of life wouldn't kill them.

She looked back at her list, wondering if she had gone a little overboard. She'd thought it was a wise strategy to hide her main demand among a series of others. But now she worried it would get lost, that they would seek to negotiate and merely grant the easy ones.

It all depended on her ability to stay strong, to believe this was what mattered most.

Marisa needed now only to wait. She popped open a Tupperware full of pita chips and hummus and watched as Amira Wahid exited the auditorium, running.

The girl was a blur. She sprinted the length of the hallway, down and back, her feet barely making a sound, as if she only needed to touch the ground with the tips of her toes. Then Amira stood with her hands on her hips, catching her breath for just a moment before taking off again. She seemed to get faster with each sprint, as if she knew the limits of her body were distant, but was nevertheless committed to one day reaching them.

A few weeks ago, Marisa had caught wind of Amira's dismantling of gendered categories in the decathlon, and it was one of the few repercussions in her plan that gave her pause. She hated ruining things for other girls. It didn't help that, all school year, she'd become increasingly intrigued by this hijabi girl with the green eyes and the jaw that seemed always set in determination. They were in the same AP Composition class, and Marisa had grown to anticipate getting to read Amira's writing, the glimpses of herself that were otherwise hard to come by. Amira was passionate and could wax poetic about everything in her writing, whether it was a persuasive essay decrying the inhumane treatment of refugees or an earnest ode to nasi lemak for breakfast. Every week, Marisa seemed to flick her eyes across the room more often, and she found herself trying to time her exits from class so she could small talk with Amira in the halls. Though it hadn't developed into anything beyond those walks, the occasional conversation in the cafeteria or on the after-school bus, and though Marisa had become swept up in her plans for the lock-in, her interest held steady.

It was hard to think of herself ruining the decathlon for Amira, the thing that seemed to matter to her more than anything.

But in the end it was only athletics, and in the face of the reefs, the fading oranges and purples, the murk spreading throughout the world, well, Amira's goals felt like silly, human matters. Marisa's crush, or whatever one might call it, was small, too.

Still, when Amira stopped running, took a sip of water from the fountain and looked down at Marisa from over the banister, Marisa felt herself nearly grimace. Instead, she pressed her lips into an apologetic half smile and raised her hand to wave. Amira, her breath deep and measured, did not wave back. She stepped out of Marisa's sight.

Marisa looked down at the Tupperware of hummus and chips in her lap, unable to keep herself from feeling a little embarrassed that she had ruined things for Amira. Seconds later, though, she heard the soft pitter-patter of someone coming down the stairs, and she knew Amira was coming toward her. By now, the whole school knew who was to blame, and Marisa had mentally prepared to bear the brunt of her peers' frustrations, wrath, begging. But Marisa couldn't read Amira's expression when she appeared, and despite AP Comp, despite clicking over to Amira's social media more often than she'd like to admit, she didn't know Amira well enough to predict what was coming.

A thin sheen of sweat shone on Amira's forehead, and Marisa watched as a single drop scurried from her sport hijab down her temple, past those fierce green eyes. She stood in front of Marisa, her hands relaxed at her sides. Marisa marveled at how Amira's breath had completely subsided now, reverted back to the calm, forgettable mechanism it usually was. If Marisa had run half as long and half as hard as Amira just had, she would've been on her knees, gasping still. The girls watched each other for a while, not sure who should go first.

So instead, Marisa held out her Tupperware, offering it as an olive branch, or an invitation, or just a postrun snack. Amira stepped forward and grabbed a pita chip, dipping it shyly in the hummus, not wanting to take too much. "Thanks," she said in English, CIS's neutral ground as far as languages were concerned. They both spoke Spanish, too—Marisa because of her family, Amira because of her time in Colombia—but their first interactions had been in English and they kept reverting to it, though every now and then one of them would throw in a Spanish word when none in English would do.

Amira took a seat in the eerie but calming silence. The auditorium's door was shut and soundproofed, so if there was more shouting going on, they were isolated from it. Even outside the building, people had stilled. They were getting updates from those inside and were now aware why no one was allowed in. They had the food trucks out there, sure, and whole tubs' worth of filled water balloons, ready for the traditional underclassmen versus upperclassmen war. But most everyone outside was milling about sullenly, as if waiting to board a flight that had been continuously delayed. Every now and then someone would come by and give the doors another tug, not willing to believe they'd really been locked, simply because they couldn't see Marisa and her chains. Marisa heard the scraping sound their rubber soles made as they shuffled away.

"What was it like in there?" Marisa broke the quiet, reaching for another pita chip, then passing the whole container to Amira.

Amira shrugged. "Ms. Duli's taken over as boss, no surprise. Master Declan was so happy she did he practically hugged her. She says we have to wait and see what the board decides. Peejay said they should give you what you want." She didn't mention Jordi's opposition, for no other reason than she found it distasteful.

"Is everyone pissed at me?"

Amira leaned back to rest against the door. She thought of Omar, and whether she would get the opportunity to dunk on him, sweet though he was. She thought of the decathlon's cancellation, and though part of her was, yes, filled with anger, part of her was relieved, too. To not have to hide the plaque or trophy or whatever she'd win from her mom. To not have to lie about how she'd spent lock-in night. It was a silver lining at least. For now, the anger didn't direct itself at Marisa. She knew why Marisa was here, after all, had heard the murmurings in the auditorium, had read the demands on the poster. She couldn't fault Marisa for raising her voice. After all, Amira had fantasized about doing just that countless times. "I think right now they're just nervous," she said.

Marisa didn't have to ask what they were nervous about. She looked over at Amira, reading her body language. She suddenly recognized how long Amira must have trained for the decathlon. All those hours Marisa had spent researching, planning, thinking; Amira had spent those hours and more, likely, honing her skills. And Marisa had ripped it all away from her.

"Are *you* pissed at me?" Marisa asked.

Amira crunched on a pita chip, then handed the Tupperware back. For a moment, Marisa took this as Amira's response, and her muscles relaxed slightly (though they were already tensing with the strain of moving beneath the chains), but then Amira turned to look at her, her expression not changing. "Not yet."

Back in the auditorium, most of the 276 students locked inside the building were talking about one of two things. They were either discussing everything they wished they could be doing at lock-in night, or they were picking sides. Peejay or Jordi—it seemed like everyone fell into one camp or the other, swayed by who knew how many societal factors to land at an opinion even before this situation arose.

The only two people, it seemed, who were entirely quiet were Kenji and Celeste. Celeste looked around at everyone speaking and thought if she was seated next to anyone else, anyone at all, she would find the exact same silence. Part of her wanted to shout, "No! This isn't how Things Will Always Be." But the truth was that part of her had been wrong so many times before, and it was getting exhausting to fall for hope time and again. She had no lines anymore, no place in this world.

Celeste didn't care if lock-in night ever resumed, because it had changed nothing.

"God," Kenji said, "this has changed everything, huh."

His voice still cracked with puberty, accented in a strange place, somewhere between the adorable lilt British children had and the charming accents men grew into.

Celeste wasn't entirely sure he was speaking to her, even though there was absolutely no one else he could have possibly been speaking to. "I wish I could be playing right now," he said. On further inspection, it was completely possible he was speaking to himself.

Then he turned to Celeste and raised his sparse eyebrows over his large, clear eyeglass frames, making it undeniable he was indeed talking to her.

"Playing what?" Celeste asked, picturing video games or wooden blocks, childish things. She had learned to think of her manner of speaking as having an American accent instead of *lacking* an accent, the way she'd said a few times in her first weeks at school, drawing eye rolls from several people. Her ignorance, she felt, could fill this auditorium.

"Improv," he said, smiling as if the word were the very act itself. "We call it playing." He looked at his phone, confirming to himself the showcase should've started by now. "Have you ever done it?"

Celeste shook her head, wanting to pull her legs up onto the seat, hug her knees and draw into herself, bracing for the end of the conversation.

"Oh, man, you should definitely come. We meet Tuesdays in the green room after school. My friends and I also play on Fridays at Lindsay's house. Then most Saturdays, too, but that's usually just because we'll get bored wherever we are, the mall or waiting for a movie to start or whatever, and playing is just always more fun than not. I won't freak you out by telling you you should come to those other things, too, but I reckon after a couple of Tuesdays, you'll want to." He was breathless. Celeste wondered if she'd ever loved anything the way this boy seemed to love even talking about improv.

Then she realized: he'd invited her to join him. An invite! Casually thrown out, and perhaps meaningless, but an invite.

It was her turn, she knew. Back in Glen Ellyn, she would've had no problem continuing a conversation. She even knew the words she could use. "What are the rules?" or "How do you play?" or just "Tell me more." She'd had friends back home. She could talk to the other kids at school. But she wasn't home anymore, and somehow Celeste couldn't seem to complete the steps. To open her mouth and speak. To offer a smile and say (or scream), "Yes!" Soon, this sweet, eager boy would take her silence as disinterest or annoyance, and he would stop trying to include her. Every millisecond that passed without her speaking seemed to make the silence harder to break.

Kenji, however, was not easily dissuaded from trying to spread his love of improv. His brothers had quickly learned, back when Kenji had discovered this love of his life at eleven, dropping hints was of no use when it came to Kenji and improv. They had to ask, often plead, for him to stop talking about it. His parents hoped improv was a phase he would grow out of. His father had considered sending him to therapy, but hoped eventually the boy would find some more serious passions to pursue.

"I know what you're thinking," he said to Celeste. "You're thinking it's not for you. Everyone who hasn't tried it thinks that at first. And sure, some people don't really enjoy it much. But I want you to promise me…" He paused, tilted his head like a puppy. "What's your name?"

This, at least, she could do. "Celeste."

"I need you to promise me, Celeste, that you won't say those words—'improv is not for me'—until you try it. I'll even be the one to make sure you feel comfortable the first time." Kenji pushed his glasses farther up the bridge of his nose. Celeste braved a direct glance at him to see if he was messing with her, but his eyes were wide and expectant and benign.

"Okay," she said. "I promise."

This, too, she thought would bring about the end of the conversation. Especially since Kenji smiled, satisfied, and slunk back into his seat.

Well, Celeste thought, that was something at least. An exchanged word or two. One more person who knew her name. She could picture walking past this boy in the halls (damn, she should have asked for his name when she had the chance) and how he'd give her an enthusiastic wave. Maybe he'd call her name, putting it out there in the world so more would hear it, absorb it by proxy. Maybe he'd wave her over during lunch, seek her out next week so she could fulfill her promise to try improv. All hypothetical, of course, but it was something, a morsel to hang on to. It could be enough.

Not for Kenji, though. "So, how you play is pretty simple," he said. "The first rule is you always say yes to the situation you've been thrown into. You accept it and build on it. 'Yes, and…'" he explained with a wave of his hand, continuing on breathlessly with the rules and all the things he loved about it. Celeste sat and listened, knowing she was still silent, but no longer feeling the full weight of her silence. She'd received an invite.

Peejay, meanwhile, thought of his options. Giving up the party was out of the question, so it was a matter of bringing in the supplies, and somehow the DJ (a CIS alum who'd made it big in the past three years, and had happened to be in town for a music festival that weekend). It'd be nearly impossible to work it all out if they remained imprisoned in the auditorium, but he doubted the school would keep them confined here for long, so he worked under the assumption the building was the prison, not the room. If only she had closed the locks an hour later.

The windows, of course, were out. That left the roof. He tried to remember the last time he was up there, what its layout was, how he might be able to sneak in his contraband. He cursed himself for sticking to lunchtime routines out on the soccer field, for not memorizing every inch of the building as a contingency.

His first idea, fun though it would be, was a little too ridiculous to pull off, even for lock-in night. He had this image of Diego catapulting some supplies up, or maybe using a giant slingshot. Was it open air? It must have been. Everyone called it the roof garden, and what garden would be closed to the world?

There was, ostensibly, a way for the booze and the earphones to land safely. He'd need only enough pillows and sweatshirts and blankets, of which there were plenty thanks to the movie marathon upstairs. But even if all the fragile goods made a safe landing, surely the DJ would object to arrival via catapult. That was, if Peejay (or rather, Diego) could even find the materials to build a blasted catapult in a matter of hours.

A not completely implausible solution might be a helicopter. Peejay was a scholarship student, and obviously had no access to one. He would bet, though, that among his classmates, someone was a phone call away from a chopper. After all, Hamish wouldn't have been able to pay off the bribes or hire the staff to dig his secret party room without the help of some CIS endowments.

Whether a chopper could land or deliver supplies or be paid for somehow were all bridges to cross at a later time.

"Does anyone here have a helicopter?"

The question took those in his vicinity by surprise. Not that they all thought it was ridiculous—they could immediately name someone they knew whose family or whose parents' corporation or place within this or that government gave them such access—but they were surprised Peejay's mind was elsewhere while they all discussed what should be done with Marisa.

He could have easily rolled his eyes and said, "It's for the party," and they'd all pull out their phones or make their way around the auditorium tapping on shoulders. That was exactly the problem, though, word spreading that the party was potentially in jeopardy. These blessed Sea Cucumbers needed to hang on to some hope, and being reminded that the party might be canceled, too, might be too much for their poor hearts to take.

Peejay hadn't believed Ms. Duli's threat of being sent home for a single second. He had watched the lunk/hunk swallow the keys, had seen the steadfast belief in Marisa's eyes. Barring some sudden onset of food poisoning, or forcing laxatives down the protestors' throats (which the board would never approve), they were going to be here for a few hours at least. So the party would happen. It had to. The longer they stayed here, the more people would need the party. If lock-in activities were suspended indefinitely, it was the only thing that could possibly salvage the evening. And Peejay's plan still allowed for that to happen, if the supplies were around. It'd be more difficult, sure, but that would make it all the more satisfying.

But if these heartbroken masses caught wind that the party had been stripped from them, they might lay down and die on the spot, or kill that poor girl at the entrance. Peejay would not be able to control them. He was about to say, "Forget it," when someone tapped him on the shoulder.

"My family does, why?" It was Robby Maldonado, whose dad owned a series of sugar refineries.

Peejay leaned in and whispered what he was thinking, taking careful note of Robby's expression to see if the plan was genius or crazy. But the damn, sweet heir to the sugar throne had a good poker face until the end, when he furrowed his brow. "Dude. Isn't the roof completely covered in glass?"

6

9:25PM

Word began to spread: the school had decided to break the chains.

Excitement built in the auditorium as teachers mobilized up and down the aisles, searching for tools. The students were going to be freed.

With each teacher who left the room, the murmurs grew, as did the anticipation, and the guessing. The proclamations got bolder. A blowtorch had been found. The doors had already opened. Marisa was under arrest.

They didn't care that there was no evidence of any of this, that the teachers kept coming back empty-handed, disappointment all over their faces. It was going to happen. Any minute now, they'd have lock-in night back.

Ms. Duli, though, expected her coworkers would all come back with nothing; she remembered Marisa's papers were well-researched, and had assumed the girl had done her homework for this caper, as well.

And indeed she had. Hours earlier, while everyone was distracted with the opening ceremony, Marisa and her cronies had collected every tool that could be used to force their release before her demands had been met.

The fact that they looked for tools inside showed they had no idea what they were up against. They thought Marisa had done this on a whim, was simply throwing a tantrum that could be resolved by picking her up off the floor or letting her tire herself out.

For weeks, Marisa had been sneaking into supply closets, snooping in teachers' desks, making an inventory of hammers and chisels, the blowtorches locked away in the kitchen for when the advanced cooking classes made crème brûlée, and yes, the bolt cutters. The chains and locks Marisa had bought were top of the line and advertised a resistance to the kinds of bolt cutters thieves (and probably janitors) might use. Still, Marisa had taken the extra steps of gathering all these tools while everyone was busy with lock-in night excitement and hiding them in a duffel bag, then tossing it in the bushes by the elementary school's yard.

The minutes passed.

The rumor deflated, less like a cartoon balloon farting its

way around the room, and more like an inflation vest used in scuba diving: the bubbles rose to the surface and disappeared, leaving the students alone to sink to the bottom of the murky ocean.

They checked the time against the schedule, and started, alas, to cross things off the list of possibilities. There went the food fight, which could no longer happen without changing the schedule of the cooking competition, which would alter the fort-building challenge, all to take place in the cafeteria, beyond the locked doors.

A few students, Jordi Marcos and Dov Nudel leading the pack, started discussing that the locked doors should not have any bearing on the course of the evening. If they couldn't leave in the morning, that was up to someone to figure out later, a solution to be found in the light of dawn. For now, shouldn't they be allowed to at least huddle on the roof and watch movies? Or learn how to spray paint, showcase their improv skills, have a highlighter war in the chem lab? Sure, the decathlon would be hard to complete without access to the track, the field and the pool, and it was an outrage not to have the water balloon fight. But did they have to lose it all? Couldn't they salvage some of the night?

The teachers wanted to say yes. God, that would have made it so much easier. Keep the students busy while the teachers tried to solve the problem. But the president of the school board, Nigel Appuhamy, had passed along his ruling: more kids might join the protest, they might (a good guess here) take it upon themselves to break down the doors or the chains, harming others in the process. The board couldn't stand for that. No, the students were to be kept in sight until further notice.

Meanwhile, the students stuck outside the building sprang to attention when a van pulled up. Even those who'd never encountered a locksmith before, had never heard the word in any of the languages they spoke, understood what it was there to do. They grabbed at each other's shoulders to get a better view, or to contain their excitement. They were getting back in.

Men piled out of the van, holding tools. There we go, the CISers thought, stepping closer to the doors, wanting to be there as soon as they opened. One of the food truck employees looked up from her phone, the only entertainment she'd had in the past hour or so. She wasn't sure why the business had slowed so much, but this offered a clue.

The food truck employee waited for the sound of the tools. Lindsay waited, too, hoping she could still play improv tonight, still hang out with Kenji. Her other team members waited. A hundred or so people waited. But instead of buzzing or hammering, instead of some special tool they had never heard of which made a sound they wouldn't be able to identify, they saw the crew inspecting the doors for about five minutes. Just looking at it. Muttering. There was one tease of a clang, the sound of a wrench accidentally banging against the door handle.

Then the tools hit the ground.

Two men lit cigarettes, a third pulled out a phone.

"It's not going to happen," the students outside heard him say. Lindsay heard him, and texted Kenji. Marisa heard it, too, smiling as she waited for Amira to hate her or forgive

ADI ALSAID

her. "This thing's reinforced to high heaven," the man said. "Only way it's coming off is from the inside."

Amira stood, reading Marisa's poster. There was a brief hubbub outside, but things quieted down. Her muscles were stiffening back up, the blood flow slowing. She could only stretch for so long, though, and Marisa's confidence in the lack of tools made her feel like there was no use in keeping herself limber all night. The decathlon wasn't going to happen anytime soon.

They were numbered like tasks to be completed. For months, a similar list lay crumpled in Amira's desk drawer, hiding among receipts for earphones and the boarding pass for the flight that brought her here. It was written in blue ink, with some unreliable pen that had failed to fully transcribe every letter. In other spots, the ink seemed permanently etched in, as if no matter what Amira accomplished at the decathlon, the goal to win would always stare back at her.

1. One-on-one basketball tournament
2. 400-meter dash
3. 400-meter freestyle night swim
4. Archery
.
.
.
10. Rock climbing

Amira's mother had seen the list one day, a month or so ago, while going through Amira's desk as if it belonged to her, too. "What is this?"

Amira had wanted to answer honestly, proudly. And if it

86

had been her dad, her sisters, Omar Ng, anyone else, maybe she would have. Maybe it would have made her blur the lines between her school self and her home self. But because it was her mother, and because her mother believed certain things about what girls could or could not do, Amira bit her tongue, hating herself for saying, "Nothing." At least she could train on her own time, compete without her mom knowing.

Although now none of that made a difference. All that time training for what? One dunk? She kept her eyes on the list, not wanting to look at Marisa for fear of a sudden surge of anger.

1. Single-use plastic ban on CIS grounds.
2. Every student must sign a petition asking for the ban of single-use plastic throughout the city.
3. School motto will be changed to reflect new envi-ronmentally driven curriculum.
4. Curriculum from primary school through high school will include environmental sciences.

.

.

.

30. CIS bus routes will operate only with electric buses.

Amira pictured Marisa at work on this poster, at home, keeping it secret from her parents, from her brother. Though in the end, Amira guessed, Marisa wouldn't be able to hide it. It was already too late for that. Whatever her parents would say or do, Marisa had moved forward, willing to face the con-sequences.

"Will your parents be angry at you for this?" Amira asked,

imagining what would come down on her head if she'd fallen into a path of protest instead of athletics.

"I don't know, probably. Don't think they'll be surprised, though. They know how much the reefs matter to me."

Marisa said this so casually, as if it didn't take a massive act of bravery to face the consequences of an action this public. All year, Amira had been in quiet awe of Marisa. Of the way she allowed herself to be as quiet or loud as she wanted to be. Of the rainbow flag sticker on her laptop. Of the way that, in class discussions, she could recognize logical fallacies, calling out people who couldn't source their knowledge. She had a biting sense of humor, and the sort of fierceness in her eyes Amira could only muster in her muscles.

Then there were Marisa's eyes themselves. How they filled Amira with glee, to see them first thing when she walked into that classroom. How they made Amira certain, absolutely certain, that eventually the gap between who she allowed herself to be in front of her family and the other version of herself would widen even further. Or cause the gap to come crashing down. She had made her peace with all the facets of herself, though there had been a couple of hard years before she could. She wasn't sure if her mom would ever make peace with it, though, and even that felt like an understatement. Her mother might hate the very idea of who Amira was at CIS— who she *really* was. The thought wrenched Amira's insides.

She suddenly realized she'd been staring at Marisa, and looked instead at her lap.

"Why do the reefs matter so much to you?" Amira asked.

"Aside from the fact that if the reefs die, people die?"

"Sure. Aside from that."

Marisa sighed. She gave the speech so often, delineated all

the ways the reefs were dying and the impacts it would have on the world. But Amira didn't seem to need that kind of convincing. "Have you ever gone snorkeling? Or diving?"

Amira nodded. She had a vague memory of being eight or so, making a game out of going deep beneath the surface, chasing tiny turquoise fish for as long as she could. Her mother had laughed at first, taking her in her arms once Amira was back on sand, saying what a happy child Amira was. Then Amira kept going longer and longer, stretching her lungs' abilities with each dive, feeling her muscles burn with lack of oxygen and trying to push them for another ten seconds, another twenty. Her mom had not kept laughing. When Amira returned to shore, her mother had yanked her down by the arm onto the sand and said, "That was too dangerous for a girl. Stay here with me."

Amira didn't have a clear memory of the snorkeling itself, or of where they were. It must have been that holiday in Langkawi, which was around the time Amira's mom had stopped treating her like a child and started treating her like a girl.

"Well, then," Marisa went on. "What you saw was probably not a fully living reef. It was choked, choking. Imagine knowing that when you were down there. Imagine loving the reefs like nothing else, your happiest moments are when you're visiting them, but then you know they're choking." She paused, not feeling like she was making her point. "It's like visiting a grandparent on their deathbed," she said. "And you know it doesn't have to be their deathbed, all they need is a little medicine. But no one's bringing it to them."

Amira didn't feel the need to respond. She finished reading the list of demands, suddenly knowing the decathlon was never going to happen. She waited for the rage to come, waited to feel the injustice of her dream getting ripped away by

Marisa. All she felt, though, was the rage against her mother, who would've been glad Amira was denied the chance to compete. Then there was the guilt at the rage, guilt at the things she kept hidden from her mother, who was not abusive or cruel but simply held different beliefs.

Like always, the rage-guilt was followed by the urge to run. She turned to say something to Marisa, but just then a teacher approached them. His hands were in his pockets and he was walking calmly, as if they were in class and he was just coming around to see if they needed any help with their assignments.

"I've been sent to, um, negotiate." He made a face like he didn't know why everyone was taking everything so seriously. "Is this a good time?" He eyed both of them as if both should answer.

Amira gestured vaguely over her shoulder. "I'm gonna go."

Marisa watched her go before turning to Mr. Gigs. "I don't understand, what is there to negotiate?" She motioned with her head toward the poster behind her. "I get those things or no one leaves."

"Sure," Mr. Gigs said. "I get that. But I don't think they want to give you all of it."

"Why not?"

He pulled his hands out of his pockets and put them up, hands out. "Whoa, whoa, whoa, I haven't been authorized to speak on their behalf. I'm just the messenger." He smiled, eyeing the poster. "But there is kind of a lot on that list. Some of these items could take time." He pointed. "Like, number twenty-two? 'Ensure that all school suppliers comply with—'"

Marisa cut him off. "'With the highest industry standards for waste disposal.' I don't think that's too much to ask for."

"Well, sure, I agree," Mr. Gigs said, not sure if he was breaking some sort of negotiator/messenger rule by agreeing with the hostage-taker. Probably. "But that kind of thing takes time. There's contracts in place, probably. Lawyers will have to look at those if they have to get broken, someone's going to have to do research to find suppliers who meet those standards. That all takes time."

"I didn't set a timeline for them."

Mr. Gigs chuckled. "Fair enough. But if you scratch that one or, I don't know, tell them they have to promise to do it within a certain time frame, it makes it more likely that they'll say yes to the others soon."

Marisa sighed. She'd expected this approach from the school board, and knew maybe as time went on the offer would sound more tempting. That it was a reasonable thing for them to request. But she was prepared to hold out for weeks if she needed to, and she was almost disappointed they had tried this tactic this early. She'd *just* snapped the padlocks shut.

She reached into her duffel bag to pull out a book. "These aren't up for discussion and I'm in no rush," she said. "If the board is feeling pressured to get these done quickly for some reason, that's on them, not me." Marisa opened the book to her bookmark—a postcard from Palawan in the Philippines, a reminder of bleached coral—and looked down at the pages, signaling to Mr. Gigs the way a number of teachers had signaled to her throughout her academic career that the conversation was over.

From where he was sitting, Kenji could just barely see the green room through the wings of the stage. It was busy with teachers and definitely not with improv.

Lindsay was still outside. In the group chat some of the other players on the team announced they had called their parents for a ride. Scene! Kenji texted, wanting to smile at his joke but feeling its rough landing. No one responded, and Lindsay privately messaged him, I thought it was funny, though she didn't accompany the text with an emoji or gif or Haha, and Kenji could picture her out there staring unsmiling in the dark.

It was amazing and terrifying just how easily his thoughts could make him feel like he was at home again. Home, for Kenji, wasn't a warm, welcoming place you stepped back into comfortably after a long hard day in the outside world. Home was a dreaded place he returned to after getting his fill of joy at CIS. At home, his father patrolled the hallways for joy, ready to stamp it down. Joy in and of itself did not lead to success, and therefore it was pointless, it was a cancer that stifled more productive emotions. The outside world had improv, it had jokes, it had people who said "yes." It had Lindsay. Home was the place where "no" reigned supreme.

What are you doing out there? he texted Lindsay, wanting to get away from his thoughts.

Waiting. What else could I be doing?

Fashioning a bouncy house out of gym mats.

Don't be ridiculous, all bouncy houses have to be approved by the school board, and I hear they're busy.

Celeste watched Kenji texting, and pulled out her own phone, too. That seemed to be the socially appropriate thing to do, although sitting there in the auditorium, Celeste couldn't think of a single person to text except her mom. She could text her friend Jamie back home, but ever since the move, their communication habits had fallen by the wayside, and it could be hours before she heard a response.

Her family, at least, still felt like home.

Hey, Ma.

How's it going, hun? Having fun?

What are you doing in there? Lindsay texted.

Shouting at people, begging them for a suggestion. I miss improv.

Any luck?

Kenji looked up from his phone. He wondered if it was too soon to ask Celeste to play, if he would scare her off. Not just from improv, but from his company. Kenji typed out a few jokes as a response before settling on, I might have a lead. You know Celeste?

New girl? American?

Yup.

Cool. Bet she'd be fun. She's quiet, and the quiet ones are always quippy.

Celeste didn't know how to respond to her mom. She could sense her mom prying about friends. It made her feel cared for, but also sad, to picture her parents cuddled on the couch, talking about how worried they were about her social life, whether they'd made the right choice to come here with Celeste struggling so much. They'd had enough of the US, and so it was right to leave, but had it been right to come here?

Yeah, I guess, she wrote. She didn't think to tell her about the protest, figuring it would be over eventually, or that she could tell her in the morning.

Well, we're having a blast over here. Your dad's been asleep since 8 and I'm sitting on the couch not knowing what the hell to watch on TV.

You guys are wild.

Shush. Go be wild for us.

The movie was over and Eli brushed away some of the happy tears that always came when he watched *About Time*. The credits rolled. Eli marveled at all the names it took to put a movie together, wondered if a movie were filmed at CIS, would it take everyone in the building to make it? More, less? He listened to the credit songs play out, to the poignant silence that followed. It felt like the movie was sinking deeper into his psyche, into his bones.

After a moment, he heard the sounds of the city, still going on with its usual business, not privy to the way things here had ground to a halt. There was a bus stand outside of the school walls, and Eli could hear one of the men who always shouted the bus's destination at passersby, as if hoping to convince them to change their plans and climb aboard.

The screen, projected from some absent teacher's laptop, went back to the streaming service's main menu, with recommendations for what to watch next. His stomach gurgled. Either he'd eaten too much popcorn, or the keys had not sat well with his system. He wished someone would come back up and select another movie.

The auditorium had fallen quietly into jittery legs and whispers. Another rumor had spread, this one much more credible, because it came from the students who were on the outside. The whispering worked its way from the front row toward the back of the room like so: a person who had just learned the information would announce the plan to a nearby friend, and that friend looked around her vicinity to find someone else to pass the knowledge on to. Finding none, she looked for someone she knew from class—perhaps that alluring redhead who'd one day lent a pencil?—and if no close acquaintance was visible within a two-row radius or so, she'd simply wait for the first person who made eye contact with her. She'd lean toward the eye-contact holder, beckoning them to do the same. Then, not caring that they'd never exchanged a word before, not caring that they were several seats apart, leaning across other strangers, she'd announce the information she had gleaned. The listener would then look around his vicinity for a friend, as would those who had been leaned over and heard the information, and in this way the news spread: the school had tried to break down the doors, but even the experts were at a loss. A locksmith van had arrived on campus, and after a few minutes of running around to all the exits, it had simply left again.

Here or there, someone had fallen asleep, and they whimpered like puppies with nightmares. Some people just stared off in the distance, as if recovering from some trauma, reliving some horror in their own minds, or fighting internally to stay away from its visions. Perhaps they were just bored.

Some, like Jordi Marcos, stewed in their anger. He knew they should have broken the chains right away. The fact that the tools were gone from the building as soon as the night began was lost on Jordi, and he thought that, somehow, if they'd acted when he said they should, something could have been done.

While his anger had initially been pointed at the administration, and at Peejay Singh, now it redirected itself toward Marisa Cuevas. How dare she throw this tantrum in his face and on his time. What gave her the right to step into lock-in night and steal the joy from all these people? Jordi, his brief glimmer of hope in taking the doors now cast aside, was unable to keep from focusing on the unfairness of it all. He crossed his arms and grunted as he shook his head. For now, he didn't know what to do with his anger, how to have it come down on Marisa's head.

While Jordi wasn't the only one stewing, there were a few students who'd decided the best use of their time (other than lock-in activities, of course) was, aptly, to learn. They were in school, after all.

Omar Ng was one of them.

So the doors wouldn't open and the decathlon was doomed,

what with many of the events scheduled for the outdoors. However, Omar's first reaction wasn't disappointment. Rather, as he absorbed the information and looked across the room at where Peejay sat ensconced in a beam of light from an unreasonably bright bulb overhead, Omar felt a tug of excitement in his belly (and perhaps, if he were being honest, a little lower than that). This night no longer had a surefire end time, and that meant the hours to come might be spent in Peejay's company. Or, at least, with Peejay in proximity. The decathlon's busy schedule now loosened, and rather than turn to the bleachers to see if Peejay was nearby, now Omar might spend the whole night knowing exactly where he was. Dear God, he might sleep in the same room as Peejay would. Lock-in night was still sublime.

Occasionally glancing over the edge of his phone screen at Peejay, Omar wished he knew how to calm the storm of emotions crossing Peejay's face, wished he knew how to approach Peejay at all.

Since he didn't know and couldn't fathom how he would learn such a thing, he instead was reading about coral reefs. Not necessarily because of Marisa, but because his sister had cared enough to tie herself (pun intended) to Marisa's cause. He hadn't had a chance to talk to Joy in the gym, and for the time being she wasn't answering Omar's text messages.

It'd surprised him to see her there in the midst of all the fracas. Omar and Joy had been friends when they were little, as can be expected for siblings only two years apart. Somehow, though, they had hung on to their friendship through the tumult of adolescence. Omar rejected his friends' temptations to pick on his younger sister; Joy resisted the urge to isolate herself and think no one understood her. Omar understood her. He always had, and pubescence wouldn't change that.

This, though, Omar did not understand. So he went to the internet to try.

Maya Klutzheisen and Michael Obonte, too, were learning about the reefs. They were sitting side by side, drawn to each other and to the oceans by their newfound love of Marisa. Whenever one of them found some interesting article or tidbit—coral reefs grew up to four inches a year, twenty-five percent of the world's reefs were dead, certain sunscreen harmed reefs and shouldn't be worn while snorkeling—they would tilt their phones to show each other, making soft disapproving noises, which they thought Marisa would approve of.

Near the front of the stage, Zaira Jacobson typed on her laptop. She was doing some cursory research on ocean pollution as well, but she had dozens of other tabs open, too, each one representing a stray thought, some information she needed corroborated, or a possible detour for her article.

Zaira was assigned to cover lock-in night for the school newspaper, and had taken plenty of notes when the evening was still going well. Though she was an expert at maintaining her objectivity in almost all the stories she covered, Zaira was just as susceptible to getting swept up in lock-in night's charms. She'd written over two thousand words waxing poetic on the wonders of the night, not to mention all the audio interviews she'd conducted already—at least twenty. Each year, the story wrote itself, a fluff piece that was less journalism and more one writer's chance to flex their hyperbole muscles.

But Zaira no longer had a fluff piece on her hands. She knew it as soon as she'd seen Marisa swallow those buttery keys. In the auditorium, Zaira had switched off that CIS part of her that demanded deference of lock-in night, and she handed the keys over to her journalistic tendencies. She'd already found the names and phone numbers of all the board members and reached out for comments both via phone and email.

Soon, she'd find some excuse to leave the auditorium and interview Marisa. For now, she learned about the oceans, the reefs, the planet's warming, CIS's current environmental policies, its past controversies. Marisa would soon tell her all her reasons, but as a journalist, Zaira liked to find as many facts as she could on her own. There was a joy to research few of her peers seemed to appreciate. What a thrill, to learn about the world and piece together its facts to create a story.

She learned as much as she could, thankful she had a way to distract herself from the hurt of the canceled night.

Malik Harris closed the book he was reading, propping it open on his leg with the spine out. He looked around the green room at all the teachers gathered, obviously trying to avoid him. Many were on their phones, more teachers staring at screens than Malik had ever seen at once. Their eyes were glazed over with scrolling. Over in the corner, three teachers were starting to play a poker game. He kind of wished he could join them, but didn't know how to ask, or if it'd be weird. The chains were really starting to dig into his ribs and armpits, and he shifted this way and that for temporary comfort. Several heads turned his way. He couldn't tell if they were reproachful, accusatory or what. Most of them looked kind of bored. Malik could relate.

He'd volunteered himself to be one of Marisa's chainees, and part of him had really been looking forward to the night itself, to killing time for a cause. Yes, he'd attended the meeting advertised on the little slip of paper Marisa had tacked onto the message board outside of the ecology club because he wanted to save the world. But he'd felt uniquely qualified to sit in one spot for an indeterminate amount of time.

Malik loved airport layovers, waits for trains and the morning bus ride to school for the opportunity they provided to consume media guilt-free. Books, podcasts, music, movies. He loved to sit still and not be expected to do anything other than wait. Right now, though, he couldn't focus on anything.

After Peejay had yelled at Malik and the assembly had been called, he'd listened to ten minutes or so of a podcast before the teachers showed up and stole his attention. He'd even been tempted to answer his phone when his parents called, even though Marisa had predicted that was one of the first things the board would attempt to do: get their parents to talk them out of it. Malik wished he were in the gym, or on the roof with no one around. He wished the teachers would interact with him in some way. He wished enough people had volunteered so two of them could be at each door.

Joy wished she could pee. She knew she *could* pee, but she just couldn't bring herself to use the bucket, even though it was the one good thing about the empty gym. Joy was creeped out by the silence, creeped out being here on her own. It made her feel disloyal to the cause, disloyal to Marisa, but she was regretting signing up. She was regretting not peeing when she had the chance.

Meanwhile, Omar's texts stared out at her from her phone's lock screen, adding shame to the regret pressing in on her bladder. When she picked up her phone, it was to text Lolo.

Have you peed yet?

Ha. Yes.

How? I'm nervous.

Why? Are people around?

They could be.

Girl. Don't give yourself a UTI. Pee in the bucket.

Remind me why we're doing this again?

Because Marisa is going to save the world.

Joy looked at the text, considering whether she agreed. After a few seconds, she thought: Why with buckets, though?

The students at CIS kept expecting something to happen that would change things. Surely this situation could still be salvaged. It wasn't supposed to happen like this, so it wouldn't.

Lock-in activities, at the board's insistence, were still suspended, since the teacher chaperones were all busy researching how to meet Marisa's demands.

The clock gave way from nine to ten and the doors remained chained shut.

7
10:01PM

Jordi Marcos had had it.

He wasn't going to wait for something to happen. Peejay, scammer in chief, was clearly okay sitting back and not doing anything. Jordi was not. He leaned over to his friend Dov, and to a handful of others sitting in the vicinity. "Follow me," he said, trying to make it sound the way Peejay would.

There wasn't very much space between rows, so the seven of them made quite a racket as they made their way to the center aisle. Jordi stumbled a few times over people's legs but refused to say, "Excuse me," though some of his cronies didn't have it in them to ignore social niceties. Ms. Florgen, sitting at center stage, about to nod off, snapped to attention at the apologetic exodus.

"Hey," she shouted.

But Jordi had cleared the row of classmates' legs, and anger had made him move quicker than he ever had before. He was nearly at the exit, and the teacher stationed there, Mr. Jankowski, was not one to stand in front of an exit. It was, in fact, one of his pet peeves. So he stepped aside, sentry duties be damned, and Jordi and his followers were out.

Once they were gone, there was nothing holding anyone back anymore. More people stood. They stormed the aisle, a building hubbub as everyone figured out how easy it was to escape. Ms. Florgen and Mr. Jankowski shouted for help, but it was too late. The students were free.

Amira had found her way back to the gymnasium and run a few sprints up and down the bleachers. Then she'd spotted the basketballs that had been used in the tournament on a rack pushed up against the wall, and she'd been shooting around since.

Amira was used to keeping her own company. Training led to a lonely life, and though Amira was friendly with most people at school, and would even call some of the teammates on her various teams friends, she wouldn't often go more than a few hours in people's company. It wasn't that she had an introvert's urge to recharge her batteries on her own, necessarily, nor that she had agoraphobia that built up over the course of a day. It was merely that there was always another bit of training to complete. She always felt compelled to step away and improve herself. Since she was used to spending time alone, after a while in other people's presence it felt right to revert to that standard. Which wasn't to say that was her ideal situation, per se.

She found herself thinking of people often, almost longing for them. Sometimes while running around her neighborhood, or along the pathways in the city's large central park, she'd have these little daydreams that someone was running with her, and in between breaths they'd talk. Freely, about the two worlds Amira inhabited, and how she might get them to meet without a catastrophic result. The other person, in these fantasies, sometimes listened with a sympathetic ear but never seemed able to offer the advice she needed to figure out how to make it happen.

Other times, the fantasy could turn romantic.

It wasn't common for her. Even if her mom's voice wasn't constantly in her mind dissuading her from even thinking about it (a girl could not), Amira had no time to worry about someone else's body. She was too focused on taking control of her own.

Still, she was human, and despite the guilt that came with it, sometimes it was where her mind went. Sure, she wasn't allowed to date, much less someone outside her religion, and definitely (she guessed) not of her gender. But that's exactly what Amira was doing at the moment, surprised that the fantasy was so vivid now of all times. Yes, yes, her eyes and how they made Amira feel whenever she walked into class in the mornings. Yes, there was Marisa's ability to speak her mind, and there was the way she did it with a smile. But before, her guilt at defying her upbringing and her family would muddle the fantasy before it could fully play out. Her mother's voice would echo in her head, interrupting Amira's thoughts, stopping the imagined joy in its tracks before she could begin worrying about the consequences she might endure if that joy ever left the realm of the imaginary.

So why was that defense mechanism failing her now?

This was how it went: Amira dribbled the ball twice (thunk thunk), then rested it against her right hip. Two deep breaths, then another quick one before shooting. The whole while, her mind was taking laps around a mall with Marisa.

Both were dressed up in a similar manner, as if they wanted to impress the other without making the intention perfectly clear. Amira couldn't fathom what people talked about on dates, so she tuned out that part and instead focused on the visuals.

If you make fifteen in a row, she'll hold your hand (thunk thunk), Amira thought to herself, goose bumps shooting down her arms as soon as the fifteenth shot swished through. They walked through the mall like that, taking laps hand in hand, smiling at each other, making each other laugh. At thirty, she'll sit in a dark movie theater with you and lean in and kiss you (thunk thunk). A ball clanked off the rim, and Amira started the date all over again.

Amira could still feel the tingle on her arms as she walked over to the water fountain near the bathroom, which put her in view of the girl chained to the exit.

She went over to Joy, slightly off-put by the lingering desire and wanting to put it out of her mind. The gym was quiet now that her dribbling had ceased, and it felt like it could have been any other evening of training.

"You're Omar's sister, right?"

Joy nodded. To Amira it seemed clear the girl was in deep discomfort, or pain, even. "Guessing these chains aren't comfortable."

Joy breathed through her pursed lips, almost sibilant. "They're not." Her lips were dry and starting to crack. The whole night, she hadn't had a sip of water, afraid a single drop would be the one that caused her to burst. Eventually it would be the bucket or her leggings, Joy knew. But even the thought of lying there in urine-soaked leggings for who knows how long didn't help her.

"Do you need anything? You don't look like you're doing well." Amira dribbled the ball, just once, tucking it right off the bounce against her hip. The reverberations on the wooden floor rippled out across the court, echoing in the empty gym like the lonely drips of water filtering through stalactites in a cave, plinking down into puddles hidden in the dark. It was one of Amira's favorite sounds.

The feeling, however, was not Joy's favorite. She felt the ripples of energy on the ground go through her legs, a soft but unbearable knock on her lower abdomen. She breathed again, her exhalation so shaky she knew tears were coming the moment she spoke again. Maybe they would help her get rid of the liquid in her bladder, she thought, knowing it was ridiculous but hoping all the same.

What a stupid night it had been so far. She hadn't felt like a rebel or a badass, hadn't felt like she was helping the world in any way. She hadn't had an ounce of fun except for her texts with Lolo. It'd been lonely and painful, and she hadn't even spoken with Omar the whole night. So she looked up at Amira and nodded.

★ ★ ★

Amira knew what her mother would say to this. Not lady-like, not becoming for a girl. It was maddening how persistently her mom's voice rang out in her head, even though every part of Amira disagreed. She climbed the bleachers and reached for the large plastic banner commemorating the CIS girls' volleyball team for a championship in a tournament of other international schools in the region a few years back. A girl would not damage property, a girl would not chain herself to a door, a girl would not fantasize about a girl who chained herself to doors. A girl would not pee in public, even with the public's absence. It all made Amira want to dunk again, want to do every single thing her mother had told her she could not do.

She tugged at the banner until the strings holding it in place snapped. Then she found a couple of orange cones beneath the bleachers and propped them up around Joy, weaving the banner through the cones so it formed a protective wall around her.

Tears welled in Joy's eyes again when she thanked Amira, and it almost felt like the tears did bring relief, however slight. Amira nodded, then dribbled away, shrouding Joy with noise for complete privacy. It was right after Joy had popped the lid off the bucket and began to feel exquisite relief when the gym suddenly filled with more noise.

Now that they'd declared their freedom, the students ran through the halls like criminals on the loose, like champagne bubbles popped free from their bottle.

Granted, official activities were still suspended, and the

teachers were running around to make sure no real shenanigans broke out, but the students didn't care. They had lock-in night again. At least a version of it.

Jordi Marcos ran straight to the spray paint tutorial. If Ms. Tekin was too busy or concerned with protestors to teach them how to spray paint, they still could go and spray paint poorly, tagging the canvas that'd been hung up around her classroom. Their names were sloppy, the paint dripping down in a way she would have taught them to avoid. They got paint all over their fingers, splattering, not creating anything remotely cool. But why not just that, their names sprayed haphazardly on canvas, proof the night, to an extent, had happened. Proof he had not let those damn protestors have their way and ruin his evening.

Others went into the library, because they'd been promised a game of charades via Skype with that famous actor who was someone's uncle. While they'd been sitting in the auditorium, they pictured him in a mansion in Los Angeles, waiting for their call, and their hearts broke at the thought that they had left him waiting. Now they found the girl who was his niece, and though she wanted to be elsewhere, six of them gathered around her, like beasts they usually were not. A teacher tried to intercede, but when she went to get help to break up the altercation, the charade hopefuls marched the girl into the library and made her call her uncle. The uncle, though, had better things to do than wait around for a Skype call that hadn't arrived on time. He didn't answer.

They threw her phone at the wall. They deserved the charades they'd been promised.

★ ★ ★

Some students didn't know what to do with this stolen freedom. They grumbled as they filed out of the auditorium without their friends, most of whom were still outside. All they had wanted to do was participate in the student cooking competition. The school had brought in various local chefs as judges, but would those judges still be patiently waiting in the cafeteria beyond the locked doors, recently cleaned from the food fight, when all this was over? (No, they would not. The judges were gone already, having slunk away as soon as Master Declan called to say there had been a development.)

Some wandered in and out of classrooms set up for lock-in night, waiting for an activity. The teachers leading them, though, were meeting in the green room trying to figure out how best to proceed. Or they were locked outside the building, yawning and wondering when they'd get to go home.

Others didn't take the disruption well. They took to the windows, struggling to find a place that could be opened. They all knew it was pointless, but still, it was hard not to try. Some grabbed chairs, then looked over their shoulders to see if an adult would stop them. When none came by wagging fingers, when their friends egged them on, it felt so obvious this was what they had to do. If there was any way in or out of the building, lock-in night would be back in full. The irony wasn't lost on them. Shmuli Rogers, the largest of Jordi Marcos's friends, ended up tossing the first chair. It bounced back uselessly, the glass giving a comical twang as it laughed off Shmuli's attempt, the chair clattering back at him and forcing him to jump away.

Many students, not quite up for causing mayhem, preferring to wait for permission, settled into their usual nooks and crannies around the school. Muscle memory led them toward their daily meet-up areas in front of so-and-so's locker, or their lunch spots up on the roof garden.

The bookworms followed the library's magnetic pull, where they holed up on various beanbags or chairs for the remainder of the night, occasionally stepping out to stretch their legs and take stock of the situation. A few students who'd been hurt in the fray of their peers' rush out the auditorium went to Nurse Hae, though they knew she'd simply offer a cup of tea and send them on their way.

The basketball team went to the gymnasium, as did those hopeful Amira admirers who still clutched their posters in their hands and wanted to see her take Omar down. (This was the crowd who walked in on Joy midstream, and though embarrassment flushed her face red, no one noticed what she was doing, thanks to Amira's improvised barrier.)

Pok Tran, a sophomore, was close to having a nervous breakdown, and so he found a comfortable nook in the corner of Mr. Sanchez's closet and curled up in the dark, away from the noise and the mayhem.

For some, it was as if nothing had changed, as if the disruption was just a brief and inconvenient pause, nothing more. The Spice Scream Social resumed and, emboldened by the circumstances the way a near-death experience might make people live more freely, seven different students tasted the Carolina Reaper hot sauce. The organizers of the Lock-In Night Escape Room, who'd been giddy the whole night, now rushed around the school, searching for clues on how to get out, sure that Marisa and her cronies were just fellow escape-heads, that this was a mystery they alone could solve.

The couples who'd resisted touch in the auditorium while under teacher surveillance escaped to the roof garden, slinking into the covers of night and blankets to press close together and kiss and feel what was left of lock-in night's effects on their affections. They'd never found each other so beautiful before, never enjoyed each other's conversation or presence quite so much. Eli munched on the last of his popcorn silently, trying not to disrupt with his chewing or the creaking of his chains.

Maizey Krokić and Anwar Gomez exchanged "I love yous" for the first time, shortly after their release from the auditorium, and they spent the next few hours up on the roof making out and trying the words out on each other, over and over again, marveling at how true it felt to say them, how much they believed them.

There seemed, for a moment, for some, to be a little bit of the lock-in night magic left in the air.

So the party was on. Peejay had never doubted it for a moment. There was still the issue of the supplies, and the DJ, and the teachers now running around everywhere trying to put out fires. Some literal ones, even (the highlighter war had escalated quickly and significantly). How, exactly, the administrators would miss a party right under their noses in this state was a bridge to cross later.

As his peers rushed to feel like the night was not lost, Peejay decided to visit Marisa's cronies and check the strength of their blockade. He wasn't the first person to think of this. On the roof, Peejay heard that poor Eli child swear to the soccer team he had swallowed the keys. Not believing him, they rummaged through his pockets, upturned the bag he'd brought with him, checked under his tongue.

In the green room, Malik was being interrogated by teachers' questions in a similar albeit less invasive way, and he was glancing at the novel by his side so longingly that Peejay had the urge to shoo the teachers away and throw a bedspread over Malik's hulking form to let him read in peace. Omar Ng's sister in the gym was so nervous looking everyone had mostly left her alone by the time Peejay arrived. He felt like the poor child might explode from nerves when he finally examined the door she was obstructing. Without tools, there was no breaking the door itself. The chains, too, were heavy and industrial looking, and even with the right tools, it'd be hard to make them come off without hurting Joy.

That left the basement.

Lolo Dufry perked up at the sound of another visitor. She was sore in so many places already, and though it was an honor to fight for the reefs alongside Marisa, she was bored out of her damn mind and wished they'd had time to set up a couch or something. Her text conversations with Joy had devolved into strings of nonsense emojis. When Lolo saw it was Peejay in the basement, a bittersweet feeling ran through her.

She was so happy to see him—she was not just immune to his charms, but considered him a close friend, had even come by the hospital a few days ago to pay her respects—but it pained her to think she'd been down there all alone while everyone else got to spend their time in Peejay's company. When their eyes met, Peejay smiled, his face lighting up. "I should have known you were part of these shenanigans," he said, one cheeky eyebrow raised.

Lolo gave a faux-nonchalant shrug. Then she bit her lip, dropped the facade. "Sorry about your party. I really am."

Wonderful as he was, Lolo had seen Peejay's mood turn in an instant, and she braced herself for his expression to turn dark. Malik had told them in their group chat about the tirade, though Lolo could tell he'd tried to sugarcoat it.

"What do you have to be sorry about?" Peejay said, walking over to some boxes stacked up by the shelves Mr. Gigs had rummaged through while looking for tools. Had they been there before? Lolo had barely noticed them, couldn't remember if they'd been there when she and Marisa had snuck in the day before, rehearsing. Peejay grabbed the top box and lowered it to the floor, tearing open the tape on the top flaps.

He squatted on his haunches as he sorted through the cellophane-wrapped earphones Diego had managed to bring in before the literal lock-in began. Two boxes had made it in, which was less than half of what they needed for a truly inclusive party the way Peejay had dreamed. But so many students had been locked outside the doors, he now realized, they might have enough to carry on. With the raised alertness around the school, handing them out would have to be a little more surreptitious than originally planned (truth be told, that part of the scheme had always felt lazy to Peejay, just throwing the earphones over the second-floor railing and assuming the teachers would simply not understand what they were for), but that would come to him.

"There's no chance I could convince you to open up this door for me, is there?" Peejay asked, running his hands through the earphones, listening to the satisfying crinkle of cellophane. "Or did you swallow the keys, too?"

There was a long pause, which Peejay hoped was Lolo weighing her loyalties to him and Marisa. Perhaps he had a chance here, to persuade her to just open up for a little bit, let him sneak out and come back in with the DJ equipment, the booze, the DJ himself. He thought for a moment he could go see Hamish, too, just make sure he hadn't woken up. But no, not before the party. Best to see him with good news to tell.

He would promise Lolo not to flee, or tell anyone how he'd procured all the supplies. Then she said his name, in that way someone does when they're trying not to disappoint you, all drawn out and tender, like hearing your own name could hurt. "Peejay..."

"Yeah, I thought so." He looked up at Lolo and smiled. A beat passed, and Peejay tried to push himself to get a move on, to return to the world above and figure out a way to make this thing happen.

"Any news on your brother?" Lolo asked.

Peejay lifted the boxes of earphones back to where they were, doing his best to tuck the flaps back into each other. The question was trying to burrow itself into his gut, make its presence felt. Peejay didn't have time for that, though. Hamish would want him to throw the party, anyway. He gave an almost imperceptible head shake, which, in the dark, Lolo could have easily missed. "Do me a favor, and keep those safe until I come back to get them," he said, then he went back upstairs.

★ ★ ★

Kenji and Celeste were two of the last students to leave the auditorium. They paused by the door, watching their schoolmates wander off as if there was still some schedule to adhere to. How did they know where to go? Kenji wondered.

Celeste stood quietly by him. He glanced over, not wanting her to say goodbye but wondering how soon it'd be until she, too, heeded some unknown call and left him alone. Before she, too, said no.

Celeste, though, didn't want to say bye. Of course she didn't. Goodbyes were so much harder than hellos, because they stole away the chance of anything else. Goodbyes in Illinois were how she'd gotten here in the first place, desperate for attention, desperate for a place to feel at home.

"So," Kenji said. "What should we do next?"

The question hung between them for a moment. Kenji had no idea what the options were. Without improv, without Lindsay, he was lost. Celeste was giddy at the "we," but terrified whatever she might suggest would reveal her great singlehood, reveal whatever it was that had kept others at CIS away from her. So neither said anything for a while, until Jordi Marcos started running down the hall in their direction, two spray paint cans in hand, spraying into the air behind him.

There were a handful of others trailing him, making whooping noises and occasionally coughing if they happened to inhale some of Jordi's colorful exhaust. Celeste and Kenji pressed themselves against the wall and covered their mouths.

Then it was as if the whole school was again just waiting for Jordi to lead the way in mayhem, and other sounds of chaos erupted. Glass broke, furniture squeaked against linoleum as a group pushed Ms. Duli's desk across her room. Someone started playing punk music on a portable speaker, perhaps for the sole reason that it was a fitting soundtrack.

Celeste and Kenji widened their eyes at each other and wordlessly walked the hall in unison, scoping out what their classmates were doing. Not too far up ahead Matias Merkling was standing at the railing, looking down and shouting directions. Celeste and Kenji paused and saw some kids making a pile of backpacks and sweatshirts on the floor below.

"That's a terrible idea," Celeste said, more to Kenji than to Matias.

But Matias gave her a look, as if just now considering the possibility that something could go wrong. He looked back down and, suddenly dubious, called to his friends to find a mattress.

"I think you may have just saved his life."

"I know I'm new here, but is all this normal?" Celeste said.

"I mean, I haven't heard about stuff like *this* happening. I know it's supposed to be unpredictable and a little kooky, but no one's ever protested on lock-in night before, from what I know. So I think we're in unexplored territory."

They turned the corner to go down the stairs, and saw two boys sitting at the landing weeping into each other's shoulders.

"That's Cory and Shem," Kenji whispered. "They do cry pretty often, though I've never seen them do it on the stairs, so that's inconclusive vis-à-vis all this being normal." They kept walking, almost tiptoeing to give the boys space.

When they reached the bottom of the stairs, they found about a dozen students hauling a mountain of chairs out of classrooms. A crowd had gathered to watch. This time Kenji tapped someone on the shoulder. "What's happening?" he asked.

The girl who responded was Ceci Torres, who Kenji'd had a brief crush on at the start of the year until he realized she was not an adventurous eater. She seemed to have a pretty fresh nose-piercing, although Kenji couldn't remember her having one before, or if there'd been any piercing booth set up before Marisa's lock-in took effect. "Building a bonfire!" she shouted, a little too excitedly for comfort.

"Yeah, I don't think this is normal," Kenji said to Celeste, backing away from Ceci with a tight-lipped smile.

"What do we do? Should we, like, tell someone?"

At that moment, a kid near the mountain of chairs started shouting out for matches, right as Ms. Florgen, the gym teacher, came bounding down the stairs. It looked like she'd been running around for some time now, sweat gathering at her hairline and sticking to her chest. The wild look in her eyes told Kenji that, though she couldn't believe what she was seeing, this was only the latest in a long line of unbelievable sights the poor woman had been subjected to.

Several bonfire builders scattered when she yelled out, but others just kind of eyed her up. The same kid who'd been asking for matches asked nonchalantly if she had a lighter they could borrow.

"What?" she screamed. "No! No, I do not have a lighter, Mr. Strovanoff. You are not allowed to set these chairs on fire."

The kid, Karl Strovanoff, as it turned out, rolled his eyes as Ms. Florgen yelled that a lot of people would get hurt. Karl was already walking away, as if she were ruining his fun for no reason. Across the foyer, Marisa watched with a bemused smile.

"I'm so conflicted right now," Kenji said. "This is everything I've dreamed of. The world is saying yes to every conceivable situation. But it's not improv, and I'm kind of scared."

Ms. Florgen took her phone out of her pocket and called someone. After a moment, she said, "I have to stick around here. They're trying to set the whole place on fire." She took a few deep breaths, making brief eye contact with Kenji. "No, I don't think intentionally. I think they've just lost their minds. Just be on the lookout for flammable materials is what I'm saying." She paused. "Yeah, sure, whatever, I'll do research on meeting demands. But I'll do it from here." She eyed the pile of chairs suspiciously, although since it reached about fifteen feet in height, not without some admiration.

This was not lock-in night.

What Celeste and Kenji were witnessing was 276 students waking up to this realization. They might have been free to roam the halls, free to eat hot sauce and make out in the dark, but they had lost what was, in that moment, most important to them. The magic was absent from the few activities available.

No amount of unsupervised spray painting, or throwing chairs at windows, or general *Lord of the Flies* behavior was going to change that.

The chains weren't budging, the hinges were resisting any tinkering they attempted. Someone had even knocked over Joy's bucket and sifted through the clumped sawdust with the tip of their sneaker, looking for a key. Joy hid her face, quietly thankful that it had only been pee.

They hadn't wanted to believe it was true. That whole time in the auditorium, those brief moments of joy when they'd broken out and the school was available to them again, they'd all thought it would end soon. That the teachers hadn't tried hard enough to get them out, hadn't been as desperate as they needed to be. Now they saw no amount of clawing would undo the chains, bring down the doors. That it was pointless to pretend things could still be the same.

They didn't know how near or far the board was to meeting Marisa's demands, whether there was a chance the doors would open this way. They barely knew what her demands were. That hardly seemed to matter. They knew only this: Marisa had stolen the lock-in from them.

8
11:34PM

When Marisa saw them coming, she tucked her book in her duffel bag and pushed the bathroom bucket out of the way. She'd expected them earlier, to have already been dealing with their anger for the past few hours. The assembly had provided an unexpected respite, and that added rest now made Marisa feel like she'd easily withstand whatever the mob would throw her way.

Despite the escalating madness, her fellow students didn't rush at her, didn't declare all-out mutiny quite yet. It was menacing enough for them to stomp their way from all around the school and gather en masse.

At first it was just a bunch of dirty looks. Most of these kids lived privileged lives, and the anger they'd felt was mild and temporary. Those who had felt true anger, deep and all-consuming, the kind that wrenched your stomach until you wanted to scream, had mostly been angry at the universe for the death of a parent or grandparent or friend, angry at politicians who were ruining lives (though not these angry students' lives, since their rich and privileged lives were generally untouched by public policy), and they had never stared the object of their rage so directly in the face before.

Some were scared by the thoughts that cropped up in their heads, scared of the violence their imaginations were capable of, even if they could quickly reject it. They were afraid of what they had in them, what might come up to the surface if they weren't vigilant.

Many of them staring her down had liked her since she arrived at CIS, had admired her intelligence and confidence, her passion. They liked being in class with her, liked the way she spoke her mind, but not every time, only when it seemed to matter to her. Almost everyone at CIS wanted to be closer to her than they were, even those who considered themselves her friends. They liked the way she smiled at them in the hallway when they passed her, brief and meaningless, sure, but a true smile, not the halfhearted tightening of lips most people offered to strangers.

Others, Jordi Marcos among them, relished these thoughts, even if they didn't all have it in them to actually turn to violence. Here was the sole reason for their misery, the single person who had stripped lock-in night from them. (Though

Jordi himself was confused about who, exactly, to direct his anger toward—Marisa or Peejay. Peejay, who had everyone's love without earning it. Peejay, who had become the party host and hadn't saved them from this hostage situation, who hadn't delivered on his obligations. Or Marisa, who stood in the way of others' fun, who shouted her causes in the faces of those who didn't care.)

Marisa lifted her chin and waited to see what would come first, insults or rocks, or an attempt to rip the doors down. She wouldn't try to talk them out of it or fight them, would only defend herself and her stance. They had a right to be angry. But so did she.

For a while it seemed like there might simply be tears. Some people in the mob clenched and unclenched their fists, but the gesture seemed more of an attempt to hold on to their own emotions than a threat. A lot of these same students had witnessed the strength of the chains, and though they wanted to test it for themselves, they knew already it was no use. They wondered what to do with their anger now that they knew where to point it.

Nothing had happened yet, and there was no music playing from the speakers that could have served as a cinematographic aide to increase tension (the background music that played on every lock-in night, a playlist of students' favorite songs, curated by the students themselves, had been paused when Master Declan made the assembly announcement, and was now forgotten). Despite this, everyone in the room felt their heartbeats pounding in their ears, building up to what was sure to be a boiling point. Marisa held her ground. Not that she had much of a choice.

Finally, from the back of the crowd, Guillem Kim shouted what everyone in the foyer was thinking. "Why today?" There was such hurt in his voice, Marisa couldn't help but picture him as a child who'd lost a precious toy.

"Because it would hurt you," Marisa said.

"I'm not a sadist or anything," she followed up, before the shock would make her lose their attention. "I did this because your pain might make you listen. Because I've been wanting to shout about this for a very long time, because others have been shouting for even longer, and it seems that no one is listening. This is the loudest I could be." She shrugged, which further infuriated half the crowd.

The gesture, coupled with her speech, caused two others to completely lose their rage. Instead, they were filled with warmth when they looked on at Marisa, an admiration so deeply rooted that it was hard not to think of it as love.

How had they not known before? How had they ever looked upon her with even a hint of distaste? This girl wasn't just hypothetically going to change the world. Here she was in front of them, actually doing it. She would make no excuses for it, wouldn't lie about the fact that it was disrupting others' joy. She was here standing up for what she believed in, what she loved. There was no doubt in their minds that if she ever came to love them, this is how she would act on their behalf. She would chain herself to protect them. Even if they would never be worthy of her love, they knew all of a sudden there was no one more deserving of whatever love *they* had to give.

Both newcomers to love, Lou Chaminowitz and Lydia Chang maneuvered their way up to the front of the crowd. They could feel the anger growing in the rest of her audience, and could imagine a situation in which they might need to protect Marisa.

"We don't give a shit," Jordi yelled. He stepped forward, too, a violent step if there ever was one. Those angry people in the crowd uncomfortable with their imaginations' violent impulses tensed, not sure what to do.

"Well, then, soon you will," Marisa said. A couple of people oohed and aahed, as if she had delivered some biting trash talk.

"That's not what I meant. You can scream and shout all you want. But if you keep doing it in my face you'll be sorry."

"What are you going to do, beat the shit out of me?" Marisa said, the calm in her voice astounding to everyone listening. "That won't open these doors."

Jordi growled. He thought of his father again, thought of a truck plowing through people on a highway.

Three more people fell in love with Marisa and stepped toward Jordi, willing to restrain him if they had to. "You want to help yourself get lock-in night back?" She motioned with her head at the poster behind her. "Here are your instructions."

Kenji's eyes went straight for number seventeen. *Cancellation of construction project on Lokoloko Island.* He gulped, though he wasn't sure if he did it as a joke. The name of the island wasn't familiar to all at CIS, but Kenji had heard his father talking about it countless times. With Kenji's mom over dinner, over the phone constantly during the past two years or so, with who knows how many business people or government officials. Kenji had never given the name much thought, except that it was a little silly, and whenever his father talked about it, he tended to go on long, righteous rants about how he was bringing joy and tourism to the people in the area.

"Diesel boats?" someone muttered from the crowd. It was one of the freshmen who'd gone in to the showcase to see Ludo and had heard Peejay deliver his tirade against Malik. Speaking of which, here was Peejay now; he'd just left the basement to try to negotiate a little more with Marisa.

"Why should we help?" Peejay said. "Why wouldn't we just sit here and bide our time until you shit out a key?" A few people in the crowd who'd missed the dramatic key swallow raised their eyebrows. "Or until we run out of food and you have to let us out?" Then, the possibility just now occurring to him, he said, "Why wouldn't we just let this night get canceled and wait for the school to reschedule another one?"

The audience murmured. Why hadn't they thought of that already? When Marisa smiled, though, Peejay knew he'd fallen for a trap. "I'm glad you asked," Marisa said.

The majority of the crowd did not seem to be paying much attention. Marisa was explaining future scheduling conflicts and the likelihood, based on previous CIS scandals (the shampoo bottle booze incident on the ski trip, the dozen broken bones during the human bowling event only three years ago) that lock-in night wouldn't happen again in the month or so remaining in the school year, possibly ever again. The longer they stayed in there, the less likely it was that the administration would be able or willing to find a new date to make it work.

This fanned the crowd's rage all over again. They didn't want to hear the logistics spelled out for them. Those still paying attention were the ones who had thought at some point, like Peejay, that they could sit back and wait for this to blow over and then wait for a second chance. They only got angrier.

Marisa had known there was no way CIS could reschedule the night, had known her actions might lead the school board to scratch the whole thing for good, and still she'd done it? A handful of students began to cry—frustrated, angry tears of the kind they hadn't cried since true childhood, when a sibling's senseless destruction of a toy awoke within them the great sense of injustice they couldn't put into words and therefore put into tears.

Again, from the back, near the almost-bonfire pile of chairs, Guillem Kim, the question still not satisfactorily answered, like a lump still stuck in his throat, shouted, "Why?"

Marisa didn't bother answering him this time.

Jordi Marcos clenched and unclenched his fist again. He thought, *Protestor.*

From Kenji and Celeste's vantage point spot in the back of the foyer, they could see a number of people shuffling toward the front of the crowd, moving away from the chairs and toward Marisa. Kenji assumed that Marisa, as she packed away her presentation materials, was saying something else, but too quietly, and others were just trying to hear her. Celeste, on the other hand, worried for Marisa, because she was a girl and on a platform and, at least at this particular door, was on her own. Without thinking, she reached out and tugged on Kenji's sleeve, a gesture she'd soon be examining in her mind over and over again, fascinated that such a casual touch was within her realm of capabilities.

Like a couple of concert-goers, she moved them toward the front entrance, not knowing what might happen, or what she would do if anything were to happen. But the mood in the air propelled Celeste forward, and it was only when she and Kenji were at the very front of the crowd, practically separating one from the other, that she let go of Kenji's shirt, suddenly aware of her boldness and retreating from it.

Kenji had barely noticed her fingers there, used to the way friends reached out to one another. He merely assumed that Celeste knew something he did not, had finally known where they were supposed to be, and he was happy she'd thought to bring him along.

As soon as Marisa packed away her presentation materials and faced the crowd again, the first item came hurling toward her. She couldn't tell who had thrown it, only that it was a shoe, and it was poorly aimed. The crowd had been shuffling about throughout her explanation; she had sensed their restlessness, sensed that though some were deflating hopelessly, she was only fanning others' flames. The flames had already been burning before they gathered.

So it wasn't a surprise to see the shoe sail a few feet past her head and strike a nearby column. She'd expected to come to some harm and had ice packs, gauze and painkillers in her bag. Plus, she knew the nurse was in the building (had made sure of it before the doors closed), so whatever danger came her way could be dealt with. What she didn't ex-pect was that, as others followed suit—throwing shoes, pens leftover in pockets from the school day, loose change, sets of keys—some people would step forward and form a protec-tive barricade around her. Sure, she had thought she might win a handful over to her cause. This, though? This faction within the crowd who, with no apparent prior communica-tion, with no apparent hesitation, put their bodies between a barrage of items—here came a backpack now, maroon, straps splayed out in the air like a flying squid—and herself? She had not prepared for that, and felt a lump rise in her throat as she watched them rush to protect her.

Even if it *was* a second too late. Everything went black.

9
11:45PM

Peejay was surprised to find himself among those keeping the mob away from Marisa. She was unconscious, hanging limp against her chains, which held her weight without loosening. The crowd stopped throwing things for now, stunned momentarily that their actions had consequences, that one of them had thrown a textbook-laden backpack and hit Marisa in the head, and as a result, she was now a rag doll. Peejay, unable to help himself, thought of Hamish. He felt a momentary desperation to flee, to get out of this damn building and stand at his brother's bedside. He could wake up at any moment.

Amira Wahid had stepped forward and was coaxing Marisa

back to wakefulness. Some in the crowd looked at Peejay like a traitor for standing there, some just looked confused, waiting for him to point out why he was there, waiting for him to speak so they could follow. What he would soon tell them (after he recovered from the transportation to his brother's bedside, after he recovered from wondering how long it would be until he saw his brother again, standing or not) was that throwing shit at Marisa would get them all locked up in the auditorium again. If there was any chance of them partying tonight—and didn't they all want that, didn't they desperately crave something good happening?—they couldn't just riot.

The truth, however, was that Peejay had acted thoughtlessly and selflessly. He had not thought about the party when he stepped toward Marisa, raising his hands to his head to protect himself while protecting her. He hadn't thought, *This is for the party*, or, *This is what Hamish would want*, when an apple hit him in the stomach, or when a metal ruler whizzed by his ear, slicing the air before crashing loudly to the floor. And now, while he formed part of the half circle of people keeping the crowd from Marisa, his arms out, stiff, pushing encroachers away, he wondered why.

Why, when this girl had taken away this opportunity from him, stolen everything he'd fantasized for this night; not just the joys of partying itself, or the looks on the faces of everyone at school, not just the pleasure of getting away with it, but all those fantasies he'd played for himself of the aftermath, the texts and congratulations he was supposed to receive for years to come. The chance to do what Hamish had done, gone. In one fell swoop, Marisa had erased the memory of his party in these few hundred minds, and supplanted it with something of her own. So why protect her? Why wasn't he siding with Jordi for once?

He looked at Marisa, whose eyes were fluttering open. Then he looked back at the crowd, meeting Jordi Marcos's eyes, wondering what separated the two. They both thought they were right, in the end. Both were fighting, in their own way, to get what they wanted. One, however, was selfish, the other was global. One had been violent, the other merely disruptive.

Amira rested her hand on Marisa's cheek, tilting her captor's head gently upward to check for signs of a concussion. She tried to focus on the size of Marisa's pupils instead of the mahogany shade of her irises. She felt her insides swirl.

"What do you think?" Marisa muttered. "Am I going to live?"

Amira smiled, pulled her hand slowly away. "I'm sure you'd survive anything they throw at you."

"Do me a favor and don't tell them that."

Amira chuckled, then looked over her shoulder. It felt like the crowd was pushing in on the ten or so people forming the barricade, but at least the projectiles had stopped. "No concussion, then?" Marisa asked.

"I don't think so. But I should probably find the nurse and have her check you out."

"You really want to go through that crowd?" Marisa and Amira turned to look at their peers, still shouting among each other.

"I guess not." Amira looked back into Marisa's eyes a moment longer, this time only pretending to examine her pupils.

In that moment, she decided she wouldn't leave Marisa for the rest of the night. The crowd had officially turned into a mob, and mobs were dangerous. Marisa could handle a backpack to the head and more, and Amira knew Marisa was willing to suffer for her cause. Those chains alone must already have chafed and pressed painfully on her body. With Amira at her side, though, Marisa would suffer less. Amira was a neutral party in this, somewhat revered for her athletic abilities (the lore of her dunk, though unappreciated in the moment, was now growing, whispered about by those around school waiting for lock-in to resume). CIS had nothing against her. So she stayed put.

"You should be rock climbing by now." Marisa groaned. "Are you pissed at me yet?"

Amira blushed, as if Marisa was somehow privy to her daydreams. She shook her head.

Kenji wasn't sure what he was doing facing down the audience. He was mimicking Celeste and Peejay and some of the others. He thought, *Just pretend this is a scene, find the humor.* Then his mind went blank and his mouth dried up. He was so skinny, and no match for fury. Even though the faces staring back at him were people he knew, people who only a few hours earlier he'd approached with a smile and a flyer for the showcase, people who didn't mean him harm, only the girl behind him, he was still terrified.

Kenji prided himself on his quick thinking, his ability to fall into any situation his friends presented him with and not get stuck on what might happen next. Those hundreds of prior situations, though, were imaginary. Not one bit of this felt like playing pretend.

He stood frozen with his arms out and shaking, his legs quivering, wishing, for once, there was a script for him to follow. All the while, he thought of his father, and the fact that he would be the one to decide whether the construction site on Marisa's list of demands would be canceled. He was thinking of how often his father said no, and how it didn't seem like Marisa would take no for an answer.

10
12:01AM

It was midnight when those stuck outside the high school began to lose faith they would ever be allowed in.

Not all of them. Some would linger by the door and on the soccer field until the whole ordeal was over. They would have food delivered to them by increasingly worried parents, who'd beg them to come home. These lingering students would shower when the automatic sprinklers came on, or when it rained, making a little home for themselves out of tarps found in the sports equipment room between the soccer field and the elementary school. These were the children made famous by helicopter news footage, lingering on the field, using an arm to shield their eyes from the sun as they looked up to the helicopter. But that would come later.

At midnight on the first night, some who were outside simply couldn't feel the lock-in magic any longer, and they decided there was nothing worth sticking around for. The food trucks had already left, as had the laser tag organizers in the parking garage. Those with cars simply walked away, offering rides to anyone who lived near them. Some stopped at a popular street food stand not too far away, as if they were merely returning home from a late night out.

Others called their parents, who answered their phones breathlessly, as if seeing their child's name showing up like that on their screens had frightened them to the core. Among the parents, lock-in night had its own lore, and it was well known that no CIS parent had ever received a phone call from their child on lock-in night before (there were no illnesses on lock-in nights, there was no homesickness, no heartbreak painful enough lock-in night itself couldn't cure). The school hadn't reached out, either, figuring the parents weren't expecting their kids back anytime soon, and they still had a few hours to resolve this thing. A few people would lose their jobs over that decision.

The parents became certain mayhem was breaking out, that their child was hidden under a desk or in some closet, and they begged to whatever gods they believed in that the shooters or kidnappers or terrorists would not spot their child's hiding place.

When their child's voice came on the line, and rather than panicky pleas for help, they simply said, "Can you come pick me up?" their heartbeats slowed and they nearly cried with re-lief. Then they furrowed their brows and thought, *Wait, what?*

As they pulled on pants and made a quick pot of coffee, they reached out to their friends, other parents at the school. Some were likewise hauling themselves out of bed, confused over the circumstances, but thankful there was nothing tragic afoot. Others answered the phone midlaughter. They had gathered at one person or the other's house, using their kids' absence as an excuse to sit and drink and generally behave more like they had when they were younger. This, too, was a lock-in night tradition, even though parents who'd been around before never had to suggest it. Minds of parents freed from their teenagers think alike.

But these parents answering the phone now, happy drunk, hadn't heard of anything happening. "What, is Roberto sick?" they would ask, equally confused by the prospect of someone getting sick on lock-in night as they were to receive a phone call informing them of that at midnight. Then they cupped their free ear shut and pressed the phone closer, motioning for the other laughing parents to shut up for a second.

"Something's happened?"

"I don't know. I guess. It didn't sound like an emergency, but he called asking me to pick him up. Felipa is getting the twins, too. Something's up."

So it was around midnight the students gathered in front of Marisa began to answer their parents' frantic phone calls. Even while the kids told them what they knew, and all they didn't, they marveled at the fact they hadn't thought to call before, at how lock-in night or even the hope it would still happen had shaped their behavior.

Some students felt that, of course, getting the parents involved was the solution. (Amazing how the human heart latched on to any hope it could invent.) Others, embarrassed as they were to have not even thought to inform their parents, knew this parental involvement would change nothing. If Marisa didn't yield to Peejay, if she didn't yield to or even respect lock-in night, what chance did the parents have?

Sure, CIS parents could make a fuss like no other group in the local country, or even in the many countries familiar to CIS students. They'd gotten the ugly linoleum flooring changed and the hand-sanitizing dispenser installed. And God knew the poor board members were going to really get it for failing to notify the parents before their kids did. The board had known, of course, it wouldn't go over well. But they were trying to solve the issue before panicking the parents. The only ones they'd called were Marisa's and the cronies', but they hadn't managed to reach anyone but Malik Harris's parents (who took the phone call to be a scam of some sort and promptly hung up).

Nevertheless, the parents were here to yell. Marisa's chains, surely, would stand up to even the fiercest yelling.

What Marisa was counting on was that the board would not.

This is what she was telling her mom over the phone. Marisa knew her mom, knew she could forgive any crazy idea if it was well thought out. She'd come close to telling her the plan, but even her mom went around saying it was better, sometimes, to ask for forgiveness rather than for permission.

"How sure are you about this?"

"Well, Mom, it's a little late now."

"That's not what I meant. How sure are you that what you're doing is worth it all? The pain you're causing others, the potential pain you're bringing on yourself. The nuisance of it all. The consequences, hun. Because there will be some. At school, with your friends, later in life. This will stick around. Is it worth it?"

Marisa didn't hesitate. She was still woozy from the backpack to the head, could still see people in front of her wanting to tear her apart. But if the construction stopped, if she could bring back just a little color to the reefs, if she could *save* something... Just the thought was enough for her to want to tighten the chains. "Absolutely."

"Okay," her mom said. "How long do you think until they give you what you want?"

"It'll take more than the night," Marisa said, leaving it at that. She glanced over at Amira, to see if she'd heard that bit. But Amira gave no indication that she had. Marisa's eyes lingered longer than necessary on this girl who'd come to sit by her side, this classmate she'd been looking to steal a few moments with in the hallway.

"So I shouldn't expect you for breakfast," her mom said. It wasn't a question. Marisa was sure her mom could see the range of outcomes, and she would know, better than anyone in the building, Marisa would not be home for breakfast. Her daughter had the strongest convictions of anyone she knew.

"I don't think so."

Her mom cleared her throat. It might have been to hide tears, though Marisa wasn't sure if they would be tears of pride or concern.

"Good luck, honey. I love you."

★ ★ ★

Celeste's mom was not as understanding. For starters, like every other parent, she understood less. "Wait, is this a local thing?"

"No, I don't think so," Celeste answered.

"Was it on the schedule? Selena from the embassy called, and I did not understand a word that woman was trying to say to me. She sounded like someone was ripping a brunch mimosa from her hands."

"Um," Celeste said, switching her phone to the other ear so Kenji couldn't hear. "Well, what happened, I think…" She lowered her voice, thinking there was a chance she herself didn't understand the situation, and speaking what she thought would bring ridicule her way. "It wasn't planned or anything. Or at least not by the school. It was some students."

"Mmm-hmm?"

"They are, uh, I think, um…" Celeste was trying to explain the situation in a way that wouldn't completely freak her mom out. "I'm fine and all, there's no violence or anything."

"Celeste, baby, you've got your 'I don't wanna scare Mom' voice going. I can hear it a mile away. And the longer you go on with it, the worse I'm gonna think things are. You know how good my imagination is. So, just say it, baby. It's okay."

Celeste took a deep breath, looking for a place to step away. But the crowd, busy though they were with their own calls, was still right in front of her, Marisa only a few steps behind. At that moment, Kenji was reaching for his phone, too. Celeste could almost feel the vibrations across the little space between them. "We're kinda sorta being held hostage. I think."

There was a long pause on the other end. Then her mom

spoke, almost under her breath. "I thought we'd left this shit behind in the States."

"No, Mom, it's not like that. I'm okay."

Celeste's mom sighed into the phone. There was a ruffling sound, and Celeste's dad's sleepy voice in the background. Her mom spoke to her again. "And it's not a local thing?"

"Local thing" had become the Rollinses' term for any bit of culture shock they experienced, good or bad, fascinating or incomprehensible. They had a family chalkboard set up in their kitchen, and each day someone added something new—a slang word, or some transportation taboo, or an observation about the local people, how they all seemed to place a hand over their bellies as they laughed, young or old, a chuckle or a breathless, cackling breakdown. "No," Celeste said. "It's for the environment, I think. A climate protest. It's not violent or anything."

This time there was a pause on the other end as her mom took in that it was a protest. She'd been a community organizer back in Chicago, and had been involved in a handful of strikes and marches. "Are they harming anyone?"

"No. They're just chained to the doors and won't let anyone out until their demands are met."

Another deep breath. "Good for them, then." She said something away from the phone, presumably to her dad. "If you're safe, then I guess we'll have to wait and see what happens. We'll try to figure out what we can from here. Just let us know if anything changes, and don't go disappearing into yourself. In stressful times we need other people. Find someone good and stick with them." Celeste turned to Kenji, who was speaking in such a quiet, clipped voice she knew he wasn't talking about improv. His cowlick somehow stuck out even farther.

She assumed he was talking with his parents, and for some reason, it felt like this voice, muted, un–Kenji-esque, was the voice that came out when he spoke with them. It was an assumption, just a hunch, because it sounded so different from how he'd been speaking to her the last few hours, because it's what she sounded like at school, wholly different than how she sounded at home.

"Okay, Mom," Celeste said. "I will."

Kenji smoothed out the wrinkles on his pants while he listened to his dad ramble about things that were unacceptable. He felt the urge to do an impression of his dad's posh, stiff-upper-lip way of speaking. "I don't know, Father, they haven't given us much information. I believe they don't have much to share."

"Why are you speaking like that?"

"Like what?" A pause on the line while his dad tried to figure out if Kenji was being silly at an inappropriate time. The way the word *silly* was used at the Pierce household was similar to the way Jordi Marcos's dad used the word *protestor*.

"What are these damn criminals asking for?"

Kenji found himself gulping again. Was he a gulper? He hadn't known that. "Um, a bunch of things," he said.

"Well," his father went on, "for the tuition I pay, this is absolutely ludicrous. I'll be making calls, of that they can be certain. You will be home within the hour, and that is final." Kenji said nothing, waiting for his father's incredulity to run out. He'd heard Celeste chuckle at something her mom said, and he wondered if he'd ever laughed at anything his father said. Well, yes, he had. But in secret, after the fact, laughing at him in his mind or with his friends. He wondered what it would be like to have the kind of relationship with his father that looked more like a friendship and less like docile student–severe teacher.

When the conversation ended—thankfully without Kenji accidentally blurting out that his dad's company was mentioned in the demands—he put his phone away and took stock of the room, wondering why he was standing where he was, and how his father would react when he found out Marisa was coming after Lokoloko.

Then the parents came.

They arrived in droves, a caravan of SUVs and minivans and luxury sedans. Lupita Minji—the administrative assistant who'd been posted at the little booth by the parking garage entrance to attend to the various vendors who would come and go through the night—woke from a nap to the sound of horns. Dozens of cars were waiting to come in, and she wondered if she'd slept through the whole night before raising the barrier and waving them in.

They climbed out of their cars wearing pajama pants and hooded sweatshirts, or they were let out by chauffeurs and wobbled forward on high heels and dress shoes, popping mints to hide their boozy breath from their children.

Some were already crying; the rumor mill had been working furiously ever since the first phone call from CIS came, and now they weren't sure if they'd ever see their children again. Kidnappers, some had heard, spreading the story as if they'd seen the ski-masked perpetrators with their own eyes.

A bomb threat, others believed. Some giggled as they took the elevator up from the garage to the soccer field, having heard there was merely some malfunction with the doors and the night had been canceled. They greeted each other as they crossed the field, casually or with deep, sobbing embraces, depending on which rumor they'd heard.

Some had already spoken to Master Declan or Ms. Duli or one of the board members (whichever one they were best connected to), and though they'd been told exactly what was happening, they didn't understand. They gathered in front of the entrance, waiting for some school representative to come and meet them. A lucky handful spotted their children right there on the lawn, and managed to convince them to come back home.

Lindsay's parents (pajama-clad variety) found her cross-legged on the soccer bleachers, using her phone's camera zoom to try to sneak glances through the building's windows. Lindsay saw them out of the corner of her eye, but pretended not to. She and her mom had fought again right before the lock-in, and her dad never understood what they were fighting about, thinking everyone was always blowing things out of proportion, which of course only angered both his wife and daughter. So right now they were all mad at each other, on top of Lindsay's anger at being on the outside. Lindsay's mom nudged her husband. He rolled his eyes and greeted his daughter, who said, "Hi," back because she didn't yet know how to tell them she wouldn't be going home with them until the school doors opened.

Surprise, surprise, it was Jordi Marcos, Sr., who pushed past patiently huddled parents to try to force the front doors open. Others watched him approach, wondering why they hadn't thought to try. Some were forgetting they'd been told about Marisa and knew about the doors. Others had simply stood by, spellbound, just following the crowd.

Marisa felt the push behind her. Amira did, too, and raised an eyebrow. Moments later they heard a voice shouting into a phone, making demands. "Parents," Marisa guessed.

Granted, many parents had arrived still on their phones, waiting in a queue to speak to some poor teacher or other—the ones who hadn't been placed into the preferable role of researching how to meet Marisa's demands. Because of course the board couldn't be called upon to do the research themselves; it was nighttime, after all, and they'd been outsourcing research to assistants for decades, had no idea how to research anymore, only how to make decisions.

The remaining unfortunate souls were now cast as customer service reps dealing with angry clientele. And here were their customers now, not just shouting their complaints into the phone, but at the building itself.

"We want our kids," Dov Nudel's mom, Sharon, yelled. She was a slight woman, but loud. It was her voice the teachers heard from all the way up in the green room, from the chem lab over the sound of the fire extinguisher they were emptying, from their laps around the halls trying to keep the school together. Those on the phone with some other worried/angry/upset/demanding/pleading parent only had a second to perk their free ear up before their attention was pulled back.

Ms. Duli, on a conference call with the board, who'd finally gathered together to review the demands, switched over to speakerphone. "Do you hear that?"

A few kilometers away, meeting in a hotel conference room, with their assistants lined up against the back wall typing away on laptops, or fetching drinks from the downstairs bar, the board members tilted their heads closer to the overhead speakers, which had been wired into the call. Ms. Duli let the sound carry over for a good thirty seconds. Meanwhile, something in her pulsed, something she couldn't quite name. It could have been admiration that Marisa had done all of this, but there was something else, too, some vague ache she couldn't quite put a finger on yet. She felt young again, for some reason, holding the phone up for the board to hear. It was exciting for this to be happening, and Ms. Duli had a fleeting fantasy that she was Marisa, that she had put all this together.

"What is that, a riot?" one of the board members grumbled.

Ms. Duli put the phone back to her ear. "Parents, sir. A bunch of pissed-off parents." The board grumbled to each other now, each raised voice trying to rise above the others, creating only a din, as each voice in the room was used to being the loudest voice and did not want to cede that position.

"You might want to start taking this girl seriously," Ms. Duli said. "Or we're all going to be here a very long time."

11
12:32AM

After the parents arrived, the brief, savage attempts to reclaim lock-in night flittered away. The violence aimed at Marisa was put on hold.

A sense of normalcy, maybe, returned, although not a one of them felt things were normal. It was more that suddenly it was clear to the students they were prisoners, hostages who had no voice. Sure, it was all about them. The parents and administrators trying to get them out, Marisa keeping them in. But they were supposed to sit there and shut up and be safe. They were pawns. The only ones with voices were the adults, and Marisa herself.

Though for the time being, it felt like even she was taking a backseat to the adults yelling at each other. One of the parents outside had thought to bring a megaphone, similar to the kind Marisa had used when she gave her initial speech. Jordi Marcos, Sr., had bullyingly procured this megaphone and was now yelling into it, demanding the kids' release from the administration. He didn't seem to have a solid grasp on the situation.

So Ms. Duli was forced to ask Marisa for her megaphone so she could respond. As she did, she seemed to notice for the first time the weird positioning of the kids around Marisa, the odd array of objects strewn about. "What happened here?"

Ms. Florgen, who'd been in the foyer when the projectiles began but whose shouts no one heard, scoffed. The two teachers who'd joined ranks as protectors pretended not to hear.

Marisa shrugged. Lacking the energy to dig deeper in that moment, Ms. Duli filed the thought away, grabbed the megaphone and went to the nearest classroom. It, too, was in disarray. Chairs on their sides, and one in the window itself, as if someone was trying to rearrange physics to fit the chair through the tiny opening. Ms. Duli freed the chair leg and pulled it down, standing on it so she could angle the megaphone out the little window slit.

Ms. Duli cleared her throat and spoke to the parents huddled out on the soccer field in front of the building. "Welcome, parents. We're sorry you've had to come all this way, but we'd like to make it perfectly clear that everyone inside is safe. There seems to be a little confusion, from what I hear. A group of students have chained themselves to the doors and have effectively blocked all ways in and out of the building.

They have some demands, and the board is working to meet them in order to release the students as soon as possible. That is all the information we have at this time, but I will personally deliver any updates as they become available."

Since it seemed like she was done speaking, Jordi Sr. reacted exactly like the man Jordi had learned his behavior from, and shouted into his own megaphone. "Open the goddamn doors right now, by any means necessary."

Ms. Duli had started climbing down from the chair, but now stopped and spoke again. "Sir, the exits are blocked. We have no tools to open the padlocks or break the chains. Ways in and out of the building have been explored, to no avail. For now, we have to assume that the doors will remain closed until the board meets the students' demands."

Someone else outside grabbed hold of the megaphone.

"Well, how many demands have you met so far?"

Those weasels on the board should be answering this, Ms. Duli thought. "We've been attempting to find other ways to deal with the situation."

"How many?" he repeated.

Ms. Duli would have pressed, too. "None."

A roar of murmurs sounded out, and Ms. Duli thought how much these parents were like their children. Kind and concerned but expecting the world to bend to their will.

A few back-and-forths later, they agreed a copy of the demands would be emailed to the parents, as well as posted on the school website. Someone else grabbed the megaphone and begged Ms. Duli to "bcc" everyone or at least for the other parents to not hit "reply all," which, of course, many would. Parents stood around, dumbfounded that their kids could be in a building they couldn't access. Some whose English skills weren't great were thinking they hadn't really understood this whole time the lock-in would be literal.

Arthur Pierce now grabbed the megaphone. "This is ludicrous!" he barked. "I pay too much money in tuition to abide this behavior. Release the children at once!" If Kenji's mom were around, she might have placed a calming hand on his forearm, but she was away on business.

Ms. Duli once again explained the situation, the way she would go over the many reasons why World War I began when a class couldn't wrap their minds around the subtleties of the situation, how wars began for complex reasons, not over one tidily summarized cause. Except now more parents wanted to echo Mr. Pierce's sentiment and were either shouting out their agreement or phoning chauffeurs or significant others to go down to the hardware store or whatever establishment sold megaphones and buy them one.

Now that the student crowd had calmed and didn't seem on the verge of attacking Marisa—Ms. Duli had commanded teachers to post up in the area—Peejay's mind left his unexpected interference on Marisa's behalf and returned to the party. He chewed the tip of his thumb. He wasn't lamenting having wasted his time and efforts so far, all those hours spent planning for the perfect lock-in party (not quite as many hours as Marisa had spent, but many of them had happened at the same time. Marisa and Peejay had sat in their respective rooms in different neighborhoods, no TV on, phones resting facedown on their laps, used only intermittently to look up something crucial to the plan. Outside, similar sounds of the city welcoming in the night: honks from cars directed at scooters buzzing haphazardly around; steel curtains coming down on shop windows; food vendors rolling up their carts to popular corners, the sharp whistles of steam releasing from their make-shift boilers, which they used for yams and dumplings. Marisa and Peejay had each sat like this for hours, their respective parents passing by their open bedroom doors wondering if they were still home, so silent had the house fallen. Diego, not fully in the know, but not as oblivious as some thought, went from one house to the other, noticing the intense concentration in both these people in his life, thinking it wonderful. This, of course, before Hamish's accident at work, the last few details strung together at the hospital, unable to sleep, Peejay hoping his brother would wake up now, now, now, and help him plan out the rest).

Peejay still believed he could throw a party. Not a lock-in party any longer, but a hostage party, he supposed. Something to show CIS he was still worthy of their adoration, still worthy of the title bestowed upon him as Partyer in Chief. Something still worthy of Hamish. These kids needed it. Look at how much control they lost without it, look at what the lack of joy had wrought on their angelic little faces.

He texted Diego again for an update on the DJ equipment.

But Diego had momentarily left campus to go eat with the famous DJ and his hands were currently busy holding a plastic-covered plate while he bit down on greasy fried chicken, the spicy sauce dripping down his chin. He hadn't thought of his sister chained to the door, or how that related to the problems he was trying to solve for Peejay. Diego didn't like to make many connections between his thoughts, between any situation that wasn't the one at hand. Which made school particularly challenging, unless it was some hands-on project. He liked looking at exactly what was in front of him and making that his whole world. Right now, that was the delicious food in his mouth, and the DJ standing in front of him, telling stories of having traveled to clubs in Berlin and Mexico City. Diego was immersed. Not necessarily in the DJ's stories, but in the DJ's talking, the sound of his voice, the shape of his mouth. He was immersed and completely aware of the sauce clinging to the DJ's beard, in the guy's accent— which he couldn't place—in the freedom he himself had to be out late at a food stand on what should have been a school night and not face anyone's scrutiny (this was categorically false, since Peejay was calling him now and his mom had left three voice mails shortly after she'd spoken with Marisa). It was a perfect night out, and Diego, despite his reputation as somewhat of a dummy, or rather, for the same reasons, was perfectly suited to enjoying it.

"Diego, you gorgeous, maddening dumb-dumb, answer me." Peejay hung up the phone. He looked next to him, surprised to see Celeste Rollins, and that it was maybe the first time he'd seen her not looking completely shut inside of herself. When she noticed him looking, she even smiled a little. Not a big or lasting smile, and probably not a knowing one. But the girl had smiled.

Part of him was wildly irked by this. *Why now?* he wanted to yell, like someone else had not long ago. *What is it about this particular situation that makes you so fucking peppy all of a sudden?* But Hamish would disapprove of that approach, and his efforts were better saved for a party. Instead, he just sighed and said, "These Cuevas siblings really have it out for me today."

Celeste hadn't caught Marisa's last name, and had never met Diego, so she had no idea what he was talking about. "Hmm," she said as a response. She looked down the line of students sitting with their legs crossed facing the crowd, those she was starting to think of as Marisa's Protectors.

On her other side sat Kenji, his hands small nervous twin engines rattling. Beyond him, Maya and Lou, kids she had a few classes with, as well as a handful of others whose names she didn't know. Two teachers had joined in, as well (under the guise of protecting a student, though both Mr. Jankowski and Ms. Ficorino as science enthusiasts and environmentalists weren't just protecting Marisa, they were standing with her, arguing for her, damn whatever the board would have to say about it). For the first time at CIS, Celeste was part of a group, however informal. She thought about that other Celeste who existed in some parallel dimension still in Glen Ellyn, growing instead of shrinking. The thought alone didn't cause her to shrink further, like it might have not long ago.

Instead, she tapped Kenji on the knee, leaned over and whispered, "Tell me more."

Kenji jumped slightly at her touch, and adjusted his glasses. His heart was still thundering in his chest, though the tensions had dissipated a few minutes ago when everyone had decided to sit. The parents were yelling, and he was sure he could hear his dad's nasal, stiff voice booming through a megaphone. He looked at Marisa, then back at Celeste, panicked for a moment that someone had connected the dots between him and Marisa's demand for Lokoloko Island.

"About improv," Celeste said. She couldn't imagine there was more to say, but she'd be happy to hear every word again, happy to sit in this informal group and be part of a conversation.

He hesitated, looking furtively at the crowd as though speaking about improv might set them off again. Before Kenji could work up a response, he saw Peejay lean forward behind Celeste. "You're one of those improv kids," he said, snapping his fingers at Kenji.

Kenji stammered for a while, but then Celeste (a gleam in her eye) answered for him. "Yes, and…?"

Throughout all this, Mr. Gigs had been climbing up and down the stairs, traipsing across the school to ask Marisa questions on the board's behalf and deliver her answers to Ms. Duli. No one seemed to consider the option of the board speaking directly to Marisa, or of messaging with her via cell phone. Mr. Gigs was glad to get his steps in for the day, though, to not be tethered like his coworkers to researching some demand or another, or stationed at the library to make sure no one was doing inappropriate things on the computers.

Now he crossed the foyer again, a pep in his step, a paper scrap in his hand. Those who had paid attention to his role as messenger perked up when they saw him, taking note of his smile. Marisa, woozy though she still was, knew what was coming.

Amira rose to her feet when Mr. Gigs approached, a bodyguard at the ready, though Paul Gigs had never once in his life looked menacing. He slowed down and smiled, raising the paper up between two fingers like a cigarette. "I bring good news." Heads turned. All over the foyer, those sinking into despair and rage cocked their ears. Good news? They could hardly remember the phrase. Those who had plugged into their devices and were playing games, watching videos, posting updates, messaging friends looked away from the phone for a second, thumbs still hovering over the screen. In the darkened closet where he'd hidden himself from the night's events, Pok Tran opened a single eye, like a cat hearing something moving in the dark and trying to suss out whether it was worth getting up and chasing.

Amira turned to Marisa. Marisa nodded at Mr. Gigs's raised hand. "What's that?"

Mr. Gigs offered it gently to Amira, as if it was obvious that all communiqués directed for Marisa would now have to go through her. Amira inspected the hand-size piece of paper, clearly ripped hastily from some student's forgotten notebook. Then, realizing she didn't know what she was supposed to be inspecting it for (some sort of danger? Poison? A weapon?) she stepped over to Marisa, holding it out, surprised to find herself hoping Marisa would brush her fingers when she reached for it.

To everyone's disappointment, Marisa only raised an eyebrow at it. Mr. Gigs's shoulders sagged and he tried to sound cheerful when he said, "They're meeting one of your demands."

A jolt worked its way through the crowd, as if they'd all heard it at the same time (though there was no way, what with the parents shouting outside, the constant murmuring din bouncing off the high ceilings).

Marisa gave him such a mocking look he was instantly thankful he'd never had to stare the girl down in class. Then she grabbed the note from Amira's fingers (quick, wonderful brush of index finger against palm, the kind of touch that made hands brushing together famous) and read it. CIS held its collective breath.

It was a single demand, they knew. They'd heard Mr. Gigs. And they could see the long, numbered list in front of them. Still, they hoped. Maybe this was it, maybe it would all be over now. There were a few hours left. They would take those, be happy with them, if only she were to grant them that gift.

"Who wrote this?"

Mr. Gigs stammered. "Me?"

"Why?"

"Um. So you could see what they're agreeing to."

Marisa rolled her eyes and crumpled the paper in her fingers. To everyone watching, it felt like she was crumpling their dreams. "It's a nice dramatic touch, writing it down and handing me the slip of paper, like in the movies. But you could have just said it. Either way it doesn't mean a thing." She turned as much as she could, trying to hide the cramp that seized her lower back as she moved, and she tossed the paper into the trash. "I want them to enact the rule officially. Change the rulebook. Act, not just fling words at me."

Mr. Gigs narrowed his eyes. "A rule banning single-use plastic."

"Yes. None of my demands are going to be satisfied with a declaration on a piece of notebook paper. I'm here for ac-

tual change, and these doors will not open until I receive it."
Heads sank back between knees, into the sweet embrace of
phone screens.

Not long after, the PA system came on and formally announced the new CIS-wide rule. Ms. Duli, too, made the
announcement to the parents outside. Some applauded as if a
hostage had been released, others only shouted louder. Giving in only legitimized the protestors. Others stood in their
bathrobes, still rubbing sleep from their eyes, huddling close
to each other as if a fire alarm had pulled them from sleep
and any second now they'd be cleared to return home. Marisa
checked the website, which after a refresh or two reflected
the change.

There was such a long way to go, but Marisa couldn't lie:
this felt good. It mattered. Less plastic used meant less plastic produced meant less plastic floating in the ocean, photo
degrading and killing the fish that kept the reefs alive. It was
a blip, in the grand scheme of things. But it was a blip she'd
caused. She leaned gingerly over to her duffel bag and pulled
out a dry erase marker. Uncapping it, she turned again toward
the door where her list of demands was taped up.

Another lower back spasm shot through her, this one too
painful to hide. Amira, who was so tuned in to her body it
made her knowledgeable about others', at least knowledgeable enough to recognize muscle spasms when she saw them,
leaned down to grab Marisa's water bottle from the floor next
to her foldable stool. "You need to drink a lot of water," she
said. "It'll help with the cramps, which you're definitely gonna
get more of."

Marisa breathed sharply until it passed, then took the water bottle and gulped. "Thanks. I do remember reading that." She found *Ban single-use plastic* on her list and crossed it off. Afterward, she returned to her trusty duffel bag, slipping the marker back into its pocket, and from another zipper she pulled out a miniature champagne bottle. One of the teachers taking part in Marisa's Protectors noticed it, but decided to play dumb. There were larger fish at stake here. Namely, fish.

"Sorry, I only have one glass," Marisa said. "You can drink from the bottle if you want."

Amira chuckled. "Thanks, but I don't drink." She wasn't religious, sure, but that aspect of Islam was one she didn't care to set aside, even at CIS, away from her family's eyes. She looked over her shoulder. "You're just gonna pop that open here?"

At that moment Ms. Duli walked by with Master Declan, talking as they passed behind the crowd. Master Declan seemed to be taking notes on a clipboard, nodding pleasantly along, smiling. He much preferred being second-in-command, the responsibilities delegated to him, the weight of responsibility, loaded onto some other back. Master Declan preferred legwork, he realized. He had strong legs and weak shoulders.

"What are they gonna do, expel me?" Marisa laughed. She twisted the golden foil from the bottle, not knowing exactly what she should be doing, just that at some point there should be a—

Pop. The cork did not shoot spectacularly into the air like Marisa had expected, but it did get a little bit of airtime. Enough to catch some eyes. Instead of wondering what a champagne cork was doing in the air at CIS, they merely followed its trajectory for a moment and turned away, as if it had been one of those small brown birds that flitted into the building some mornings and perched high on the support beams beneath the glass ceiling. Some stopped following the cork when they noticed the ceiling, the spattering of stars amazingly visible overhead. By God, they thought, it's a school night and look at where we are.

"Plus," Marisa added, letting the frothy bubbles spill over her fingers for a moment. "My mom always says to celebrate small victories."

"Don't tell me you have a bottle for every one of those demands."

Marisa smiled. "No. But I bet he does," she said, gesturing at Peejay.

Kenji scratched the back of his neck. "I mean, it's not really the same thing," he said to Peejay, who was looking at him so intently it made Kenji feel he was, at least for the moment, the only person that mattered to him. "I can make stuff up having to do with, like, character motivations or adapt to weird things other people say."

Peejay snapped his fingers and beamed. "That. That's all I need."

Celeste had her doubts about Peejay and why everyone seemed to adore him, especially after she'd witnessed his tirade at the green room. But now she could kind of see what they could. Peejay treated others like people, like they mattered. Even if he was using them, even if he told them he was using them, he seemed to still see them as people.

"Pretend this is a scene and you're in my shoes. You're playing me. What do you do? Adapt to the situation, go with it."

Kenji felt a little put on the spot. The spot was usually comfortable for him, at least within certain parameters. He looked out at the audience. Some were whispering to each other, casting hateful glances at Marisa. Glances he happened to be in the way of. Being told "no" all his life had been terrible, a soul-squashing way to grow up, sure, but he'd become accustomed to it. This? This sheer hatred? It rattled him. He didn't like to be reminded of its presence in the world, much less be in its path. It was so much worse than his dad not understanding him.

"Forget them," Peejay said, confidently reaching to turn Kenji's chin back to meet his eyes. "You're a guy trying to throw a party at a school with no entrances, and the supplies for your party are mostly outside. That's the situation. What do you do?"

Kenji studied Peejay, disarmed by the reminder of the party. He hadn't planned on attending, since all he'd thought about was the showcase. But he knew that, all around, people must be whispering about it. That it was fueling their anger, had led them to escalate from thrown pencils to backpacks.

"Okay," Kenji said, meeting Peejay's warm eyes. He stared into the distance, letting his vision blur the way he always did right before starting a scene. It was his way of softening his mind, making it malleable, preparing to accept any situation. He nodded to show he was about to start, that he had entered the magical world of pretending. Then, in a convincing, albeit cartoonishly heavy Italian accent, he yelled, "It's a pizza party!"

Immediately he waved his hand in front of his face, as if trying to erase the words from having been spoken. "God, no. What. I'm sorry. Ignore that, I don't know what that was."

Celeste clapped a hand over her mouth to keep the laughter from spilling out (all the while recognizing that she had laughed, that the sign for the improv showcase she'd seen hours ago promising this had not misled her). Peejay pressed his lips into a tight line and blinked slowly. A few of the angry people were staring at Kenji's outburst, waiting for an explanation.

"Sorry," Kenji said again, this time to the crowd, for the moment forgetting the dynamic at hand. He apologized to Peejay, and one more time to Celeste, who could only shake her head, her hand still clamped over her mouth. "Let's start over?" he suggested.

"Let's," Peejay agreed.

Kenji stared off into the distance again. Peejay and Celeste braced themselves for what was to come.

They waited for nearly a minute, exchanging glances, not wanting to pressure Kenji. His eyes refocused, and his lips parted, ready to impart his imaginative wisdom. Then he closed his mouth again and pulled his glasses off so he could rub his eyes. "I need a scene partner, or something."

Peejay sighed, running a hand through his dark hair, mussing its usual perfect coif. Diego was still not answering his calls and time was ticking away. Sure, Peejay had arrived at parties at 1:00 a.m. before; not all was lost. But time was marching, the anger in the foyer was stewing, a party's ability to ease their pain was fading. Some people might even be forgetting about the party. He'd seen it on Kenji's face, clear as day, clear as the darling goofball's blemish-free skin. The "oh, yeah" in his eyes. Peejay needed to find a way right now. "Sure," he said to Kenji. "You be me. Who am I?"

The smile spread Kenji's lips before he even started speaking. "The king of Spain!"

Peejay mussed his hair again. "What would the king of Spain be doing here? Why would he be talking to me?"

"Oh, right," Kenji said, "we're here."

"Of course we're here, where else would we be?" He pointed at Marisa.

"Okay, we're here," Kenji agreed. "You're still king of Spain, though."

Peejay opened his mouth to protest, but Celeste interrupted him. "You have to say yes. It's a rule. Accept the situation and add to it."

Kenji beamed. Nothing from Peejay's phone yet, nothing on his mind, no clue how to get the booze in the building, how to get music in the building, no idea how to have his perfectly planned party under these circumstances, no ideas at all. He took a deep breath, thought of Hamish, whose life mantra happened to be "Say yes more." "Okay," he said.

He unfocused his eyes the way Kenji had, opened himself up to the world created for him. Then he dropped his voice and moved his arms as if he were walking. "I'm the king of Spain!" he shouted. "What is the meaning of all this? I came here for a party."

People within earshot thought, *Peejay's lost it.* They knew someone would eventually. Although it was a surprise (to everyone but Jordi Marcos) it would be Peejay Singh, they'd heard him say the word *party* and it made sense all of a sud-

162

den. Now they remembered. Their rage toward Marisa increased. Of course Peejay would be the one to lose it. The first Partyer in Chief to fail in his duties. Possibly the last one, and this was how he was going out. What a whimper with which to end lock-in night's greatest tradition.

12
2:15AM

It was around 2:15 a.m. that the hunger pains really began to take hold. Everyone in the building had had the thought, of course. How will we get food? The cafeteria was outside of the high school, out of reach. It served such terrific French fries, fantastic chicken wings, and goulash, too. It hurt their stomachs just thinking about it, and they couldn't help but count the hours until lunchtime came around (or maybe they'd even get out in time for the elementary kids' earlier lunchtime, since the whole school shared the same cafeteria and traded off lunch schedules).

They'd pushed the thought away throughout the night, replacing it with the assurance that they'd be out of the building well before hunger would be an issue. Now they weren't so sure. They imagined they could smell the salt wafting over from the cafeteria, somehow traversing walls, slipping in through those damn window slits. Their mouths were in a constant state of watering.

The ones who felt it worse hadn't taken advantage of the food trucks in time, too wrapped up in lock-in activities to tear themselves away. Those who'd been upstairs watching movies, too, felt the unmistakable pang. They'd held off dinner with popcorn, and now their stomachs grumbled, having done away with all that could be absorbed.

In the green room, Malik reached for his kebab. He unwrapped it, instantly salivating at the sight. The smell wafted over to the teachers still holed up in the green room, as they answered phone calls or were called away by Ms. Duli to patrol. All four teachers in there now looked away from their phones and craned their necks toward Malik, nostrils flared to let in as much of the smell as possible. One of them let out an inadvertent whimper, and though all the others heard it, no one had the heart to laugh. They felt like whimpering, too. God, food. When would they have it again?

It had only been eight hours or so, at maximum, but it felt like they might never eat again. If they'd known that sad PB&J hastily made in their kitchens that morning and consumed in the hallways on the way to a meeting scheduled for some blasted reason during their one free period of the day, that a goddamn hallway PB&J would be a last meal of sorts... well, they would have done something else. They would have woken up earlier or stayed up later to cook something real, something substantial, something lasting and delicious. Something like what Malik had.

He unwrapped a second tin foil packet, this one smaller, containing a sliced pickle and a dollop of schug, a Yemeni chili paste. His mom knew him so well, how he hated the pickles making the pita bread soggy, how his taste for spice came and went, so he liked having the option of how much to add. He took the first exquisite bite, a little bit of tahini dribbling out onto his chin. He used his finger to scoop it back into his mouth, not wanting to waste a single drop. A soft moan escaped his lips, similar in sound but wholly different in feeling to the teacher's whimper. Every stomach in the room grumbled in response.

Omar Ng's stomach grumbled, too. His metabolism worked like a clock, or rather, like a metronome. If he had just played a sport, hunger came. If he had just woken up, hunger came. If he had simply spent an hour or two not eating, that pendulum swung back and Omar had to eat. He wasn't in the foyer. He'd quickly figured out there was no food in the foyer, and had been scouring the building. The roof garden had provided some popcorn dregs, but he hadn't been able to figure out how to work the fancy popcorn machines (lent to CIS for the evening by a parent) to make more.

In the basement, Lolo Dufry had offered him an apple, but to Omar's six-foot-three seventeen-year-old frame, an apple was the equivalent of a single French fry. He'd taken it in greedily and gratefully, but as soon as it was gone, it was as if he hadn't eaten anything. The one place he hadn't explored yet was the gym. His sister, Joy, hadn't responded to his texts, and he worried that if he came storming in before she was ready to talk, she would clam up. But after seeing Lolo, Eli, Marisa and Malik pull out various foods, he knew Joy, too, would have planned accordingly. He hung just outside the gym door and texted her again.

I'm coming to the gym. Don't have to talk yet if you don't want, but I'm so hungry I just ate a freshman.

He waited for a moment, smacking his phone against his hand.

But I'm a freshman, she wrote, and he knew it was okay for him to come in.

It took him a few seconds to find her sitting on a stool behind some sort of improvised room divider. Funny how he'd already forgotten where the exit to the gym usually was. She pulled out a container filled with rice and curry. "I forgot about having to heat it up," she said.

He popped the lid and grabbed the metal fork she handed to him, then squatted down beside her. He studied the fork as if it was some unknown device. Joy wondered what was on his mind at that moment, why he wasn't scarfing the food down already. Was he angry at her? Would he demand she open the padlocks? She glanced over at the bucket. If Omar asked her to she would want to, she would do it in the moment. If it were entirely up to her. She pushed away the mental image of a half-digested key.

Finally, Omar spoke. "You haven't been using plastic utensils," he said. They spoke in Spanish to each other, having spent five years in Madrid before starting at CIS. "I can't be-

167

lieve I hadn't noticed." He turned his attention to the food, took the first heaping bite. It was their dad's curry, always a little bland the first day, but amazing the next, the mysterious alchemy of a night in the refrigerator. Any time Omar heard his dad say the phrase "letting the flavors marry," he pictured actual weddings, cloves walking down the aisle next to ginger, bird's eye chili clad in a Catholic priest's uniform waiting to recite a psalm. In thirty seconds, half the food was gone.

Omar resisted the urge to finish the food and put the container down. "Joy, why didn't you tell me?"

She bit her lip, wishing for a second barricade around her, something for the shame. "Marisa made us promise. She couldn't risk anyone finding out."

"Not about tonight," he said. "About this." He raised the fork. "You didn't tell me you cared about all this so much." Joy didn't know what to say. It was the first thing she'd never told him, and she was scared it had irrevocably changed things between them, that she would keep not telling him things.

"I've been drinking two Gatorades a day out of plastic bottles." He sighed.

"I've been posting all those articles as a hint. I just got into it, and by the time I realized you didn't know, it started feeling awkward to bring up how deep I was in it. I didn't know how to bring it up directly."

Omar chewed his lip. "Well, now I feel bad for only reading the headlines." They both laughed a little. "I've been reading tonight, though. I'm going to do better."

This maybe made the whole ordeal worth it. "Thanks," Joy said.

He stood, looking out at the gym over the barricade. It felt like it'd been days since the start of the decathlon, since he'd stood at the top of the key on the basketball court studying the crowd out of the corner of his eye, searching for Peejay. "There's something I haven't told you, either," he offered. "I have a crush on somebody."

Joy's head shot up, her eyes widening and filling with light. "What!" she shrieked. "Who? Tell me, tell me, tell me!"

Everyone in the gym turned in their direction. They'd forgotten they were locked in, and seeing the barricade, re-membering that's where the doors were, each of them had a brief pang of sorrow, which left as soon as they returned to what they were doing.

Omar laughed, running his hand over his close-cropped hair. He couldn't believe he was about to say it, but it made him happy to have a reason to say the name out loud.

Peejay was thinking this had been a stupid, desperate idea. Playing improv to try to coax a solution from this innocent, ridiculous boy. Trying to salvage a party that couldn't hap-pen for a person who couldn't experience it.

Then it all changed. Without possibly understanding the magnitude of what he was saying, Kenji Pierce saved the lock-in night party.

Peejay, as the king of Spain, hadn't really been doing much pretending in their scene. Mostly he was just adding an oc-casional lisp while explaining the obstacles in his way. Kenji, for his part, though he was disappointed this wasn't the show-case, that it wasn't what he was hoping for, that his father was right outside and might lose it if he saw him Being Silly dur-ing a Serious Time, had a giddy inner monologue running through his head: *How cool! I'm in a scene with Peejay Singh. A Peejay Scene-gh! Lindsay would love this.*

This, even as he solved all of Peejay's problems, one by one.

Few people around them were paying attention, most thinking Peejay was becoming untethered and dragging Kenji with him. They didn't want the same happening to them, so they turned away. Thankfully, none of the teachers were paying attention, as it would have jeopardized the whole thing, giving Kenji's solutions away.

The two teachers who'd joined ranks with Marisa's Protectors were deep in conversation with each other, discussing whether young people had the ability to stand for what they believed in and whether adults should support them or applaud their initiative and take the reins away.

So when Kenji, as Peejay, shrugged his shoulders and said, "So we get another DJ. There's gotta be at least ten in here," only the two of them in the scene, plus Celeste, Amira and Marisa heard. Peejay couldn't believe that he hadn't thought of that. It was so simple. But of course he hadn't. He couldn't have. His mind had been mired in the old rules of the world, trying to fight his circumstances instead of working within them. All this time he was thinking, "But...how?" when it should have been "Yes, and...?"

"Don't you worry your pretty little Iberian head, King. I know exactly what to do."

"You do?"

"Look at social media, one in every three people in here is a DJ. We'll find someone who can do it. And the AV club must be bored out of their minds. I'm sure they'll help set everything up." Just like that, it was coming together.

All the solutions felt so simple when Kenji spoke them. Distribute the earphones without their wrappers, connect them to a computer, get an amateur DJ to provide the music. Peejay had been married to the idea of having the old DJ perform, since he was a borderline celebrity, and a former CISer. Peejay himself had had a few classes with him, when the DJ was a senior just starting to play the local clubs. Now he was on billboards. But he wasn't in the building, so who cared. Peejay had wanted to one-up Hamish by including more people. Well, here was how he could include more people.

"And the booze?" Peejay whispered, hope rising in his throat like acid reflux.

"Well, the drinking fountains, of course."

"The drinking fountains," Peejay repeated.

Kenji realized that Peejay was saying "yes" quite a bit but not adding much "and" to it. A little frustrating, but not surprising for a first-timer. "Sure, my lord. The water source is outside the building."

"I'm not following." Celeste wasn't, either, but she was enthralled watching Kenji become someone else, speaking as if he were Peejay, as if he knew exactly what Peejay would say. Better than Peejay, it seemed, whose mouth dropped every time Kenji spoke.

Kenji threw an arm around Peejay, a move so emblematic of the other boy that several kids around them pointed and smiled at his mimicry. "Then let me lead you, Your fabulous, slow-witted Highness. The cistern, right behind this very building. It feeds the water fountains, mostly with rainwater. The teachers never drink from the fountains because they don't trust the filters, so they'll never suspect a thing. Plus, it's dry season, so there's not much in there, anyway. All we have to do is get my man on the outside to drain whatever's left in there and pour the booze inside. Then we start drinking from the fountains."

Peejay blinked. It could work. Hamish would be laughing that gleeful guffaw of his if he were here. He always loved when people surprised you like that, offered help as if it were the easiest thing in the world. It was, Hamish said, often. We just don't ask often enough, don't allow others to help.

"How do we keep from getting caught? If we get caught the party's no use, and we all get expe—" He paused. "If I get caught feeding booze to a bunch of foreign children, it'll create an international debacle."

"Ah, you sweet, royal bumpkin. The teachers will see we're desperate for water, sensible after this much time, after all. But they'll run to the teacher's lounge for their fill, since Ms. Duli herself sees to the filter's periodic replacement. The booze is in the building, they are none the wiser. The party goes on."

Peejay wanted to kiss Kenji. He settled for mussing his hair and saying, "Scene."

A moment later, Diego, his meal done, returned Peejay's call.

Marisa had started to sense the hunger building around her. Small friend groups snapping at each other and forgetting to glare at her. People getting up to go rummage through their lockers for hidden granola bars and forgotten apples, perhaps not yet moldy. One boy, a senior, came up to petition Marisa to add a vending machine to her list of demands.

"And how, exactly, would that benefit the oceans?"

The boy blinked a few times, as if he'd just now heard this

was her cause. Then he muttered a "Whatever" and sulked away, a hand on his belly as if at any moment his stomach would shoot out in search of food.

When Peejay got up, at first Marisa assumed he was seeking food, too. Soon, the school board would send Mr. Gigs to ask how she intended to feed people, and only then would she reveal that of course she'd already thought of that, too. Until then, they could suffer a little.

A minute or so later, though, Kenji stood up, too, giving Marisa a tight-lipped smile that must have meant *I'm sorry.* She didn't know what he had to be sorry about. Then she noticed Celeste—a girl whose voice she'd never heard, a girl who slinked the hallways on her own, ate lunch on her own, longingly looking at different cliques—making her way through the crowd, approaching others to whisper a question, and she knew something was up. Her first thought was that Peejay was trying to organize a breakout. The champagne had made her head light and loosened her hold on her emotions, coming close to tears every time she looked at the human barricade around her; nearing rage when she saw the angry crowd beyond them, how little they cared for what she cared about. When she looked at Amira beside her, though, she got a flood of joy that she felt like she could literally swim in.

So the thought of everyone getting away from her, all these bargaining chips she'd planned so hard to gather scurrying away due to some oversight she may have made, shortened her breath. *No, no, no*, she thought. *I haven't done enough for the reefs yet. I haven't saved the island.*

Behind her she could hear the parental crowd getting larger, could sense their restlessness as time went on. She hoped they were calling the most important people they knew, heads of corporations and ambassadors, reading the list of demands and begging, "What can you do to help?" Now it was pride flooding into her, and she tilted the last of the champagne to her lips. She forgot about Peejay.

A moment later Zaira Jacobson appeared before her. *"Sea Cuke Gazette,"* she said, brandishing a phone tuned to a recording app, her thumb hovering over the screen, impatient to get on the record. "Can I ask you a few questions?"

It was on her third shoulder tap that Celeste realized she was making the rounds successfully. She was talking to people like it was easy. Like she used to. She wasn't opening up, wasn't making new friends with the ease she'd imagined before lock-in night began, before her family moved here and she'd lost part of herself. But there was Kenji and there was Peejay now, and she could see doors opening. Not *the* doors, of course. But maybe some.

As she asked the next group if they knew anyone who was a good DJ, Celeste caught herself thinking something that would've never crossed her mind a few hours ago, something that had been thought over and over again on every other lock-in night, and on this one, too, before Marisa snapped her padlocks shut: *I hope this night never ends.*

Kenji wasn't sure the improv had really helped. He didn't have that feeling he normally had after playing, and Peejay hadn't really seemed to get the true spirit of it all. Sure, Peejay had seemed really happy, and he was happy the party had been saved, but Kenji couldn't imagine Peejay doing improv ever again. He'd certainly gotten his fill quickly, rushing out of character after that one scene. But this was kind of fun, he guessed, climbing the stairs to the second floor, toward the tech room, where surely at least one member of the AV club would be hanging out. He'd never tried to transpose a scene onto reality before, had never even considered it. Peejay had insisted, though, and maybe when they were done with this little plan Celeste would want a turn.

Reaching the tech room, Kenji knocked on the door, which was halfway open already, soft sounds filtering through computer speakers from within. He peered in and saw Sylvia Lin and Olaf Padilla each looking at a computer screen with video footage of what seemed to be the two of them looking at the computer screen. They were trying to test their editing skills to sync up their blinking on the footage. The sounds Kenji heard were background noises from lock-in night, the far-off parental chants that were only getting stronger. Compared to Sylvia and Olaf's original plan to create a mockumentary-style movie based on lock-in night, this was considerably less fun.

When Kenji knocked they quickly swiveled around, hoping for good news, for Mr. Peterson to tell them to grab their cameras. "Hey," Kenji said, and their hearts sank until he followed it up with: "You guys want to help Peejay with the party?"

This, at long last, was how Peejay managed to keep the lock-in party tradition going.

Celeste found their DJ: sophomore Nadia McIlveny, who was originally from Singapore but had spent the past three years at a music boarding school in Slovakia, learning musical theory and playing warehouse raves her classmates and the locals all attended. Music was Nadia's obsession, leaving so little room for other pursuits that it wasn't even fair to call music her passion: it was her whole life. So of course she had her computer with her, and the hard drive that contained her entire digital musical archive. Of course she wanted to DJ until sunrise, even if she lacked the proper equipment. Music didn't need a turntable or an amp to have a heartbeat. "I'll figure it out," she'd said.

Nadia had been sitting on the floor in front of the library, her headphones on, her computer plugged in. The only thing she would have to do differently was sit in the foyer to better read the crowd.

Meanwhile, outside the building, Diego sneaked around the sudden conference of parents to retrieve the booze. He'd left half the boxes stacked by the back staircase while everyone slept, the other half by the basement entrance. Then he found the cistern behind the building, a large, dark green tank with tubes coming out of it heading into the building. He was on the phone with Peejay, reporting his progress, following directions. It had been just as easy as Kenji had predicted. Peejay made a mental note to ask Kenji how the hell he'd known about the cistern. There had even been a little spout on the side to drain the cistern and not water down the massive cocktail.

Peejay had found a recipe and multiplied it, the description online promising it was sweet enough to hide the scent of alcohol and go down easily.

Anyone familiar with the careless leanings of teenage drinkers might be shaking their head in anticipation, but Peejay was confident this one other lock-in tradition might survive: no one had ever lost enough control of themselves during a lock-in party to get caught.

Half the fun was getting away with it, and everyone knew sloppiness was a surefire way to ruin everything. So people maintained their tipsiness without escalating it, and those whose drunk trains did not ever stop at Buzzed Station but took them express to Hammered Town, cut themselves off at the first sign of light-headedness, at the first slurred word or unbridled expression of love for their fellow man, at the first inappropriate dance move.

Every now and then someone would overdo it, of course, what with the amount of freshmen or sophomores who'd never had a drink before, or the amount of juniors or seniors swimming with fake confidence they could hold their liquor, but simply couldn't hold their excitement. In those surprisingly rare cases, though, CIS had always rallied to keep the party safe by keeping the drunken culprit hidden. They'd take care of their drunken friends and hide them in the corner beneath a mound of blankets, or they'd sneak them off to the student-only showers and wash them sober. Once, famously, three incoherent sophomores had been taken to the classroom-size ball pit (another lock-in tradition), where their drunken frolicking looked exactly like sober frolicking. Faculty had been none the wiser, and the lock-in party tradition lived on.

Peejay went back to the basement, texting the group he'd recruited before this whole madness began. They were each from different social groups, people who'd be able to keep a secret, but who could spread the word to their respective friends, bring in the whole of CIS with them.

This tip he'd taken straight from Hamish without building upon. Without the advice, Peejay would've just found anyone willing to be at his beck and call (read: anyone). There were ways Hamish couldn't be outdone. He wished he could tell him these things, now that the party was coming together. He wished he could tell him the story of the night.

"You're back," Lolo said.

He smiled. "Have I told you the universe has a strange and wonderful sense of humor?"

"That doesn't sound like something you'd say. Have you been reading inspirational memes again?"

"As if I need them." He returned to the boxes of earphones and started tearing through the wrappers, so the crinkling wouldn't call attention to them as he handed them off to his minions.

Lolo eyed him, confused, before the meaning sank in. She could see the joy in his movements. "You've found a way, haven't you?"

Peejay could only smirk in response.

Lolo made Peejay swear to never again mass-order something wrapped in so much plastic, and to make sure it all got recycled. He nodded solemnly.

After he'd divided up the earphones into manageable piles and handed them off to the half dozen CISers he'd chosen, he bid Lolo adieu and went over to the water fountain tucked away near the library, where teachers hadn't been monitoring much.

Part of him hadn't believed it would work, hadn't believed the cistern would be there, hadn't believed Kenji knew what he was talking about, not even a little bit. Once things were snatched away from you they weren't given back.

He looked around for teachers, saw only bookworms splayed across library furniture, one couple cuddled on the floor watching a movie on a phone. Peejay reached for the faucet, turning it a fraction of an inch. Nothing happened. Despite people's rare ability to keep it together and refrain if they needed to, alcohol was necessary at the party. Without it, they wouldn't be getting away with anything. A groan from the pipes behind the walls. Peejay turned the handle another fraction of an inch, and then it came, the gurgle he'd been waiting for. He leaned in and opened his mouth, and a few seconds later came the steady stream.

Even before it hit his lips, he could tell it wasn't water, could smell the tropical juices he'd bought. He swallowed, celebrating the small success. When he returned to the foyer, he emptied his pockets into Kenji's and Celeste's waiting hands. The earphones slipped perfectly into most eardrums, clear to avoid detection. They only had to hand them out to the crowd without arousing suspicion, bringing a few people with them down to the basement to fill their pockets, too, and spread the earphones around.

Then Sylvia and Olaf used their AV expertise to sync them up with Nadia's computer. Sylvia also managed to find the master list of school email addresses, and narrowed it down to all upper school students. From Peejay's account, she sent the following email, which he'd dictated.

Good morning, ladies and gents and all other Sea Cucumbers. Sorry for the delay. Party's on, drinks are served. Your discretion, of course, is appreciated. Kind regards, Your Partyer in Chief.

13
3:00AM

The students who'd left the CIS campus were in bed already, wondering why sleep hadn't come for them when their phones buzzed. Happy for whatever it was that would pull them from the vicelike cycle of their thoughts, they reached to their nightstand or beneath their pillows and swiped their screens alive. They read the email in an instant, after which their stomachs began to ache, their sinuses pressed with the threat of tears. Even if they knew the lock-in night they'd been denied hadn't been granted to the others, not the way it should have been, the email confirmed something they'd been fearing this whole time: they were missing out. Some tossed their phones across the room and buried their faces into their pillows to stifle a sob or a scream. Others brought their phones over their hearts and closed their eyes, waiting for the hurt to pass or sleep to come erase this wasted night from existence.

Lindsay, who'd resisted her parents' attempts to coax her from the bleachers by simply not saying much, looked up from her phone and to the building. She almost expected to see it drastically alter before her eyes: to see the lighting change somehow, shift from mere fluorescence to the hypnotic pulsing of strobe lights and laser-like green beams shooting out of the windows. She waited to hear music thumping and voices carrying through the walls and over the field, the way parties her neighbors threw always did.

Obviously this wasn't going to happen. The only change was the feeling Lindsay had. The ominous aura that seemed to surround CIS now faded away, though Lindsay guessed her parents and all the others gathered on the field couldn't sense a thing. Good, she thought. She was glad for Kenji, glad for her other friends still inside.

"Honey, this is ridiculous," her mom said for the eighth or ninth time. "What are we waiting for? Let's go home." Lindsay was briefly tempted. Why gaze on at a party she couldn't attend? Why witness—kind of—joy that didn't include her? She couldn't answer, only shook her head again.

Then Diego Cuevas came by, and dropped some earphones in her lap.

Amira saw Peejay approach Marisa, and somehow sensed this was a conversation not for her. As she stepped away,

Peejay pressed something into her hand, the movement so seamless she hadn't even noticed him reaching for her hand. Earphones? she thought, looking at her hand, which she kept cupped. She hadn't yet checked her email.

Peejay did the same with Marisa, slipping the earphones imperceptibly into her hand like a magic trick. Marisa had read the email, and understood right away what the earphones were meant for. "I'm sorry we're going to have some fun," Peejay said. "I hope that doesn't kill your hostage situation vibe." Marisa laughed. "You won't tell anyone?"

Marisa thought for a moment. She made eye contact with Amira, who was just a few steps out of earshot, then glanced around the foyer at all the faces she'd made so miserable. Behind her, the list of demands remained uncrossed save for one. Mr. Gigs hadn't come around in half an hour, which meant either the board was working on the next demand or they were patting themselves on the back and waiting for her to yield. She felt for a moment like none of it was worth it, like this had been some temporary insanity and she should end it right away. Lokoloko was going to fall apart in front of her eyes.

Then she remembered her call with her mom, and the sight of reefs in all their true splendor, and she shrugged. "No reason for me to do that. Truth be told I've been having fun, too." She slipped the earphones in, undid her ponytail so her curly hair fell over her ears. Everyone had been watching the exchange. Even those still irate at Marisa, not wanting to concede anything to her, not even an acknowledgment of the power she held over them, understood the gesture for what it was: the emperor's thumbs-up. The party would live.

Peejay smiled at her and gave a slight bow. Then he looked

across the room at Nadia and nodded. She moved her finger across the keyboard, and CIS exploded with music.

It remained perfectly quiet, of course. Or, at least, as quiet as it normally was in the groggy weekday morning preamble before classes started. There was chattering and some laughter. Maybe a little more laughter than could normally be heard on a school day, but that could easily be attributed to late-night looniness, to sleep deprivation and the madness of their circumstances. Footsteps still echoed in the hallways, the clang of a locker opening and closing still resounded on the opposite end of the building. If a teacher focused enough, they could hear the water fountains churning into action, liquid bubbling through the pipes. Whenever they did happen to catch the sound, though, the teachers would shudder with the thought of those unchanged filters. Maybe we should tell them, some teachers thought, but then another teacher would read their minds and say out loud, "Let's not give her another battle to fight. Some other time."

There began a general shuffling-about. People moving from one room to another. The adults were surprised it hadn't started earlier. The kids were just stretching their legs, loosening their stiff joints. Of course they were. The teachers themselves were starting to feel some cabin fever, a weariness in their muscles from all the inactivity. They saw lines of students gather at water fountains and they checked their reusable water bottles and saw they were empty. They started to gather in the teacher's lounge, hiding from the students, hiding from Ms. Duli and Master Declan, who kept assigning them little tasks they didn't know how to achieve. Someone made a fresh pot of coffee, laugh-complaining about the call they'd been told to make to a manufacturing plant that made the rubber bands the school used in order to check their environmental qualification. Mrs. Wu brought up the possibility of a party, wiping her lips after a long drink of water. No way, the other teachers said, standing in the doorway and looking out at the second-floor hall, and below into the foyer. Sure, there was some more movement than before. But a party? Please. There wasn't even any food in the building, how would there be booze?

You really think there's no food in the building? those who'd eaten only a sad PB&J asked. The conversation tilted in that direction, leaving the party behind.

For the next few hours, at least, everything was fine. More than that; it was special. After all that time hoping, mourning, raging, pleading, waiting—the waiting may have been the worst of it, waiting for something good to happen, waiting for the night to be over—here it came, a morsel of good luck, a helping of joy. Not that everything was forgotten, nor that they suddenly believed themselves to be free. But some amount of fun amid all of this; what a gift to receive.

The music! How had they forgotten how good music was. It had only been a handful of hours, but it felt like months.

They danced. Obviously they couldn't dance the usual way, pressed together, letting their bodies do whatever they pleased, at least not just anywhere. This sort of dancing still happened in unsupervised corners of the library, beneath the bleachers, in the shadows on the roof garden. But in their glee, the slightest movement felt like dancing. Two fingers tapping soundlessly on the ground beside them. Couples tapped one finger on their partner's hand, rubbed a fingernail down the wrist like necking during a slow song. Others danced by walking to the bathroom, the dance coming through in each step. An imperceptible shoulder shimmy, a twitching calf muscle, the steady rhythm of lungs and hearts; it was all dancing. The students at CIS had been granted permission to dance, so dance they did.

Diego had even tracked down those who were outside the high school doors but still at CIS, handing out earphones under the cover of night and a fairly huge distraction. They danced, too, while parents yelled at the dark about Marisa's plan, about their disrupted evening, their own concerns. Lindsay closed her eyes to the music and pictured she was at Kenji's side, for once not just laughing but dancing with him.

What a thrill it was to have a secret. To have something for themselves without having to include the adults. They'd gotten away with certain things in the past, of course—sneaking out of the house, borrowing the car without permission, arriving home past curfew with alcohol in their bloodstream but none on their breath—though nothing of this magnitude.

They swayed their heads to the music this way and that, even as Ms. Duli and Master Declan walked past them. They stood for another drink from the fountain, only slightly worried they would rouse suspicion. It felt like their joy would protect them. And indeed it was as if a protective layer shrouded the partyers; the bright orange tiki drink sprouting into their mouths went undetected, as did their earphones, which every now and then caught the fluorescent lighting and glinted tellingly, though no teacher ever noticed. Oh, to have something the adults in their lives could not touch.

Maya, Michael, Lydia, Lou and all the others who'd fallen for Marisa over the course of the evening gathered together, her magnetic hold still strong around them. They glanced at her out of the corner of their eyes and thought about asking her to dance. This was a stupid thought, they told themselves, although their admonishments had nothing to do with the fact that she was chained and everything to do with the fact that they couldn't possibly be worthy of her time, much less her love. They swallowed their mouthfuls of cocktail and felt their heads swim with affection. To be alive at the same time as her was enough. To be here, with her, as her hostages, and in this small but important way help her cause. What a thrill.

Since rooftops were perfect areas for partying, the roof garden filled with more people than it had seen since the movie marathon began shortly after the opening ceremony. Mrs. Wu did notice this while she made her rounds, but she conceded that it was a beautiful night out, and despite the glass enclosure on the rooftop, the fresh air seemed to pervade on the garden more than anywhere else. A good amount of the students there seemed to be sleeping, anyway. Her allergies started to kick in from the flowers, so she failed to pick up on the fact that the pockets of students standing were huddled a little closer than anyone would just to talk, that the students were moving ever so slightly, but as if to the same beat.

Eli looked on, listening to the music through earphones Peejay had been kind enough to provide. He was happy to watch this instead of the movie, happy to watch his classmates party so quietly, to let loose so fiercely and yet so subtly. Happy that the cause he had attached himself to had not entirely ruined their night. Someone came by and dropped a pencil case full of a fruity, orange liquid for Eli, and though he had no idea who had brought it or how clean the pencil case was, or what it felt like to drink alcohol, Eli felt like a part of the crowd, and so he drank.

For the time being, they were all part of the same crowd.

The parents outside shouted for Ms. Duli and the board members, shouted at each other, arguing about what should be done, ignoring the way the kids still gathered around the soccer field had grown quiet and happy. The teachers in the lounge argued about what food to order via delivery apps or phone calls. The adults in the world, for the time being, lived in a separate world, the same one they'd all existed in before.

But the students dropped the distinctions that placed them on different sides of a fight. It wouldn't last forever, but it would last the night. Peejay's party succeeded in the goal most parties, at their core, aim for: to erase differences and bring people together to celebrate a fleeting moment of joy.

Since there were no apparent dangers, Marisa's Protectors momentarily disbanded. Those in love with her moved as one to the other side of the room so they could look at her and whisper to each other about the heartache they felt, how she both caused their pain and soothed it. If anyone had thought to tell them, *It's only been a few hours*, they would have sighed and said, "I know."

The teachers who had formed part of the protectors now went to the lounge, sensing an odd desire to step away from the kids for a while, maybe foment some support for Marisa among their friends and colleagues. This left Kenji, Celeste, Peejay and Amira sitting in front of Marisa.

The joker, the wallflower, the partyer, the athlete, the provocateur, someone might have called them. Peejay leaned back on his elbows and crossed his outstretched legs at the ankle, looking out at what to a teacher looked like a mellow gathering of students, but to him was a rager, an improbable and therefore all the more beautifully orchestrated party. He took it in for a moment, soaked in the joy that had flushed in through his system, washing away all the anxiety that had clogged his veins in the previous hours. If only Hamish could see it.

Before he could break down in tears, he turned to Kenji, pulling out one of his earbuds and tucking it into his palm to keep it hidden.

"You, my friend, are a lifesaver."

Kenji couldn't help but smile. "Just wait until the pizza gets here."

Now that the scariness was over, Kenji was much more in his element. He wished Lindsay was around to see him play with Peejay. Peejay! He could hardly believe he'd recruited Peejay Singh to play improv.

Celeste already had one earbud out, not wanting to miss any conversations. She hadn't been to a party since her thirteenth birthday in Glen Ellyn, and that one had been in her backyard during the day.

There'd been a barbecue and cake, and since her parents wanted the trampoline to remain intact and the whole grade was coming over, all those eighth-grade boys, they'd taken its legs off and laid it flat on the grass. It had felt like a childhood party, with water balloons and the smell of sunscreen, no drama about who would get invited or if anyone would get drunk and make out. Even though they were freshmen, even though it had only been a few years, Celeste couldn't imagine the same word—*party*—applying to both scenarios. This one felt so much older, less innocent. It wasn't surprising she didn't know how to act. She'd been glad Kenji hadn't made any move to get up.

"I can't believe you held in your laughter when this one went cartoonishly Italian on us," Peejay said, this time turning to Celeste. Marisa's Protectors notwithstanding, she still got butterflies in her stomach when she was spoken to directly. Not from nerves, but from joy. She was not meant to be invisible.

"Look, just because I kept it in doesn't mean I wasn't laughing," she said. "I actually think I pulled an ab muscle trying not to let the laughter out." They chuckled, and a little later, when the not-quite silence was about to take hold (they all still moved their heads to the beat), Marisa spoke from just behind them.

"Aren't you gonna go enjoy your masterpiece, Peejay?"

He tilted his head, shifted his body to open up the barricade they'd set up so he wasn't giving Marisa and Amira his back. "Oh, I am."

They fell silent, waiting for him to say more. But he didn't know how to put it into words, or rather, didn't exactly know why he was enjoying it from the sidelines, why he wasn't deep in the fray. Yes, yes, he was thinking about Hamish, but that should have just been sadness, easy to recognize. There was joy here, too, and he didn't understand it.

Instinctively, Kenji and Celeste angled their bodies, too, scooting along the floor so the half circle they sat in became convex instead of concave, and included Amira and Marisa.

Marisa loved this aspect of parties, the unexpected groups you sometimes found yourself a part of, even if it was just for a moment. She was exactly this kind of dancer, too, preferring to stay away from the sweatiness of the dance floor itself and move at her own rhythm at the edges, maybe while standing in a group, dance moves woven into the conversation, just the slightest bounce in her feet and in her shoulders. She was perfectly suited to this party, and even though she hadn't granted Peejay any concessions to be able to throw it, now that he had managed, it felt like a waste not to allow herself to enjoy it. The champagne had loosened her stiff muscles, and warmed her to this random little group. "Will someone get me a sip of water?" she said, emphasizing the "water" so they all knew what she meant.

Amira hesitated, wanting to do Marisa a favor, but wanting also to keep watching her dance in her seat, to tap her feet on the stool's footrest, sway her hips. She wanted to see what it looked like when someone was loud about what they wanted and got it, wanted Marisa's strength to carry over to her. In that little pause, Celeste got up, reaching for Marisa's reusable water bottle, which was opaque and would hide the tiki drink well.

When Celeste came back she said, "Mind if I share?" and that's how they all came to pass the bottle around, feeding their buzz together. Amira passed on the drinking but felt her mood lift all the same. The decathlon was far in the back of her mind, forgotten but not gone. Same for Kenji and the showcase. All around the school, people had forgotten, for now, their largest complaints.

The energy inside the building had changed, Ms. Duli was sure of it. She'd taken the last two shifts making the rounds of the building, opening doors quickly, certain each one hid the party and she was about to catch them in the act. A few kids were taking their chances with the water fountains, returning to them often. But Ms. Duli supposed it made sense. She looked around the foyer again, trying to pick up on what exactly felt different.

In the photography lab were Gina Trang and Suni Jones, who'd been dating for the past few months and were unsure what to do with their relationship, since Suni and his family were moving to Las Vegas in a month. They took their clothes off in front of each other for the first time, not knowing what it said about their relationship or future, but knowing it was what they wanted to do. This is how they would remember the other in the years to come, bathed in a soft red light, the smell of chemicals in the air, experimental black-and-white pictures hanging from clotheslines on the wall. They had no idea what the future held, but they knew they had each other. They kept their earphones in.

Jordi Marcos was one of the few who resisted dancing. He stalked around the building scowling, feeling the urge to run into the green room and tell the teachers what was happening, but unable to bring himself to do it. Even he didn't know why. Especially every time he passed by the main doors and saw Peejay with that smirk on his face, saw Marisa sipping from her bottle in that self-satisfied way of hers. Ruining their joy would be sweet, and befitting. But it would bring the wrath of CIS down on his head. As much as he wanted to plow right through their joy, he didn't want to cause himself more pain. So he continued past the foyer and stalked off to the library, pausing by the water fountain to take a long, spiteful pull from the sweet cocktail coursing through the building.

Omar and Joy video chatted with Lolo to keep her company. A few of her friends had come down after Peejay picked up the earphones, but they didn't stick around long enough for Lolo to feel like she, too, was getting to party. Thankfully, one of these friends had left her a pleasantly sized cup full of lock-in brew. Omar, too, had had a few drinks, substituting the sloshing in his belly for actual sustenance. Eventually he would wake up starving and angry, weak from the sugar and alcohol wreaking havoc on his empty stomach, sad for Peejay. The drinks led him to confessing his crush to Lolo, as well, and in the course of the night, Lolo told Omar about Hamish, how much he meant to Peejay, and his current condition.

For now, though, he drank pleasantly, thrilled to have his sister there. They had learned something new about the other and were now championing the other sibling's ability to save the world's reefs and to marry Peejay, respectively.

Omar rolled his eyes. "Who said anything about marrying?" Though he agreed with his words here, his stomach fluttered at the association. Joy and Lolo giggled.

One would think the gym would be filled with laughter just based on that little corner of it. It was built to echo crowds cheering, after all, and no one ever thought to whisper in a gym. But even with the two or three dozen kids using it as their dance floor—here was Zaira Jacobson, her computer down and charging for the time being, her eyes closed and head swaying to the music, taking mental notes of the party's mood, not for the article she meant to post in the morning, but for herself—or their general party room, their make-out room, Mrs. Wu passed by the gym and sensed nothing out of the ordinary. A bunch of bored teens with unspent energy. She yawned, thinking maybe she should just go back to the poker game in the teacher's lounge.

This was how it went until sunrise. The adults went on trying to figure out the demands and how to meet them. Most required phone calls to businesses, a lot of which weren't open yet. Like with so many aspects of their students' lives, the grown-ups missed what was really going on, assuming they knew exactly what it was: teenage restlessness. The adults didn't forget their circumstances, or their hunger, but they didn't feel the full weight of either.

The kids drank. They danced in the hallways. They hid their joy, which only heightened it. They flirted in the foyer in plain view of everyone but no one noticed because they were busy dancing or flirting themselves with the alluring redhead from class. Could it be? Was this the day something happened to elevate their relationship with this most enticing of classmates? Yes. No room for doubts anymore, no reason to wonder if lock-in night magic remained. The redhead unmistakably moved closer, pressing a knee against theirs. What more could they want?

In hidden nooks around the school, couples professed their love, discovered their love, set the foundations for a love that might come later. Friends who'd fought before lock-in night put their troubles behind, mended the bruises between them with a quick albeit profound apology, the forgiveness just as easy and true as the plea for it. Then the friends didn't lose sight of each other the rest of the night, sharing in the joys together.

They felt as if the whole world was made for them, not just theoretically, but in practice. This night was literally just for them. They forgot about their friends on the outside, forgot about all that was out of reach, enthralled like Diego Cuevas usually was only with what was in front of them.

Diego himself, as might be expected, was in some back corner of the soccer field, hidden in the shadows, dancing to the music, at the very edge of the Bluetooth signal's capabilities. Unlike those inside CIS, Diego did not need to contain himself.

14

6:00AM

At 6:00 a.m. the first signs of sunrise colored the sky over the rooftop. Nadia, who loved sunrises and was constantly aware of when dawn broke, even if she didn't always get up to watch, put the music on autopilot—a playlist of sweeping, cinematographic droning songs that perfectly suited the kind of sunrise you stayed up to watch (as opposed to the kind you woke up for, which called for quiet, gentle, pretty music). She went up to the roof garden, which had already drawn in a few more partyers ready to wind down the night.

The first few yawns broke out in the crowd just as golden orange bursts of color appeared on the scattered clouds. Kids gathered by the glass enclosure, looking out at the city coming alive in the morning light. Some laid down on the ground or on blankets leftover from the movie marathon, exhausted from hours of nonstop dancing. Subdued though it may have appeared, their muscles were exhausted. They craned their necks, wanting just to see the sun climb over the horizon through the glass before allowing themselves to sleep.

Traffic began its assault on their senses, climbing over the school walls and up the side of the building, through the glass enclosure on the roof garden by way of the tiny window slits. A man with a high-pitched voice called out the number of a city bus route to passersby. A garbage truck parked nearby and the men who worked it rattled through the glass bottles in the dumpsters, sorting them aside.

For now, though, Nadia's music drowned out the cacophony. The orange rays poked out over the horizon, bringing to light the vast city expanse, the ocean in the distance.

Downstairs, Marisa insisted to her Protectors they should go watch with everyone else. They had spent what was left of the night talking, joking around. It hadn't been improv, but Kenji was happy. It hadn't been a sport, but Amira was happy. It wasn't a place in the world, but Celeste was happy. It hadn't been the party he'd planned for, but Peejay was happy. Her demands hadn't been met yet, but Marisa was unflappable. She was patient.

The sun rose. Thursday night unmistakably gave way to Friday morning. Parents who hadn't come in the middle of the night for their children came now. Lock-in night was officially over.

The doors remained locked.

PART II

ONE WEEK LATER

1
7:13AM

Marisa woke up to back cramps again. It was only thanks to
Amira's exercises and stretches that Marisa could still stand,
that her legs had not withered away. At least, that's what it felt
like. She gritted her teeth and reached for her toes, keeping
her knees slightly bent like Amira had taught her, pushing
the stretch to the seizing muscles in her back instead.

The foyer was awash in dawn's weak gray light. Rainy season had rolled in the day after lock-in night, about a month
earlier than usual. "Proves my point," Marisa had said with
a shrug, though she then had to go into a five-minute ex-

planation of how inclement weather was all part of the same problem as the reefs.

Even now she could hear the drizzle pattering on the skylight overhead. Those sleeping around her on blankets shoveled in through the tiny window slits seemed like injured victims after a disaster, overflow patients hooked up to IVs in parking lots. Of course, they were all healthy. Marisa felt lucky for this, lucky that anyone who needed medication had enough of it, the insulin and pills kept at the nurse's office, routinely refilled and passed through the slits. If anyone had been sick or hurt, Marisa would have to produce the key. And she would. Of course she would.

Thankfully no one had needed it, or thought to fake an illness. A slight flu had gone around a couple of days into the lock-in, but it had passed quickly without spreading too widely. There'd been a bout of food poisoning, too, but that hadn't been serious, either, and affected only a couple of kids who'd ordered delivery paella, which included some bad shrimp. The delivery guy had had to pass the rice on a tiny plate, piling it only an inch high at a time so it could fit through. It had taken him fifteen minutes, and the promise of a solid tip to keep him from fleeing, though Marisa suspected the delivery guys loved to come to the school and take selfies with the students through the windows.

That wasn't the only source of food, of course. There was a kitchen in the building, and during her planning, knowing full well the school could not meet her demands in an evening, Marisa had slowly brought in days and days of supplies of canned food and dried goods, as well as menstrual products and other hygienic necessities, so she could not be called shortsighted, or cruel. She'd hidden it all in her locker, in her cronies' lockers, in any forgotten closets and drawers she'd discovered while inventorying the tools in the building. The day of the lock-in, she brought another duffel bag full of eggs, milk, flour, sliced bread from the deli. All of that disappeared in a matter of days, but it'd been something. And she knew food was well within reach of all these kids with smartphones and chauffeurs, anyway. A text message could feed anyone in the building. They had the technology and the funds. Their privilege made it a nonissue.

Now, concerned parents brought fruits and veggies, too, sliced to the appropriate dimensions. The school board had begged them not to, at first, sensing Marisa might cave if people started starving. The school board member that suggested this lost his job afterward, and the parents were allowed to keep feeding their children, but that meant the board was at eight members instead of nine, and many decisions now lacked a tiebreaking vote, slowing everything down.

Marisa put her hands flat on the floor. She'd never been so flexible before, and she had Amira to thank for teaching her the art of pushing her body's limits. Marisa had thought a body was a solid thing, but it really was amazing how easily its edges and boundaries could be rearranged. When her cramp was gone, she popped open her Tupperware filled with sliced bananas and checked her messages.

These weren't on her phone, but in a repurposed tissue box they'd tied up to the wall. Mr. Gigs came by several times a day to deliver news, ask questions on behalf of the board, show drafts of the demands being met. A lot of this took place via phone and email, too, but Mr. Gigs had stuck to the lock-in routine, happy to step away from the other adults, to be useful in some slight way, to be the bridge between the students and the adults (he'd started thinking all the students were on Marisa's side). He'd left a few notes over the course of the night: *Habitat for Humanity trip changed to Rescue the Reefs. Accommodations in eco-hostel. Boats to use eco-diesel. Mineral sunscreen only on reef rescue dives. Okay?*

Marisa patted her pockets for a pen, frowning when she felt nothing against her thighs. No sooner had she frowned than a pen appeared before her eyes. Amira.

Marisa felt a deep swell of gratitude for her, though it came with a feeling of uselessness, too. What could she possibly give Amira in return? What good was she, chained to a door, always needing? What could have this fiasco looked like without Amira?

It would've had a great more deal of suffering, to be sure. That's what Marisa had planned on, it's what she'd told her cronies: prepare to suffer for this. They might not have found anyone sympathetic to their cause to help empty their buckets if they got full, they might not have found privacy to change into fresh clothes. They might have to make do with the supply of canned food they'd packed into their bags, if no one offered to run to the window slats for them.

And, to their credit, the cronies had all prepared to suffer. They were only following Marisa's lead.

But with Amira there, it had felt so…easy. Like Marisa could do this for months to come. However long it took.

"Thanks," she said quietly, relishing how common it was for their fingers to brush now. She scribbled some notes on the back of Mr. Gigs's paper—*carpool to airport, percentage of proceeds to local environmental group, check that eco-hostel's practices actually align with conservationist efforts*—then placed it on top of the tissue box for Mr. Gigs to pick up later. "How'd you sleep?" she asked Amira.

It caused a rush within her to realize how many days in a row she'd asked this, the casual domesticity of it. It was what her parents asked each other every morning. Marisa had never been in a relationship, so she didn't know all of its benchmarks. This, premature though the thought might have been, felt like one.

Amira yawned, laughing through it, since her body had responded to Marisa's question for her. She did a halfhearted full-body stretch, not awake enough yet to recognize what her body needed. Not that she listened anymore.

She sat up, scanning the foyer, counting the seconds that had passed since she'd looked at Marisa. If you wait ten more, she thought, Marisa will smile at you. If you wait thirty, she'll ask you to knead the knots out of her shoulders. If you wait forty-five, the conflicting facets of your life will easily fold into each other, and your mother will accept you.

The wind howled, and the rain drizzle turned to downpour. Amira used to love running in the rain. (It felt dramatic to phrase it that way, but it'd already felt like another life to be out there, in the rain.) She'd loved the blanket of sound it put between her and the rest of the world, had loved the hot showers after a long run in a cold drizzle, had loved the mere act of running when someone else might not be disciplined enough to. She loved telling her body what it could do. Now, though, the rain depressed her, made her want to blow raspberries in boredom, as if it was somehow limiting her options.

★ ★ ★

The early storm roused a few kids in the foyer from sleep. Some tossed off sweatshirts or thin sheets that served as blankets and headed straight for the bathroom. Others grabbed towels—thin, quick-dry travel towels, which were the only ones that could be shoved through the windows—and shuffled upstairs toward the gymnasium locker rooms to shower before the morning rush.

Amira noticed Kenji was awake, too, scrolling through his phone, his eyes half-open but his glasses already on, cowlick as prominent as ever. He had earphones in, black, corded ones, not the lock-in earphones, which were in perfect working order but hardly anyone used anymore. It was as if the students had had the best possible experience with the earphones and didn't want to sully the memory of the lock-in night party with everyday use. He spotted Amira and gave her a little wave, and only then did Amira allow herself to look back at Marisa.

She was chewing on her thumb and staring absently across the foyer, her eyes unfocused like Kenji's before his improv scene with Peejay. Amira rose to her feet, her heart suddenly thumping so hard she felt it in her stomach, too.

"Morning run already?" Marisa asked, feeling ridiculous for the whine in her voice. Amira spent such a huge chunk of her day by Marisa's side, she was entitled to time away, entitled to spend her mornings working off her considerable energy, working off the frustrations of being stuck in here because of Marisa.

Amira nodded and tried to smile, not sure why she was feeling hurt. The game—counting seconds and creating thresholds and rewards—was entirely in her head. She couldn't be mad at Marisa for not following rules she didn't know existed. She waved goodbye, then walked around the strewn, sleeping bodies toward the stairs, shaking her arms out and pretending to loosen her muscles.

Each morning she supposedly went to work out. To run, like she used to. To do yoga, play basketball, lift weights. This is what Marisa assumed, and Amira never corrected her. Instead, she went and sat in the gym and watched others do yoga and felt a deep and confusing anger at Marisa. Marisa, who had taken away from her all the training, had taken away her own version of protesting against her mother. Marisa, who had taken the decathlon away from her, and in its place left daydreams and butterflies, sweaty palms, tingles. Something even more complicated than what she had before. Amira had been in control of her body for so long, and in more ways than one Marisa had taken the control away from her. And Amira didn't know which was louder: the anger, or the butterflies.

Her mother's voice reverberated in her head: a girl could not.

Kenji hadn't been sleeping well. He knew few people who'd been getting much sleep on the floor. Even Shmuli Rogers, who'd claimed dibs on the couch in the library, slept fitfully, waking up from dreams that he was late to class, and needing to pee every two hours. Kenji wasn't doing himself any favors by listening to podcasts in the middle of the night or as soon as he woke up. He found himself focusing too much to fall back asleep once he'd done this, enthralled in that world he loved so much, often having to stifle his laughter so as not to wake others.

Which was better than the alternative: to not sleep, anyway, and to think of his father.

It felt inevitable, really, that he would have to be the one to call his father and tell him to cancel the construction project he'd been speaking about since they moved here. The whole reason they moved to this place, the whole reason Kenji lived in a world of lock-ins and Lindsay and "Yes, and…" Kenji would have to speak to his father and tell him to pull its plug.

Eventually, Marisa would figure out Arthur Pierce was in charge of the project, and he was Kenji's father, and she would tell him to call. If she herself didn't do it, the rest of the school would. They'd beg him to, they'd force him to. They'd pull the phone from his pocket and dial, pressing it against his head until he spoke and asked this huge thing of his father.

And when his father said no, because of course he would, Kenji would know finally, in no uncertain terms, how little he meant to him.

It was already sneaking in, anyway, that realization. Creeping around, like dread itself, like every image of dread Kenji had ever seen in movies, fog curling its way around dead tree trunks, a shadow lurking in a hallway.

During those sleepless nights on CIS's floor, Kenji thought about how, even if he hadn't told his father his company was named in the list of demands, surely his father already knew. And yet the demand remained uncrossed. Which meant his father had already weighed the question of helping, in whatever way he could, to help set his son free from a hostage situation, or canceling a work project, and he had chosen the latter. Day after day, for a week now, he had chosen the latter.

So of course Kenji listened to podcasts. At night, and throughout the strange new days at CIS—as the teachers tried to teach classes almost no one attended, as they struggled to meet Marisa's demands, as they exhausted themselves haranguing kids from going *Lord of the Flies* all over again—Kenji turned to improv. He didn't want to think about inevitabilities, about how much he was hiding from his new little group of friends, about his father. He just wanted to laugh.

One exception to the sleep deprivation was Peejay. He seemed to sleep all day, hidden and huddled beneath the cheap pashmina his mother had brought for him shortly after lock-in night.

No one had caught the whole exchange—they were busy collecting things from their own parents, or claiming corners of the school, or once again trying to find some air-conditioning vents to climb into action-movie style to finally flee from this scholarly prison—just that she handed the pashmina, and spoke for a little while, and then the life drained from Peejay's face. He'd practically been asleep since then.

When he did wake, he kept the pashmina wrapped around him. Kenji had no idea how to help him outside of continuing to invite him to play improv, and to every now and then refill his water bottle while he slept.

It was almost as if Peejay was soaking up all the sleep his classmates lost, as if all those hours of slumber were bouncing around the building unable to escape, and Peejay had taken it on himself to absorb them all. Just like he'd absorbed the responsibilities of the party, or how he seemed to carry within

209

him, before, enough life for the whole school, Peejay had taken it all on his shoulders.

What Kenji didn't know, couldn't know, was that the morning after Peejay had thrown the best party CIS had ever seen, Hamish succumbed to an infection he'd developed during his coma. Peejay had still been feeling the buzz of the rum in his blood, the buzz of the party itself, when his mother reached her hand up to attempt to offer her consolation through the window slit. But it was beyond her reach, beyond Peejay's, and after a few moments she had recovered from her bout of crying and told him she would let him know when the funeral would be.

Kenji stared at the perfectly still mass hidden within the blue pashmina, wishing Peejay would at least snore, show some sign that he found peace and pleasure in sleep. He reached out, resting his hand on Peejay's back for a second, wondering if it provided any comfort for Peejay or if it was a gesture he made only for himself. Then he rose, grabbing his toothbrush and toothpaste.

Kenji kind of loved these mornings. He would never say it to anyone but Celeste or Lindsay (although, these days, he hated mentioning anything about what went on inside the building to Lindsay—there was a strange longing in her texts, an obvious sense she felt she was missing something, as if he hadn't been locked inside but rather she was the one who'd been locked out), but it felt like summer camp. Or it was like long-form improv they'd all accidentally fallen into, the whole school playing pretend. It made him feel like he could stay safely within the school for a long time.

With that thought he resumed listening to the podcast he'd paused as he gathered his toiletries, passing, as he pressed Play, Omar Ng.

Peejay watched the world through the navy blue haze of his mother's pashmina. Everyone seemed to think he was sleeping at all times, and though he was dozing much more than normal, he spent much of the day simply looking out at the school. He watched Marisa, Amira, Kenji and Celeste get closer. Physically more than anything. It was amazing to see them return to their places around Marisa again and again, each day tightening the semicircle a little more. It was as if they felt someone had assigned them the spots, and they weren't allowed to change, weren't free to go where they wanted. Or rather, it was as if they'd all secretly wanted to be assigned the same group project, had been longing for each other's company all this time, and were thrilled now for the excuse.

Somehow, despite his retreat into his pashmina, despite his lack of interest in interacting with the world, despite the little he gave them on the rare times he stood or sat near them with his pashmina draped around his shoulders, they seemed to include him in their makeshift group.

They ate together, always, like a family, though not exactly the liveliest family he'd seen, what with Celeste's silence and Kenji's lost laugh and Amira's soul trapped in inactivity and Marisa staring off into the distance and thinking obviously of the sea, holding her breath as if she were snorkeling, diving down to see the fish feeding on the reef's many tiny branches. And Peejay was the depressive they never talked about but cared for, anyway. They left him little plates on the floor when he slept, like offerings at a shrine. Since he couldn't bring himself to go to the kitchen three times a day, he took them gratefully, like a stray cat lapping at a bowl of milk, though he didn't always remember emerging from his soft-clothed shell to eat.

Hamish, had he been around to see all this, had he survived long enough for Peejay to exit the building and tell him the story of lock-in night, might have loved this part of the story more than anything else. This had been the happiness Peejay had felt on lock-in night, the reason he'd watched from afar and not joined in. The joy was in bringing joy to others.

Omar had emptied the trash bin onto the floor and was using a broom handle to sort through wadded paper towels. He found another plastic bag, ripped open, delivery food containers shoved back inside, Styrofoam and vastly unrecyclable no. 6 plastic sticky with soy sauce. The bag couldn't have possibly fit through the window with containers inside, so why take it into the building at all? He didn't understand the people around him anymore. He shook his head and flipped the broom around, sweeping the plastic into a separate garbage bag.

People had taken to calling him "Sweep" as in "Did you see Omar 'Sweep' Ng again?" It didn't bother him. In fact, he was happy that, in his athletic life, no similar lazy nickname had ever stuck around (a few teammates had tried to take a similar approach with his last name and dubbed him Omar "Score" Ng, but it was impossible to use the ill-conceived nickname anywhere near the basketball court without creating mass confusion, so it had quickly died out). He wouldn't mind being known for this, though, he thought as he righted the trash can back up.

Then he looked over toward Peejay, to see if he had emerged. He had not, and it made Omar think of Hamish, whom he had never met, but whose well-being he wished for more than anything else.

From the foyer, watching Omar passing by, Celeste sat up and yawned, wondering what he did with all that plastic he collected. She checked her hair covering to make sure it hadn't moved throughout the night, then looked down at her phone and saw text messages from her mom (How's prison?) and from Jamie back home. Ever since the lock-in and the news segments, Jamie and a few others had started texting again, though lately less and less, just like it had been when Celeste had first moved. Eventually the fact of the lock-in would no longer be enough to maintain conversation, just like the fact of the move hadn't been enough to fight off time zones and absence.

For now, though, her heart pulsed with joy at having something to latch on to. She responded to her friends first (not much still here. lol. how are you? what's going on in illinois? have you gone into the city much lately?). Then she responded to her mom (still no outdoor time :/) thinking Kenji and his improv had turned her into a funnier person, though why

213

she couldn't be funny with her old friends or out loud was a question she didn't have an answer to.

For her morning routine, Celeste had taken to heading to the gym for a yoga session. At first Celeste had only followed Amira there, feeling much like she had with Kenji the night of the lock-in, a hopeful puppy wanting scraps of affection, not even begging for them, just happy for whatever fell to the ground.

Then, after a couple days, Ms. Duli started a yoga class in the gym, and rather than sit quietly next to Amira every morning, Celeste joined in. People's joints were hungry for the movement, their muscles aching for work. Celeste was merely hungry for conversation. For somewhere to stand and feel at home. She was starting to get little nods in the halls from other people who attended—Zaira Jacobson, Dov Nudel, even Ms. Duli herself, who missed her daily yoga sessions too much to care she was blurring teacher/student/hostage lines—and she cherished these hints that it was still possible, she could still find friends here.

Kenji had seemed like the answer, at least for a little while. The wider group of the Protectors, too, that first morning. After the sun rose and warmed the inside of the building, as the whole school started dozing off their drunkenness, their exhaustion and their glee, their disbelief, sitting among them all, Celeste had even had that thought: finally. Here was her place.

But then Peejay had disappeared beneath the pashmina, and Amira had started slinking away, supposedly to work out, though she was rarely in the gym, or she and Marisa were in some world that existed only between the two of them, and Kenji had started slipping his earphones in all the time.

Celeste now had a place to sit and sleep, and some people occasionally deigned to look at her, but a home this was not.

On the good days, she exchanged a handful of words with Kenji. She ate with him, and she shared a laugh or two with him, listened to him talk about a podcast episode he'd found funny. A couple of days, though, she didn't speak at all, just sat and listened and sometimes escaped to whatever quiet corners of the school she could find and made little noises to test whether she'd lost her ability to speak.

Now she kicked away her bedsheets and ruffled around for her workout gear, which her dad insisted on coming by to pick up every afternoon to wash and dry for her mom to return clean and ready to use that evening. She grabbed her hair cream, her lotion and her toothbrush. "Just 'cause you're locked up doesn't mean you stop taking care of yourself," her mom had said, passing the travel-size containers through the window slits.

Then Celeste gave Marisa a little smile and a shy wave before heading to the locker rooms to change and get ready for the day.

Marisa missed the reefs.

With her planning for the lock-in, the lock-in itself and the week that had passed since she'd closed the doors, a full month had gone by since she'd seen a reef in person.

It'd been a long time since she'd gone a month without snorkeling, even if it was a sad, dying stretch of bleached reef inhabited only by a handful of miserable-looking faded groupers. She couldn't remember the last time she'd gone more than a few days without so much as seeing the ocean.

She missed that other world, the gurgling hum of life below the waves, the wonders of her own breathing in the water, those strange and beautiful creatures going about their strange and beautiful lives, the vast expanse of blue, of blues, rather, so many rich shades, darker the farther you looked, the deeper you went, each shade hiding its own range of creatures most people were completely unaware of, completely uncaring about their existence. She missed the magic of diving below that blue mirror, like a character in a fairy tale discovering a hidden world. She missed how the ocean still inspired awe and fear in her, its looming powers and dangers becoming more apparent the more she became familiar with it.

She missed just being near the ocean, hearing all the different ways waves could crash upon the shore, all their rhythms. What she wouldn't give to feel an ocean breeze on sun-kissed skin, to watch the orange shimmer of the setting sun dance on the surface of a calm day while she tried to suss out the currents and riptides. Her feet buried in the sand while her parents sipped on cold beers, drips of condensation gathering sand each time they lifted the bottles up to their lips. She allowed herself to include Amira in this little fantasy, reading a book at her side. She could picture Diego on a lounge chair next to her, eyes hidden behind sunglasses, taking everything in, his shirt off and swim shorts hiked high up his thighs, soaking in the tapered evening sun.

She missed him, too, and wondered what he was doing at that moment, wondered what his past week had been like. Marisa typically admired her older brother's ability to ignore his phone for days at a time, but right now she wished he was better at returning texts, at having phone conversations that felt real instead of just brimming with the need to hang up. What was the world out there saying? The real world, not the one Marisa could see on her phone. Were things changing? Did anyone actually care?

As she was thinking and stretching her right calf out like Amira had taught her, two things happened spontaneously. The first: the bell rang. It was the first morning bell, one maddeningly used not to tell kids to get to their first class, but a sort of warning bell—The Snooze, they all called it— which indicated another trilling bell would ring in another thirty minutes, this one, yes, meant to push them toward their classes. Though for the past week, neither bell had been very effective, succeeding less in directing the kids around the building and more in annoying them.

The second: Dov Nudel, part of the Jordi Marcos–led group organizing a breakout, who'd all this time been climbing a rope the group had managed to tie to the rafters by lassoing it from the second floor in the middle of the night, fell two stories to the ground, directly onto Marisa's leg.

2

7:35AM

Marisa's leg jutted out at a strange, worrying angle. She got the sense that she should be screaming.

Footsteps pounded on the floor and skittered to a halt. She felt people gather around, and heard them speak, though none of their words sank in. Nor did she turn to look at them. She was transfixed by the angle her leg had taken, the fact that it wasn't bleeding. "How is it not bleeding?" she asked no one in particular.

Then the pain came.

First in her shoulder, strangely, nowhere near the break. It was where Dov made contact first, his elbows up instinctively, prepared to fall. Then her entire left side, where he'd started to flatten her, easing his own fall. Finally, the sharp, bright agony from her leg, a searing flash unlike anything she'd felt before.

She wanted to scream, but didn't, choosing instead to breathe. Nearby, Dov brushed himself off, chuckling, pretty sore. Though his plan was to fall, or at least make it look like he had fallen, it hurt a little more than he'd been expecting.

Then he realized he was supposed to fake an injury to force Marisa to open the doors, and here he was brushing himself off. Right. He realized he'd accidentally fallen on her. The rope had swung from his clumsy climbing and his clumsier jump. He turned to see if she was okay, and caught sight of her leg.

This was definitely not how things should have gone. He screamed.

All around school, people heard Dov's screams. Lolo in the basement, Eli on the roof, Joy in the gym, Malik in the green room, of course, but also the kids arriving to school just then, and all the parents in their cars, waiting for the line to inch forward toward the front gate so they could let their kids out. They turned down the volume on their radios, asking, "What was that?" To kids too sleepy to respond, or who were wearing earphones to block attempts at morning conversation.

Out on the soccer field, Lindsay and the others who'd stayed behind poked their heads out of their tents (makeshift ones, or those brought in by parents, after hours of trying to convince their children to come home, that it would all be over soon, that they were silly and unreasonable. So many parents had been there on the soccer field the morning after lock-in, still begging their kids to leave, finally going to the store to buy the tents, sleeping there with their children, even, trying to convince them hour after hour that there was nothing to stick around for) and gave each other looks that said, *I don't know anything, do you?*

The early arrivals who'd come on the buses before The Snooze ran to the high school building, their umbrellas turning inside out in the wind. The middle school kids raced over, too, as did all those poor souls who'd been locked out a week ago, and who since that day had felt strangely absent in the world, as if they were watching a movie of their lives instead of actually living it. They gathered by the windows, something they'd tired of quickly the first day back, since there didn't seemed to be anything of note going on, just kids sitting and wandering the halls. They'd kept doing it in the days since, of course, but it'd been boring. No one had screamed before. The elementary children had stayed away entirely, not quite understanding what was going on in that building, terrified of it. The cameras, the reporters, the world's prying eyes, too, had turned away a couple of days ago.

The story had hooked the public right away, especially when Zaira published her piece that first Friday morning after the lock-in, when the parents were all still gathered in their evening wear, their voices gone hoarse from screaming. Major media outlets syndicated the story, and around the world people tuned in, CIS on everyone's lips. The world waited for a dramatic conclusion—police storming in, a major environmental revolution, the parents rioting? Who knew how it would turn out. But the days went by and nothing happened—the school changed its motto to reflect its newly adapted environmental curriculum, big whoop—and people turned their attention elsewhere.

Local stations and some major international outlets still sent an affiliate junior reporter to update the story. And of course, scientists, who had much longer attention spans, continued to be riveted, rooting for Marisa and knowing that to wait a week, in the long stretch of time, was a brief snap of the fingers. Not such a big deal to wait for actual change.

Soon, like Lindsay and the other free CISers, the reporters would be standing back in the shrubs surrounding the building, pressing their faces against the glass to peer in and see what was causing those screams.

As Marisa breathed through her pain, wavering on the edge of consciousness, listening to Dov's incessant and dramatic screams, she thought about her list. Three demands had been met in total. She'd received so many emails from environmentalists commending her on the school's single-use plastic ban, or the petition to extend that ban beyond the school's perimeters, which had by now been signed by most students and parents (Jordi Marcos and his father were two notable holdouts), on turning the world's eyes to the cause. However briefly, their attention mattered.

But there was still so much left to do. She still had to save Lokoloko. Marisa let her body go limp against her chains, which were still taut, even if she sometimes managed to forget they were there at all (other times they were all she could focus on, as if all her nerve endings other than those in contact with the chains had gone numb). She put all her weight on her stool, not knowing if she should let her leg hang limp or if she should strain herself by raising it.

Amira wasn't around to tell her what was best. None of the Protectors were around actually, save for Peejay, who couldn't possibly still be sleeping through the noise, but who hadn't stirred at all.

The crowd, at first, rushed toward Dov, wondering how they could help, what had gone wrong, no one having seen the way he'd intentionally swung off the rope, or his relatively safe (for him) landing. Eventually his screaming stopped, though, and they saw Marisa.

They had no idea what to do. Give her room to breathe? Pop the leg back into place? Step forward and offer a reassuring hand on her chained shoulder? Anything they could think of felt equally useless, ridiculous. So they stood on the edge, alternately looking at her and turning away.

Those who hadn't grown faint took baby steps forward, then baby steps backward, not sure which would help. It would've given the impression, to someone watching from afar, that the crowd was dancing, like they had on lock-in night. Even the teachers who'd gathered around, who'd moved their way to the very front of the crowd with a sense of responsibility, recognized how helpless they were in the face of this.

The students were looking at them as if they should know what to do, but the teachers still worried themselves sicker by looking up symptoms on the internet, still avoided the doctor for fear of a diagnosis or paperwork, still texted that one friend of a friend who'd gone to med school asking for advice. The teachers knew to drink plenty of fluids during an illness and to wash their hands after using the bathroom, and that about summed up their sweeping knowledge of how to fix the wrongs that could befall a human body. Marisa's leg? That fucking thing? No way. They didn't have a clue what to do.

Amira and Celeste, who had heard the screams from the gym, now arrived to the growing crowd and felt their stomachs drop, as if they could tell exactly what had happened. Like they had on lock-in night, they worked their way to the front of the crowd, ambulance-chasing behind Nurse Hae, both of them hoping desperately she would stop moving before she got to the doors, that whatever had gone wrong had not gone wrong to Marisa.

Then they froze.

Amira resisted the urge to run at Marisa, to try to figure out how she could gently guide her body into feeling better.

Celeste assured herself Nurse Hae knew what to do; she would have the tools and medicines with which to do it in the modest pharmacy that made up her office. Sure, she knew everyone who went in there, whether it was for a headache, an upset stomach, menstrual cramps, a sprained ankle or any other ailment, was always offered just a cup of chamomile tea. Sometimes, if they were lucky, the tea came with a single sienna-colored 20mg ibuprofen wrapped up in a paper napkin.

But Celeste hoped for Marisa's sake, for the oceans', that the nurse was just withholding the good stuff, advised by the school's insurance providers to downplay all ailments.

Nurse Hae's porcelain face appeared in front of Marisa. She hoped maybe something in Nurse Hae's expression would reassure her. That it looked and felt worse than it really was. That this wasn't going to interfere with her plans, this wasn't a pain that would go on forever, a life-changing pain, but merely an inconvenience, an unfortunate speed bump that would make winning the fight all the sweeter.

However, Nurse Hae shook her head, as if knowing exactly what Marisa was hoping to hear. Comfort wasn't coming.

The word spread, jumping from one person to another like a wildfire jumping empty lanes of a freeway by heat alone. Marisa needed urgent medical attention. Her leg was broken in at least one place, possibly more. The pain couldn't be managed by anything the nurse had, and even if some morphine were passed through the window (Nurse Hae was already working on heavy-duty painkillers), there was a chance she needed surgery. No: she absolutely needed surgery or the leg would never heal. That was a fact. But there might also be other damage, a concussion, cracked ribs, internal bleeding, even. Dov had landed on her from two stories up.

Everyone gleaned the information first without immediately considering what it meant for her, the decision she would have to make. Their freedom had always been in her hands. But nothing had made her decision to keep them in hard. Because of this, after all this time, their freedom seemed to be something hypothetical and nebulous, something as hard to grasp on to as the idea of saving the world.

Now, though, it seemed clear. For her own good, she would open the doors. They were going to be free.

While Dov screamed about nothing and Marisa breathed tenuously through her pain, Peejay was beating himself up, thinking: *Get up.* Thinking: *Hamish would want you to get up.* Over and over, his body not listening to the words, the rest of his brain not even listening to the words, just repeating them.

Days of this. He wasn't even sure how long he'd been lying there exactly. He hadn't kept count. It felt like his whole life could pass by and he still wouldn't find it within him to rise. He knew only that the funeral had not happened yet, knew only that the doors were still closed.

Momentarily freeing himself from his thoughts, he came to as the crowd shuffled around him, focusing his eyes on the world beyond the pashmina. Nurse Hae emerged from a crowd. Behind her, Amira, Celeste and Kenji followed, as well as Ms. Duli, clad in yoga pants and a long-sleeved shirt.

All of them gathered around Marisa, and it seemed as if the whole school had appeared. Not just those inside the building but those outside, too, the whole school looking at her now, wondering what she would do. No one seemed to pay Peejay any mind, except for Kenji and Celeste, who knelt by his side, making sure no one accidentally stepped on him. It made him want to cry, and the only reason he didn't was to remain invisible.

Even though Peejay hadn't gleaned much information like everyone else, didn't actually remember hearing Dov fall from the ceiling onto Marisa's outstretched leg, hadn't been particularly cognizant of anything that had happened in school the past week, he knew well enough everything that had come before what was happening now had been small—shifts in routine, days rearranging themselves one detail at a time into a new normal, which might have continued on for a long time if not for this.

★ ★ ★

Everyone waited for the nurse to speak, to say what they all expected but wouldn't fully accept until the words were out there. They wanted her to really get into the details of Marisa's break, mention specific bone names, the consequences that would come. They wanted her to be gruesome, unequivocal. To tell Marisa: "You have to open the doors." Her first words, however, were, "I'm sorry."

When the nurse was done with all the medical information she had, when she'd provided Marisa with her best guesses and possible scenarios, she apologized again and stood back, near the crowd, granting Marisa the room to make her decision.

Now all eyes were on her again. Ms. Duli's discerning stare, and Jordi Marcos's smug smile, and a few tear-rimmed eyes belonging to Maya Klutzheisen and Michael Obonte, who loved Marisa so and hated to see her hurt. There were those who loved Marisa and were prepared to love her no matter what she did, but also those who loved her and felt they might love her a little less if she opened the door, as well as those who felt they might love her less if she didn't open the door. There were plenty of very angry people still looking at her the way they did on lock-in night, and those whose anger had simmered away and now felt nothing but a vague queasiness at the sight of her leg (or rather, just the memory of it, since it had now been gently covered by a blanket to spare everyone the sight).

Like she had that first night, Marisa met every single pair of eyes in the building, even momentarily catching Peejay's stare through the shawl. Her jaw was clenched, as if that could give the pain somewhere to go. Her fists were shaking, in part because of the adrenaline her body was shooting through her to help ease the pain, sure, but also because of the anger that something so stupid might jeopardize this thing she'd spent so long planning. Outside, other students strained to see and hear over the rain. They knew the next bell was coming and they begged her silently to speak before it rang. But they didn't have to worry. Here came her answer, and they wouldn't even have to hear it to understand exactly what her decision would be.

Marisa took a breath—the motion alone causing so much pain to shoot through her entire body that she nearly had to take another just to recover—and, so imperceptibly that many in the crowd who'd blinked at the wrong time missed it, she shook her head.

3

7:57AM

The air turned heavy again. It hadn't ever quite gotten light, at least not as light as it had been during lock-in night, but they'd all forgotten how much the little meaningless transgressions humans perpetrated on one another could shift the weight of air.

In the aftermath of Marisa's headshake, their lungs felt compressed, their breaths not carrying quite enough oxygen. The teachers, no less impacted by Marisa's refusal to let herself out, suddenly remembered classes were about to start. They shuffled away to their rooms, calling out halfheartedly for their students to follow. It'd felt like madness when the board had told them to continue to hold classes during the extended lock-in, and this was even more absurd. Few had actually come, and those who had only did so out of boredom. Mostly, the teachers worked on lesson plans to post online, for those students on the outside, who had never been timelier with their work.

That morning, though, the students followed their teachers. They wanted to sit, take their mind off this disappointment, despite how brief their hope had been. They'd known Marisa was committed, they'd known she was strong. They hadn't known just how much.

"We're going to be in here forever, aren't we?" Guillem Kim said to no one in particular, though his voice resounded in the stairwell. No one cared to answer him, not even Jordi Marcos, whose plan had somehow failed. He briefly considered running at Marisa full force, breaking her other leg, screaming at her to produce the key. The rage refused to move his legs, though, and he ended up getting caught up in the crowd shuffling away, wondering how he'd explain to his dad what had just happened.

The students filed into their classes, sat at their usual pre-lock-in spots. They looked out the rain-streaked window blankly, like they had so many times throughout the year out of mere morning fogginess, out of the vague dread of being at school yet again. They couldn't see the outline of the city, nor the ocean off in the distance. Everything was a blurry smear of gray. The teachers shuffled through their papers, clicked around their computers, trying to find the lesson plan they'd prepared out of sheer habit.

The only ones remaining in the foyer were Nurse Hae and Marisa's Protectors, or at least the core group.

They, too, felt the atmosphere's leaden shift. No one said a word, though their eyes kept flicking from one to the other and then to the floor, to Marisa, who was taking measured breaths in through her nose and out through her mouth, her teeth gritted as if this was just another cramp that would soon pass. Nurse Hae had immobilized the leg, and placed a few stools in a row so Marisa could have some support for it, but it was an imperfect setup, and every movement pained her. The three sienna pills she'd been granted might as well have been candy.

Peejay watched through the pashmina. For some reason, the tension almost made him want to smile. Almost. Maybe it was because it had nothing to do with Hamish. Or maybe it was because Hamish would smile at this unlikely group being all tense together.

That had been the best part of lock-in night for Peejay. Remembering the real reason he'd been so driven to throw the party. It hadn't been for the glory, hadn't been to outdo his brother. It had been to provide joy to others, the way Hamish had. To honor him that way.

But Hamish was gone now.

Peejay turned his attention back to the tension in the air.

Kenji played with his shoelaces, raising his eyes less than anyone else, distracting himself by wondering why he was even bothering to wear shoes. He kept wanting to make jokes, if only to forget the heaviness, but his inability to think of anything seemed to only add to it. He wished he hadn't pushed through the crowd and seen Marisa's leg. It was impossible to "Yes, and…" the unnatural protrusion, impossible to carry the story forward. It ended thoughts, that leg. A damn shame it hadn't ended the lock-in and absolved him of the talk with his dad.

Celeste was chewing her bottom lip, hugging a knee close to her. Marisa stared resolutely across the room, her chin up, daring someone to speak, to say she was wrong.

It was Amira who broke the ten-minute silence. "You have to go, Em."

Amazing when a nickname for someone else first slipped past your lips. Amira had been thinking of Marisa as Em for days now, and though she didn't know why this was the moment she chose to give in to the urge to say it, it felt lovely leaving her lips. A touch, of sorts.

"I'm not gonna die or anything," Marisa said. It was a wonder she had it in her to speak so resolutely. Anyone else would be whimpering just to get a word out.

"But you're suffering, Em."

Marisa tensed her jaw. She liked this new little nickname, though she didn't know why Amira was talking about giving up. Didn't she see the list of demands?

"This is his fault."

"No one's saying otherwise. Who knows what the hell he was doing on that rope," Amira said, shaking her head.

"Maybe he was practicing for one of those TV shows? You know, like *Ultimate Ninja Warrior*? Where they do crazy obstacle courses?" Kenji said. "Sorry, I'll shut up."

Amira turned back to Marisa. "It doesn't matter what he was doing. This is what you're dealing with now. And if you don't get help, the leg won't heal right. You'll be in pain for however long this lasts. Don't you care about that?"

Marisa scoffed, rattling her chains. "I care about *this*." The pain made her pause, but just for a second, just long enough to wince. "Everything else—dumbasses trying to break out through the goddamn ceiling included—is secondary. I haven't achieved everything I wanted to yet, everything I needed to." She shrugged. "They'll get me some morphine—I'll be fine."

They let the words hang in the air, waiting for Marisa to hear what she was saying. Nurse Hae, though she was overhearing everything, saved her comments.

"This whole thing shouldn't get ruined because of a dumbass on a rope. It's bigger than him." Marisa banged her head back against the doors. "That glass is just as reinforced as the windows—what the hell was he thinking?"

"It's not about him, though," Amira said. "It's about you. Your well-being. That leg is really freakin' broken."

"Exactly, it's about me. If that idiot was hurt and his health was in my hands, I'd understand. I'd open the doors. But I'm the hurt one, and I'm the one that gets to decide how much help I need. I'm the one who gets to decide what matters more."

"The reefs can wait."

"No, they can't."

"I know it feels like that, but it's not true. You can come up with another plan. I'll help you."

"Great. And then when someone runs at me and breaks my other leg, because they know I'll just stop again, I come up with another plan? These things on my list haven't just needed doing for the last week since I wrote them down. They've been getting ignored or actively worked against for decades. Every day that I don't fight for them is a day lost. I don't have the time to get dragged to a hospital over a broken little bone. I don't have the time to sit and think of some other way to hijack the world into paying attention, to make people care about saving themselves. This took months of planning. We've been sitting here for a week and look how far it's gotten us."

She reached back and slammed her hand against the list blindly, angrily, with rage that seemed to swallow her whole. All five pairs of eyes turned to the list, the measly three items crossed off, all related to the school's policies. Kenji gulped, felt his cheeks flush so furiously the heat rising off them fogged up his glasses. Nurse Hae opened an internet browser on her phone, and started looking up what she would have to do to help Marisa without the benefit of hospital equipment.

"So no, Amira. The reefs can't wait. I can't wait. The doors stay closed."

The bell rang again. The elementary students lined up and waited for teachers to lead them to class. The middle schoolers walked briskly toward their building, nervous they'd be late but still invested in what was happening inside the high school. They cast glances behind them, scrunching their shoulders as instinctive cover against the rain, worried they'd miss something. The high schoolers who'd been locked out lingered by the windows, almost like they'd hadn't heard the bell. Their teachers, those who hadn't chaperoned lock-in night and had been assigned unused classrooms in the middle school, were standing beside them, anyway.

Inside the high school, the students' legs jittered nervously as they pictured the break. Just a few hours earlier, they'd been wondering how long they'd have to stay in this damn place. Weeks? Months? How much of their lives would be lost to this? Now, though, they marveled at Marisa. The strength it took to deny herself medical attention. Did any of them care so much about anything that they would stand on a broken leg for it?

In the basement, getting texts from friends upstairs, Lolo tilted her chin up to the unseeing world with pride. This is who she'd aligned herself with, and she'd do it again in a heartbeat. Joy got choked up, Eli, too, hearing about Marisa's refusal to grant herself help. They weren't as strong, they knew. They believed in the cause, but there was a reason they'd volunteered for these other exits. They each took a breath, all three of them, more or less at the same time, a breath of pride and worry, and which they hoped would grant them enough determination to hold on as long as Marisa deemed necessary.

Amira admired how Marisa had spoken without tears brimming in her eyes, tears being the emotional response expected from girls, always. Amira had never wanted to cry in front of her mom. She wanted to do what Marisa did now: lash out. Hold her own. Though, dunks aside, she'd never managed to do much.

So she was about to say it wasn't true that Marisa hadn't done enough. That Marisa had done more than any of the kids in school who carried reusable grocery bags for their lunches but did nothing else, had done more than so many green-minded people had ever, just by chaining herself up and showing others it was something to care about. And she'd done more than that, more than the demands that had been crossed off. But before Amira could speak, Nurse Hae's phone rang. She answered, half jogging toward a classroom. "You're here?"

A few moments later she returned with a handful of orange prescription bottles, pills rattling inside. "Can you guys give me a second with Marisa?" she asked. Kenji jumped up right away, and Celeste followed suit. Peejay chewed on his lip for a while before slowly rising to his feet and crossing the foyer to join them outside the library.

Amira lingered. She wanted to hold Marisa through her pain. She wanted to shake her and cause her more, wanted to break the chains off her and force her to go to the hospital.

"Go," Marisa said to her, eyes still closed, breath shaky. "I'll be okay."

"Is she wrong?" Kenji asked. "I feel like she's wrong. To stay, I mean. But she's also right. I think what she's doing is right. I don't want her to give up."

"Me neither," Celeste managed.

"She can't just stay here," Amira growled, as if it was Kenji and Celeste who'd convinced Marisa not to go. Something inside her flinched at the words *she can't* but she ignored it.

They were gathered outside the library, and though they were in sight of a few classrooms, no teachers came out to question what they were doing. A few students looked out at the group, wondering, maybe, what they knew that the rest of CIS did not.

Peejay sat on the floor, his back against the lockers, hugging his knees. His pashmina once again covered his head. Amira was pacing back and forth, four steps one way, four steps back, her hands fluttering like hummingbirds. Kenji and Celeste leaned against the wall.

The week hadn't been particularly wonderful for any of them, but they hadn't imagined leaving. Especially not like this, following Marisa out on a gurney. As soon as they had each stepped in between her and the crowd, they all believed she would win. None of them were particularly interested in returning to life before the lock-in, either. Celeste was terrified of returning to normalcy and loneliness, Amira terrified of Marisa getting expelled, of never seeing her again, of going back to her mother and having to conceal more than just her athletic ambitions. Peejay didn't have a normal life to return to, just a funeral. Kenji had been just fine not going back home, only dealing with his father over the phone.

"What can we do?" Kenji said. "To convince her, I guess."

"We're not going to convince her." They all turned to the pashmina. Peejay sat up, pulling the shawl to his shoulders. His voice was soft, tender.

"Obviously," Amira said, less of a growl now. She wasn't sure what was going on with Peejay. He'd resisted her attempts all week to talk, had pretended to be asleep when Kenji had tried, too. But growling at him didn't seem like the right way to treat him.

"Emphasis on the 'her' here." He chewed on his lip again, like he had in front of Marisa and the nurse a few moments ago. Amira realized his mind was churning. "Our little cap-tor's strengths obviously extend beyond her willpower. We try to butt heads with her, we'll all come away with headaches. As I'm sure the school board already knows."

"What are you saying, then? We convince the school board?" Amira said. "That doesn't seem like it gets Marisa to a hospital any sooner."

"Not the board," Peejay said. He gestured toward the win-dows, where most of the people in a nearby class, including the teacher, Mr. Sanchez, had stopped pretending they were getting anything academic accomplished and had resorted to staring out at the Protectors. "Them."

Now all four of them met eyes with the class, and a brief staring contest ensued until the other students started shifting uncomfortably and grudgingly turned their attention back to Mr. Sanchez.

"Go on," Amira said.

Peejay thought about what Hamish would do in this situa-tion, how he would've done all he could to do what was right. Marisa was right. In so many ways, she was right. Hamish would've chained himself to a door with her; he would've used whatever was in his power to get others to see it, too.

All week, Peejay had been paralyzed by grief, physically revolted by the fact that he would never see his brother again, never get to tell him about the party, never get to tell him anything. And while he'd been prepared by the doctors to expect it as the range of outcomes, there was no preparing for this. Now, though, Peejay had a thought that eased his pain, however slightly. Hamish was gone, but his goodness didn't have to die with him.

He breathed in deep, maybe the deepest breath he'd taken since lock-in night, the only one that managed to really draw oxygen into his lungs in a week. "We've all been sitting around, twiddling our thumbs."

"You've barely done any twiddling," Kenji said. They all glared at him. "Sorry, not important."

"You're right." Peejay wanted to offer the boy a smile, but he wasn't quite ready for that. "*Everyone* here has been waiting for the adults to do something. Set us free one way or the other. But we have more power than that. We can at least try to push them. Our parents, the board, our famous uncles and godfathers, our embassies and governments, our goddamn babysitters. Some of this is in our hands."

He still had it. That ability to get people to fall in step, the ability to charm. In every classroom, heads turned in his direction. Even though they hadn't heard his words, it was something to see him emerge again from beneath the pashmina. Students outside the building, even, found themselves cocking their ears in his direction, though they'd only heard Dov's screams and nothing else, didn't know what had changed inside.

"And if they don't listen to us? The way they haven't been listening to Marisa?" Amira asked.

Peejay sighed. "Girl, I don't know. But what else do we have but to hope and shout?"

So it was decided they would go to their classes and think about how best to shout.

Amira went off to tell Marisa, and Peejay went in to the library to use a computer. Meanwhile Kenji put a hand on Celeste's forearm, asking if she could hang back. Unsure what he wanted, Celeste just looked at his hand and waited for him to speak.

"I have a confession," Kenji said.

Celeste raised her eyebrows.

"You know demand number seventeen?"

"Was that the one with the boats?"

Kenji shook his head. "Lokoloko Island." Celeste nodded, cautious and curious if this was going to be another improv thing, or something else.

It felt like he had no choice, like not bringing it up would be a disloyalty to Marisa and the Protectors. And unlike many others at CIS or in the world, he was in a unique position to at least speak directly to someone who could make a difference.

So he told her about his dad, and that one phone call could probably change things.

"Kenji, that's great."

"No, that's the thing." He pushed his glasses up his nose. "That basically guarantees it not getting met. My dad does not say yes to things. He says no. I just don't know how to tell Marisa, you know? It's been killing me to have this secret, and I just needed to tell someone."

Celeste was about to push him further, but the look of relief on Kenji's face gave her pause, coupled with the fact that she'd been entrusted with a secret. That was something friends did. Then before she could gather herself, Kenji breathed a sigh of relief, thanked her for listening and bounded up the stairs to go to class.

Dear ladies, gents and all other Cucumbers here assembled, Your evening's (ha!) host again. Since the doors haven't opened yet, I believe I'm still technically your humble Partyer in Chief. I come to you with another request. Before I called on your discretion. Now I call on your voice.

She's not going to let herself out, it's true. The doors remain closed. And maybe she deserves our anger for that. But you all saw that ghastly, mangled gam of hers. If she's willing to stand on that thing, then we don't stand a chance but to meet her demands. And if we're not getting out of here until that happens, don't we want to be on her side? Don't we want to be on the same team as someone so willing to fight for what they believe is right? When we look back on this ordeal from our deathbeds, if we are lucky enough to have them, how will we feel about fighting her? Or about not fighting with her?

Let's face it, Cukes, she's right. We were pissed on lock-in night, and we had reason to be. But that's far behind us. Enough putzing around, enough mourning.

Fight for Marisa's demands. Fight for our goddamn beautiful, dying world. That's all she's wanted, and all she asks now. She deserves our help. We can sleep in our beds soon and see our loved ones on the outside. If we fight.

Kind regards, Peejay Singh

The whispers were already at a fever pitch.

What could they do to help? The students had felt useless this whole time, mere bystanders caught in the fight between Marisa and the school, the world. Most had signed Marisa's petitions because they'd been asked to, because Michael and Maya had set up a table and some clipboards on lock-in night,

WE DIDN'T ASK FOR THIS

but other than that, what was there for them to do? The question had been rhetorical up until now.

They passed by the list of demands again, as if they hadn't memorized it days ago. They read the uncrossed items and racked their brains, trying to ignore Marisa's scowl.

Zaira Jacobson, for one, knew exactly what she could do. Get the press back. She opened up her social media accounts, which had been verified and seen a hundredfold increase in followers as the lone journalistic correspondent inside the building. She wrote: Marisa seriously hurt at CIS. Doors remain closed. She watched the attention grow, the eyeballs turn back toward them.

4

8:50AM

Mr. Gigs sensed something different about his first period class, then remembered the leg. It made sense that the room was full of nervous energy, especially with the reporters intermittently shouting questions from the windows, their voices faint and muffled by the thick glass and the storm, which had picked up in the last hour.

Rather than try to hold his students' attention, Mr. Gigs put on some music and told them to work on any assignments they had due soon. He turned his own attention to essays his outside-the-building students had already submitted, clicking away every now and then to search for flight prices.

He didn't care where, he just wanted to go somewhere remote and beautiful and quiet, where nothing would be needed from him other than to read his books and to enjoy sitting uninterrupted for hours at a time.

In the back row, Celeste fiddled with her phone under her desk. People were whispering to each other, had huddled their desks together in the corners. To Mr. Gigs maybe it looked like they were working on a group project, though he didn't want to know for sure, so he didn't ask. Celeste wondered what ideas they were coming up with, wondered if they were even going to help or were just gossiping. She hadn't been invited into any of these small circles, but now wasn't the time to think about the exclusion.

Mr. Gigs looked toward the class as if to shush them, but instead reached for his speakers and turned the music up a notch. This gave Celeste the permission she was looking for and she called her dad's phone. He answered on the third ring.

Her parents had stopped picking up breathlessly when she called, voices fraught with worry. They checked in by phone several times a day, along with their visits to the school to bring her clothes and food. "Hey, baby," he said. She could hear the shuffle of the metro system in the background as he made his way to work.

"Hey, Pop. Any local things from last night?"

He chuckled. "Beat the record for people on a motorbike," he said.

"No way."

"Six and a puppy."

"Where was this?"

"We all saw it while eating at that spot by the Laundromat," he said. In the silence that followed, they both sensed Celeste's absence.

Rather than fall into it, Celeste said, "Dad, I need your help."

She heard him stop moving, the background noise increasing as he shuffled around, then reducing enough that it felt as if he'd somehow found a closet at the metro station to lock himself into. "Anything, baby. Say the word."

Celeste explained the situation, since her dad hadn't seen the news yet, and her mom hadn't woken up yet to share it with him. "We've got to help her get out. And the only way we can is to up the pressure. Can you guys, like, I don't know, call the embassy?"

"Hon, we moved here to avoid our government's bullshit." He sighed. "But let me call some friends and see what we can stir up stateside. You know your momma and I know how to shout a little."

"Mostly Mom."

"Yeah, you don't have to tell me." He laughed. Another pause and Celeste thought maybe he was going to ask the obvious question about Marisa not opening the door. Thankfully, if he had doubts he kept them to himself. "You still good in there?" he asked, his voice soft. For the first time all morning, Celeste realized she would soon see her parents again, her brothers. That she'd see their faces, smell their scents, feel their wonderful familiar touch, the way her mom would give her upper arm a squeeze whenever she was happy with her, her dad's top-of-the-head kisses.

"Still good," she said.

★ ★ ★

In the library, far from Marisa and her cronies, Jordi Marcos gathered the group that rivaled Marisa's Protectors, though they hadn't thought to give themselves a snappy name. He read Peejay's email again, and tossed his phone to the floor.

"I can't believe she's not letting us out now," Jordi said. They were sprawled on beanbags, books splayed on their laps to make it look like they were in study hall. No one took attendance anymore, but appearances still mattered. "It's Peejay's fault, I bet. My plan would have worked if it weren't for him. He wants us to stay stuck in here."

There were six of them total, Dov included, still a little shaken from his fall and the sight of Marisa's leg.

"We can't let her keep getting her way," Jordi continued, every word striving for the fire his dad could conjure. "I don't buy it for a second. I think she's just trying to get us to pressure the school and the parents so she can win. But we can't let her."

Shmuli Rogers shifted. "I actually kind of agree with some of her environm—" The way the others looked at him made him reconsider. "Never mind."

Jordi was getting that look again, the one that had led him to shout during the first assembly, the one he had when he'd started throwing things at Marisa on lock-in night. The look he'd had the morning after, when he'd gathered his allies and planned a breakout. They'd talked day and night about how, until finally someone had suggested making themselves sick. Dov himself had tweaked the plan to an injury, since it was easier to fake or even cause. They'd have to make it look like an accident, of course, and had drawn straws to see

ADI ALSAID

who would let themselves slip from the rope. They hadn't expected the degree of the break, or that Marisa wouldn't give in right away.

"So, what do we do?" Anna Vuli said, a sophomore who'd joined the group simply because she liked scheming.

"Whatever we can to stop demands from getting met," Jordi responded. "Whatever we can to get out. Tell people she's hurting us so the cops come rushing in. Tell them she's planning on blowing us up. I don't know, I don't care. But we can't let her get her way. She doesn't get to do this."

Joy watched her brother bring in another bag of plastic. He alone didn't seem changed by the morning's events; he just kept taking the bags under the bleachers, where he'd been taking them ever since the day after lock-in night, re-emerging from the shadows with the bags emptied. All over school, people were scouring their phones for ways to hasten their departure.

The first thing Joy had thought of when Marisa relayed the update via group text was a bathroom. A proper bathroom, with a locked door and a nearby sink, the tangy smell of disinfectant in the air, maybe a single sunflower and a candle for decoration. Oh, to sit and not worry about where her urine was going, to be able to flush it all away (or let it sit to save water, even) instead of scooping sawdust over the semiabsorbed puddle in her bucket. To stand at the sink and wash her hands, then leave and not dread the next time the urge would come.

Joy thought that everyone in the building must have had a similar fantasy, not of a bathroom, of course, but of one par-

WE DIDN'T ASK FOR THIS

ticular thing they'd been denied the past week (though she could only imagine every girl who'd gotten her period was dying for a private bathroom, despite all the menstrual products Marisa had brought into the school). For most people this was true—a bed, a friend's company, one goddamn moment of solitude—but Omar's mind seemed to land only on collecting plastic and on Peejay.

"Can I know what you're doing with all of that?" Joy asked.

"Omar grinned, scratched his patchy beard. "Not yet."

"Then when?"

Omar shrugged. "We'll see. I'm gonna go take another lap, though. You won't believe how much still is out there." He practically ran from the gym, the reused garbage bags trailing behind him like deployed parachutes.

It was true that, when he heard the rumblings of how things had changed, Omar's mind didn't turn toward anything outside the building. That life, the one he'd had before lock-in night, with basketball practice and homework, family time at dinner and on weekends, hangouts on Saturday afternoons at Ping Xe's house playing video games, Sunday walks with Joy and their dog, Rye Bread, it all seemed left behind. What there was now was sweeping for plastic, and checking on Peejay. Being near him, in case whatever was ailing him needed an ear, a shoulder, whatever Omar could provide.

Ever since he'd told Joy the truth, an act he thought might unburden him from his crush, he'd been wholeheartedly consumed, as if speaking it out loud had somehow made his feelings for Peejay more real, more cemented within him. The fact that Peejay was now part of Marisa's crew only made him feel justified in the intensity of his feelings. Omar couldn't fathom leaving this building and not having Peejay nearby, couldn't fathom his life the way it used to be—several water or sports drink bottles before practice, not knowing if there were phosphates in the detergent his mom used.

Now he came down the stairs and entered the foyer, thinking classes must be going on, and glad to see Peejay not hidden beneath his pashmina.

Sensing eyes on him, Peejay turned and looked at Omar. He'd seen him through the pashmina so many times now, always with those empty garbage bags trailing behind him like a wedding dress. Peejay assumed Omar was looking at Marisa, or at Amira, maybe. He loved a good enemies-secretly-in-love-with-each-other storyline, and wondered how the decathlon would've turned out if the lock-in hadn't gone the way it did.

Yes, Omar wanted everything Marisa did now. Wanted all those demands met because Joy did, too. But he didn't want to leave, didn't want to get any farther from Peejay Singh. And he had no idea how to approach Peejay, no idea how to close the space between them. He couldn't even find a way to ask him about Hamish, if he was okay, if that had something to do with his descent into the pashmina. So he didn't try to help in any other way than to be near, to collect the plastic at CIS and ensure it wouldn't end up floating in the Pacific.

Kenji watched the rain come down at a slant against the window, beautiful long streaks that muddied the image of the soccer field beyond. It was funny how much like a normal day of class it could feel if he just listened to the rain and sat at his desk letting his mind wander.

They were supposed to be doing a geometry worksheet, but geometry was such a drag; the proofs and steps felt so rigid and yet so slippery to understand, like instructions on how to build something in a language he didn't speak.

That, or everyone was rereading Peejay's email, grouping together to discuss it, whispering about what they could do. Whatever fire had been extinguished within Peejay, he still had the ability to light it in others. Pok Tran suggested they find more chains and chain themselves to the closet doors. Nouth Shapiro suggested that junior year be replaced with a year of cleaning up the oceans or volunteering at sustainable farms or protesting (Nouth was really not looking forward to junior year and its academic workload). Someone unironically suggested staging a walkout, drawing two groans, five prolonged stares and one smack on the back of the head.

Either way, it seemed like Mrs. Wu wasn't paying much attention to them. Online poker again, Kenji guessed.

How are things out there? Kenji texted Lindsay, since it was what he always did when he was in Geometry, before the lock-in and after.

Her response came immediately. Rainy. Is it true? Marisa's leg is broken?

Yup.

We got the email here, too. Everyone's talking about what we can do from out here. What's it like in there?

The same. Mostly people have terrible ideas, but I guess they're just trying to help. He turned back to the window, trying to catch sight of Lindsay in the rain. There was a lot of activity already, and Kenji wondered if his father had heard the news yet, if he was laughing, thinking Marisa wasn't going to get her way. The relief he'd felt from telling Celeste about his dad was still there, certainly, but every tidbit of conversation he overheard made him feel like sooner or later someone was going to confront him.

Lindsay texted again. Which demand are you trying to help with? I'm trying to get celebrities on social media to tweet the president of this detergent company.

Wait, which demand is that?

None, just felt like a fun thing to do.

Kenji chuckled. Ha.

The voices in the classroom kept rising, suddenly so urgent to come up with ways to help Marisa ("Why didn't they do that from the start?" she'd ask later, they'd all ask themselves). Mrs. Wu barely looked away from her computer for more than a cursory glance. Outside, Lindsay tapped her phone against her leg, not wanting Kenji to fall back into silence.

He didn't answer her, though, or get caught up in the fever of helping. He wanted Marisa to win, wanted Lokoloko Island to be safe of his dad's destruction. But that wasn't going to happen. So what else was there to do, as Lindsay had suggested, but laugh? He slipped his earphones out of his pocket and put on a podcast.

★ ★ ★

Nurse Hae had given Marisa a light dose of narcotic pain-killers. She'd refused the full dose because she wanted to stay lucid to negotiate, but the morning had taken a lot out of her, and now she dozed, her legs propped up on the chairs that had been placed in front of her, her head resting on the door, cushioned by Amira's folded-up hoodie.

To Amira, she looked almost peaceful, just the slightest furrowing to her brow. Yes, her hair was greasy, and her clothes wrinkled, a few pimples popping up at the corner of her chin and on her forehead. Even now, though, under all these circumstances, Amira's body continued to rebel against her, craving not a run or a workout, but simply to reach out and brush Marisa's cheek. Marisa's strength astounded her.

Olaf Padilla, whose mom owned a hotel a few hours down the coast, called her and asked her to switch to tertiary sewage treatment, a phrase he didn't understand whatsoever, but which Marisa had written on her list.

Maizey Krokic had her father, the ambassador from Croatia, wrapped around her finger. He instantly gave in to any and all of his daughter's requests, from permission to spend the night with a friend to: "I need you to talk to your political friends back home. Get them to implement stricter controls on fertilizer runoff and incentivize techniques that use lower amounts of nitrogen, as well as more targeted application." *Of course, darling*, he'd responded, understanding none of what she'd said but making sure his assistant had written it down. He cleared his schedule for the rest of the day so he could figure out how to do what his daughter asked.

Ludovico Rigo, who'd already taken it upon himself to compost all the school's organic waste, having learned the nuances when he was younger on his island, posted a video online encouraging other kids around the world to do the same. His gaggle of freshmen immediately shared it with all their friends, and the video's views began to multiply.

All over the school, students messaged their most influential family members. They took to social media. This young generation, whose teachers and parents didn't even like to make phone calls, who had much more convenient and fun and efficient means of communication, flooded corporate voice mails and government officials with calls. They called newspapers. They called CIS alumni and begged them to demand change from the school at the threat of stopping their donations. They hadn't even been aware of the power of alumni donations in a concrete way until lock-in night, but now they suddenly had a perfectly clear grasp on the nuances of those dynamics, how money wielded influence even here. There were twenty-seven unmet demands left, and though some students sat back gleefully and waited for the doors to open whenever they would, most of them got caught up in the tide of emotions and activity.

They wished they'd known this earlier, had grasped it before Marisa's leg snapped and it was too late to find out. They'd always had a chance to get out. Like this, their voices all raised together. They had a chance to attach themselves to the change Marisa had already brought about in the world. After all this time, almost all of them had, at some point or another—while waiting for time to pass, while distracting themselves from the fact that they were missing family movie night again, or missing the neighbor kids they babysat, missing mall hangouts with friends on the outside—read about the reefs. Now they dove in.

In three separate classrooms, students convinced their teachers to show the documentary *Chasing Coral* via the projector; not Marisa's most ambitious or difficult goal, to have it shown to every student at CIS, but one the board had for some reason tabled until all the students could be in one place.

These students started to understand Marisa a little more, feeling dread claw at their chests that so many living things worldwide were dying and they hadn't cared before. Very few could pay attention to something dying and not care. Now they knew.

Some had already cared, all this time, even before lock-in night, cared deeply and simply hadn't known how to put it into action. Now they knew. Now they wanted it more desperately than they ever had, almost as desperately as Marisa herself.

Marisa's leg had broken their complacency, Peejay's email had burst their bubble, pleasant for some, unpleasant for others, that they would be inside CIS forever. They wanted to change the world. This was their chance.

10:33AM

By the time the high school's brunch bell rang, a quick fifteen-minute break between second and third periods, three more demands were met.

The first was that CIS would convert their fleet of school buses to an electric model Marisa had read was already in use in Europe. This had been in the works from day one, since the company the school hired the fleet through had them available, but the change required the approval of wary adults, and the school board had hung on to hopes that maybe they could get away with meeting only some of the demands.

The second came when board president, Nigel Appuhamy,

was seeking respite from the stressful yelling of another conference room meeting in the bathroom, scrolling through online videos. He happened across Ludovico's compost tutorial, and quickly emerged from the bathroom, the lack of a flush or hand-washing giving away that he'd simply been in there hiding. "This is what composting is? Why don't we already do that?"

The other board members shrugged and mumbled something about costs and insurance.

The third demand met, the one that spread true hope to Marisa and her cronies and the Protectors, to Omar and anyone who'd been won over to her cause, the achievement that spread a swell of pride and vicarious joy to Maya Klutzheisen and Michael Obonte and all the others who loved Marisa (who loved her still, after all this time, the love only stewing and intensifying the longer she held out), was one Marisa herself had never fully believed she would see come to fruition. At least, not because of her. She wasn't even sure why she'd included the demand. It wasn't school-specific, and it was arguably too ambitious to be met in a reasonable amount of time. It was really just to make her demand for Lokoloko Island seem relatively moderate. Malik and Lolo had both tried to talk her out of it, afraid that if they had to wait for this they might be chained up for years. "We're not gonna keep going for years," she'd said, though it wasn't enough to convince them. They could see her keeping up the fight indefinitely, until they were all old and wrinkled; they'd have to get online college degrees still at their respective doors, they'd have to get married while chained up, they'd die here, from the effects of climate change or something else.

Despite their fears, Marisa had left the demand in. And now she had an email in her inbox, forwarded to her by Nigel from the school board. She awoke groggily from her painkiller haze, at first not quite sure what she was looking at.

At the request, insistence and influence of the distinguished members who sat on the school board and the alumni committee, all those influential parents upping the pressure, the news reports starting to fire back up, the local city had vowed, perhaps a little precipitously, their critics would say, to be carbon net-neutral within the next three years. The city as a whole would not be adding to the deterioration of the environment. An ordinance had already passed through the city council after each member received an overwhelming amount of social media messages from their constituents and plenty who weren't (plus a few bots).

Three. Marisa had to ask Nurse Hae if she'd given her another dose, to which the nurse furrowed her brow and checked her notes. "No."

Some countries had promised to do their best in ten years, twenty. Three? She reread the email, saw it included a press conference that very afternoon for the mayor to make the announcement. Whether the city was capable of actually achieving it was one thing; that they would try, though? That alone might make the whole endeavor worth it. A city of that size, net-neutral. Other cities might follow suit. They might speed up their own promises at least. Her actions would not be undone by the school.

She watched as the news broke out over CIS, the way news

had been breaking all week, as if by osmosis, like an invisible wave bearing down on all of them, some with a crash. With others it gently lapped at their legs, frothed between their toes.

Amira, who'd just briefly stepped away from watching Marisa doze, appeared from the bathroom door and ran toward her, a smile visible from across the room, framed by her hijab. Marisa was shocked to realize it was the first time she'd actually seen her run since lock-in night. It seemed like she crossed the foyer in two long, measured strides, and for a moment Marisa thought Amira might take her face in her hands and kiss her and say, "This is to celebrate."

It was amazing how quickly the fantasy occurred in her mind, and how, just like that, it felt possible. It had felt all week like maybe it would happen, like there was a reason Amira was still at her side, caring for her, and the reason was something beyond mere compassion.

When Amira arrived she didn't know how to properly show her enthusiasm, so she just stopped short in front of Marisa and clutched her own hands together. "How great is this?"

Marisa paused, waited to see if there was more. Silly to think so, silly to let any disappointment take over in the face of this accomplishment. Amazing what fantasies could do. "I can't put it into words," she said.

Amira was already leaning down to the duffel bag to grab a marker. "I think it's gonna happen," she said. She uncapped the marker and handed it to Marisa, their fingers brushing like usual. "You're going to do it." Amira's heart was racing. The world now would see Marisa not just as a girl chained to a door, but a girl who could enact change. A girl with will, and the power to make it come to fruition.

★ ★ ★

"Yeah," Marisa said, almost adding a "maybe" but deciding, no, no "maybe." This was going to happen. For her leg's sake, which was in so much pain Marisa wasn't sure which verb she should use to describe it: screaming, throbbing, bursting. "Although maybe you should do the actual crossing off." She gestured at the blanket covering her.

"Right." The marker passed back, another goose-bump-riddled touch.

Amira crossed the three demands off, and eyed the remaining twenty-four.

Marisa meanwhile couldn't keep her eyes off Amira, wondering if she'd kiss her now. Now. Now.

Within moments they were joined by Kenji and Celeste, both of whom had run out of their classrooms. Kenji, one earphone still dangling from his ear, motioned for a high five after wiping some muffin crumbs off his hand.

Celeste, surprising herself, leaned down to hug Marisa, gingerly but warmly. She didn't know if it was her place to do so, and something in her stomach churned at the thought that she felt closer to Marisa than Marisa felt to her. Still, she couldn't help but whisper, "You are such a badass."

Marisa chuckled, relishing the warmth of the hug and wishing it had come from Amira. They all stared at the list of demands, wondering which would fall next, hungry, now, for the moment when Marisa crossed out the last one.

"Wait," Marisa asked, seeming to just now notice the excited chatter in the halls, the way people were looking in her direction with much less animus than before. "How long have I been asleep?"

★ ★ ★

From the second-floor banister, Jordi watched the Protectors celebrate. But he smiled, too. While his classmates took to their parents and the internet, rallying around Marisa and the environment, Jordi, too, had been at work.

In the many unsavory, dark corners of the internet, and plenty of its surfaces, there were people who hated Marisa, just like he did. Who said: she's a criminal, she's a terrorist, she's no good. They said: she has no right, she isn't right. Jordi Marcos Sr. was still muttering to himself, and to anyone in his vicinity, still whispering it into his son's ears, even from across the distance that separated them. There's no problem except for kids throwing fits, he was saying, kids who knew nothing but what was spoon-fed to them by agenda-spreading professors, artists, media, scientists. Jordi Jr. agreed with all of it, and so he made it his mission to let the world know what she was doing.

He posted that it was true students were hurt, but Marisa wasn't one of them. She was faking in order to win people over, to make it seem like she was strong instead of just a bully. She was playing the media and she knew it, and everyone on the outside, it seemed, was buying it.

At first he was taken as a troll, or was agreed with only by actual trolls. Then, as people realized he was actually inside the school, that he had been quoted in Zaira's original lock-in night article, they started paying attention. They started listening. All that time watching Peejay attract people's adoration, all that time striving to be like him, nipping at his ankles, had taught Jordi a thing or two about how to at least fake charm. Maybe anyone who watched Peejay long enough (or Hamish, Peejay would argue) could gain some of his attributes by mere osmosis.

There were angry, strange people in the world, and he'd found some eager to include themselves in the narrative. They asked Jordi how they could help. They were hungry to help, eager to pull the carpet from beneath Marisa's feet. Like him, they didn't want to see her succeed one bit.

That the board and the world had met three more of Marisa's demands was a bitter pill to swallow, but Jordi contented himself in knowing no more would be crossed off.

Some simply spread the news on Jordi's behalf, so that, by the time the city had announced its new ordinance to be net-neutral, the news networks already had experts arguing against the move on television. They were loud enough to make it seem like exactly half the people at CIS were on Jordi's side, like only half the world was on Marisa's, like the number of scientists who believed the dying reefs were a problem equaled the number who believed it couldn't be proven the problem was man-made (which were not opposite sides of the same argument).

They were loud enough, in fact, that they caught the ear of politicians who, simply because their enemies agreed with Marisa, stood against her, not having to hear anything else. They fought back against the parents and celebrities who'd raised their voices.

On lock-in night, the school had refused to get the police involved. While everyone remained safe, local politicos decided that was the school's prerogative and they could do as they please. Now, though, these politicos were hearing from the influential parents. Calls were made, and the cops assembled riot gear and loaded into armored trucks, headed toward CIS.

Others were willing to take on Jordi's tasks a little more meaningfully. Managing to sneak past campus security, Silvestro Di Maria, an Italian national always happy to take online talk of destruction from the hypothetical into the real world, found himself in front of the CIS power grid with a crowbar. Somewhere else in the world, Charles Reiber, armed with a computer and a team of fellow misogynist hackers more than happy to watch a teenage girl fail, took aim at local cell towers.

Students noticed the Wi-Fi's failure first.

Those still inside classrooms started feeling the stifling heat when the fans died out, those damn window slits doing nothing to keep them cool. They looked up from their disobedient phones, starting to sweat, despite the rain outside. Oh, well, they thought, cell data it would be.

But their phones showed spinning wheels, trying to connect but failing. Mrs. Wu smacked the side of her computer, trying to coax it back into internet range, a move no one had attempted in around twenty years. She looked out at her classroom, scanning for which one of the students was to blame.

Outside, reporters huddled beneath umbrellas took note of the network issues, then trained their sights on the building, cupping their hands around their eyes as they pressed their faces up to the glass. They noticed the lights were off, noticed a handful of kids plugged into outlets jiggling the wires and trying to coax the power back, as if it were just a naughty pet that had run away.

It'd been a busy morning for the reporters, exciting, all things considered. They'd liked this story back when it had started and when it had been assigned to more senior correspondents. They were glad it was them who got to provide occasional updates the past few days, when interest had waned. So it was them to whom the job had fallen back when the injury happened. At first they only had Zaira Jacobson's post to go off of, but they were sent to the school, anyway, to stand in the rain and wait.

Then the dramatic turn: the painkillers arriving. It was the smoke that pointed to the fire: someone actually was hurt. They looked at each other for only the briefest of moments, amazed they were here for it. Then they looked back into the school. The doors hadn't opened (a disappointment, sure, but somewhere in there, a relief, too, that the story would continue). After that the flurry of posts and messages from the students to keep up with, a treasure trove of activity to sort through in search of something good, something other reporters might miss. They felt, for those few hours, the way movies depicted journalists. This was the story-sleuthing they'd dreamed of back in school.

Now this. The internet gone. The lights out. The police scanners picking up. The reporters smiled while they watched the school, then tapped on the glass, trying to get the attention of the closest kid. "Hey," they yelled through the window, angling their voices toward those damn little slits. "What's going on?"

"Jordi fucking Marcos," Peejay said. "This is his doing." The pashmina slipped a little farther down Peejay's shoulders.

He had seen Jordi smirking from the second floor, and known right away, even before he saw the email that had come moments before the signal went down.

Hey, Peejay. Great job hosting that party no one went to. Is that why you're hiding under that stupid scarf all day? The shame? Or are you just ashamed to be on the same side as that asshole Marisa? Anyway, nice email. Too bad it's not gonna make a difference soon.

The other Protectors looked longingly down at their phones, feeling, like so many others at school, suddenly useless. They stole a glance at the list of demands (except for Marisa, who did not glance but rather stared at the list as if it were a love letter fluttering away in the wind, some necessary document she'd have no chance of recovering), wondering how they could do anything about the uncrossed items without access to the outside world.

"It could just be temporary," Kenji said. "I sometimes get bad service in here." They all turned to look at him. CIS famously had the best reception in town.

"The phone company will at least fix the network soon, right?" Celeste said, trying to remain hopeful.

"Sure," Marisa said. "But when?" She was scrolling through her phone, grimacing, though it was unclear if it was out of physical pain or something else. "Look at this, it loaded before the signal went down. People say the police are coming. People are saying they have to get us out, and now they're actually listening."

"But they can't, right?" Kenji asked. "They couldn't on lock-in night."

"The doors can't be busted down by a locksmith. But cops have a lot more gear than I could prepare for," Marisa said. "If they want to blow a hole in the side of the building, there's nothing I can do to stop them. It's not like a hostage situation where I'm threatening to hurt people if they come in."

"What do we do?" Amira asked. She hated lingering on what had caused a problem or why, cared only how to resolve the situation, cared only about what she could do. "Fix the power?"

Peejay shook his head. "I'm telling you, Jordi did this. He's a destroyer." He stood, the pashmina falling to his elbows. Without another word he went off to hunt down Jordi, the others staring as he left, wondering if they'd seen him move with that much determination since the party, but unable to feel happy at the purpose in his movements, facing, as they were, this new obstacle.

"Right when shit was starting to happen, too," Marisa said, her voice almost breaking.

"Don't start giving up on yourself now," Amira shot back. "This hasn't changed anything. We can still get the demands done."

"How?" Marisa asked. "We can't call anyone, can't email. Not the board or our parents or that goddamn actor who's someone's uncle. We can't tell our 'fans' to stir up some shit. We are completely isolated, boxed in—" she grabbed the chains around her and shook them "—locked in, as it were. At least for now." She gave the chains another aggrieved rattle, and though she was too defeated to shake with gusto, the motion was still too much for her exhausted, broken body.

Despite her efforts at hydration, despite the stretches Amira had taught her, despite the painkillers still flowing through her bloodstream, another cramp seized her lower back, and the tensing muscles worked their way into her leg. She cried out, not knowing how to stretch her body now, not knowing how to help herself. She gritted her teeth and begged for it to stop, unwilling to move for fear she would make things even worse.

Unsurprisingly, Amira was there in an instant to guide her. A hand on her back, gently but firmly pushing her body into relief. "Breathe," Amira said.

Marisa did, then opened her eyes, her muscles already starting to calm, though her leg was still this throbbing black hole of pain. She breathed again, in through her nose, exhaling slowly through her mouth, her eyes fixed on Amira's. "I'm just out of steam," Marisa said. "I don't have any ideas. Do you?"

"Do you want to do a scene together?" Kenji asked. Celeste rolled her eyes. "What? It worked last time."

Amira and Marisa shared a private smile, still looking into each other's eyes, before all four of them started chuckling. "Sure," Marisa said, "why not?"

"Actually," Celeste interrupted, "I think I have an idea." She turned to Kenji. "Sorry, we can play later."

"It's okay." Kenji shrugged, though he knew with these new developments there would not be a later, at least not here, not with them, not like this. "I want Marisa to cross them all off, too. What's your idea?"

It would go like this:

Marisa was right, they were locked in as far as their outreach while the power remained out, the networks down and the doors locked. Luckily, one of those things was in their control.

"Wait," Kenji interrupted before Celeste could really unveil the plans. "I just remembered the keys. You swallowed them." His eyes shifted toward the bucket. "Are...are they still..."

Marisa chuckled. "No, man. Those weren't the keys. Just a little showmanship. They were made from sugar. Funny, isn't it, how no one even tried to go through my bucket looking for them? As far as I know, anyway. No one's asked about the keys since, or how I intend to open the locks. Not Mr. Gigs, not Ms. Duli, not the board, not even you guys."

"My guess is it's not even locked," Celeste said.

"I bet you have some bolt cutters in that Mary Poppins duffel bag," Amira said, although she already knew the answer, having seen the glint of silver when she hid Marisa behind a bedsheet every night and every morning so she could change. She'd turned away and closed her eyes, of course, but that didn't always result in a complete lack of seeing. Sometimes Marisa said she was ready before she really was, as she slipped a silver glinting thing beneath her waistband. Sometimes Amira only tilted her head a little, so she could still see the movement and blur of flesh just beyond her line of sight. Guilt flooded through her in these instances, not just at the looking, but at the *wanting* to look. A girl should not, she thought to herself in her mother's voice, still, but without much of the conviction.

"Seriously, girl," Celeste added. "How much can one duffel bag really hold?"

Marisa frowned, looking down at her bag. "What do you mean? A regular amount, I feel."

Anyway, their guesses were wrong. Marisa and her cronies, as Amira had known for a while, had hid the keys on them the entire time, fastened in hidden pockets they'd all spent an evening stitching into their underwear—the pairs they'd planned on wearing on lock-in night, as well as at least a week's worth of changes.

Back to the unfurling plan:

One of them would leave the building through the basement to minimize the chance that others would be tempted to storm out when they saw the door cracking open. Once out, they'd go to the nearest Wi-Fi hotspot and post a message from Marisa's social media accounts (which had gained tens of thousands of followers). 2:30 p.m. deadline. One way or another, it ends today. 24 demands to go.

"Wait," Marisa protested, "I'm not opening the doors, though."

"Yes, you are, Em," Amira said, her hands still on Marisa's back. "It's going to end. If not today, then soon."

"She's right," Celeste said. "This way you at least control how it ends. Inspire some more people into action, or scare them into it. Get a few more demands crossed off."

"Yeah," Kenji said, his voice breaking. He fumbled with his phone in his pocket, thinking: *I should, I should, I should.*

The ambiguousness of the post would surely send some into a panic, especially all those who agreed with Jordi that Marisa was nothing short of a terrorist, that protesting in this way was no more valid than protesting violently. Hell, many of them said, it *was* violent. It fed right into Jordi's plan, though they didn't know this.

Fine. Let their speculation bring more attention. Let them believe what they would about Marisa. In the end, what mattered were the demands, and how many of them fell.

"Which one of us goes?" Kenji asked.

"Whoever can get to the coffee shop down the street fastest," Celeste said, which was a long, roundabout way to say Amira. They all listened to the rain, to their peers asking each other if the Wi-Fi had gone down for them, too.

"How do I get back in?" Amira asked. No one said anything, which was a long, roundabout way to say she wouldn't be coming back in.

6
10:55AM

Jordi couldn't decide if he wanted to stand over the banister and watch all his sad, sorry classmates mope about his stroke of genius, or if he wanted to drag a beanbag out from the library and plop it in front of Marisa to watch her unlock her damn chains. He wanted to see the look on her face, the look on all their faces, when they realized it was him who defeated her little plan, who'd granted them freedom. Too bad Peejay was hiding now, because his was the face Jordi most wanted to see give in to anger and disappointment. And maybe just a little admiration.

All these people would be free soon, not on Marisa Cuevas's

terms. And look at them. Were they thankful at all? Were they pleased? He hung around on the second floor waiting to see some joy or gratitude. He fiddled with his phone, wanting to brag about being behind the outage, but of course unable to because of it.

Then someone was beside him, and before he could turn to see who it was, the phone had been smacked out of his grasp, bouncing a few times on the floor, that terrifying noise when it landed facedown and you couldn't see whether it was cracked. "Why?" Peejay yelled, suddenly inches from Jordi's face. "Why the fuck did you have to get in the way? Why are you always like a cat weaving between people's legs as they walk? Don't you get that people would actually like you if you didn't try so hard to annoy them?"

Peejay felt better, just by yelling, as if that was all it took for the message to sink in. He watched Jordi's eyes, waiting to catch any signs of comprehension.

But Jordi only smirked, once he'd composed himself. He grabbed his phone, hiding the fact that his hand was shaking. This wasn't quite the expression he'd hoped to find on Peejay's face, but his anger proved Jordi's point even more. "You're just mad I'm winning."

"Winning what?" Peejay asked, yelling again already. Jordi clutched his phone with both hands. "The asshole Olympics? Winning at just getting in the way of things? Of destruction? How is that a point of pride? You're a speed bump. That's what you're proud of right now. Being an obstacle."

Jordi opened his mouth, but found even the word *no* didn't want to come out. He tried to push it past his diaphragm.

He could feel it there in his throat. He forced some air out, but all he managed was a glottal gulp. At least the smirk remained.

"You know," Peejay said, no longer yelling, speaking directly in his ear, "you don't have to be a minus in the world. Some people have a positive impact and some have a neutral existence, not harming but not helping, either. Just existing. And that's not bad, really. It was what I thought you might be able to amount to. Some annoying neutrality.

"Your life, though, right now, makes the world worse. You suck the life out of it. You make it worse. That's a choice you can undo."

Jordi tried to step away from Peejay, now forcing his smirk. "Whatever," he managed to say.

But Peejay stepped up to him again, his mouth now so close to Jordi's ear that Jordi got goose bumps when Peejay spoke. "You are choosing to actively worsen the world. You are choosing to be worse than worthless."

Jordi stepped away once more, but his back was now to the wall. He thought about his dad spewing vitriol at the television, about the week he'd spent locked in the building for some stupid reason he didn't understand. This wasn't how he'd expected Peejay to react. He hadn't expected to be confronted like this. He was a bulldozer, not a speed bump.

Jordi thought about how often his dad told him the value of throwing the first punch, how most fights were won by the person who struck first. He'd never expected to fight Peejay, but this certainly felt like what was happening. The growl in Peejay's voice, his flared nostrils, his constant encroaching.

So, though he hadn't thrown a punch in his life, though he didn't think about what would happen afterward, Jordi cocked his fist. This was what you were supposed to do with people who got in your way. That's what his father had taught him.

He was cornered, trapped. Peejay wasn't responding how he'd expected. He wasn't tearful, apologetic, groveling. He was holding strong. He'd called Jordi a fucking speed bump.

Jordi swung.

Instead of connecting with Peejay's face, though, his fist hit nothing, stopping a few inches short, as if his arm rebelled against the motion.

Neither of them had seen Omar follow Peejay up the stairs, hadn't seen him standing off to the side while Peejay yelled. Now they saw him, his arm hooked around Jordi's. In an instant he was pinning it behind Jordi's back. It was easy to forget Omar's strength while he roamed the halls with garbage bags trailing behind him. Much harder to forget when that strength was twisting your shoulder and wrist. Jordi let out a whimper.

"Should I let him go?" Omar asked, not wanting to be Peejay's savior, not wanting to decide for himself which fight Peejay could partake in. He'd stopped the fist from hitting Peejay's beautiful face. The rest was up to Peejay.

How Peejay wanted Omar to tear Jordi's arm off. How he wanted to pummel him while his arms were pinned. How he wanted Omar to let Jordi go and have Jordi attempt another swing, to have a fair fight and, however much damage he took, open himself to harm Jordi.

272

Still, though, even now, too much of Hamish remained within him. He motioned for Omar to let Jordi go with a flick of his wrist. There was something about the gesture that hurt Jordi more than a punch ever could. Dismissal, again. Cast aside as if he were nothing more than a fly buzzing around. As if he hadn't just single-handedly disrupted everything Marisa was trying to do. As if his actions were meaningless.

Omar untwisted his arm, but stood between them, in case Jordi tried something else. He thought there might be a few more words exchanged, especially now that people had noticed the altercation and were staring. Peejay, though, unflinchingly turned his back, readjusting the pashmina around his shoulders as he walked away.

Omar watched him go, wondering how far Peejay would retreat when Peejay stopped and looked at Omar. "Come with me," he said. "I need your help with something."

Jordi was left behind in the hallway, cheeks flushed with shame and anger, his brain churning.

Amira stood in front of Marisa. She was no good at goodbyes. Marisa was currently writing Lolo a note, which included a previously agreed-upon code word that meant whoever held the note should be trusted. Amira was to take the note down to the basement, and become the first CIS student or faculty member to exit the building in a week.

She didn't know how to process that information, so instead she calculated the distance to the nearest coffee shop (two and a half miles or so) and how long it would take her to reach it, if she still remembered how to run (twelve minutes).

Marisa was still writing, her dark curls hanging down as she leaned over. She balanced a book on her knees as support for the paper slip. Her handwriting was messy and beautiful, urgent, as if the ink itself knew her power and couldn't wait to act as her instrument. Amira watched Marisa's strong hands grasp the pen, hold the paper in place. Her nails were understandably ungroomed, a slight layer of grime that, to Amira, felt more earned than any grime she'd ever seen. After all, Marisa was clawing at the earth, fighting for dirt's right to exist among so much human garbage.

How could Amira leave this girl here? How could she tear herself away, even if it was for her? Not knowing how or when she'd see Marisa next, how their interactions would change hereafter. Amira knew that, at least until another wild event came up (Alien invasion? Birthing octuplets? Confronting her mother? Coming out? What could compare?), she'd forever think of her life as Before, During and After.

Just another day, she silently begged as she stood waiting for Marisa to finish her scribbling. How much could the note possibly need to say? Amira didn't care. She wanted to stretch the moment out forever. Let Marisa write for hours and hours so Amira could stand with her that much longer.

Just like that, though, Marisa stopped writing and proffered up the note for Amira to take. Did she not know? Could she not tell how little Amira wanted to go?

Again, their fingers brushed as Amira took the note. This time, neither of them moved away, though Kenji and Celeste were right there watching intently, though Amira's mom was ever present in her mind. The two girls looked into each other's eyes, the warmth in their fingers sending jolts down their spines so obvious it was a wonder neither of them could sense the other's shudder, that they still had questions about how the other felt.

Not knowing what else to say, Marisa managed to whimper, "Take care."

Amira curled her fingers around Marisa's, which is both exactly what she wanted to do, and not it at all. She expected herself to give just one brief squeeze, before turning away, and speed-walk toward the basement. That may have happened when she was more in control, but that wasn't the case anymore. Now Marisa seemed to dictate what her body did, and as her heart pounded, Amira held Marisa's hand tighter and said, "Now I am mad at you."

Marisa, unsure if she could focus both on Amira's words and on the feeling of her fingers wrapped around hers, said, "What? Why?"

The other Protectors averted their eyes, trying to give the girls privacy. All around the foyer people staring desolately at their inactive phones glanced over, wishing that they were part of that inner circle, privy to its conversations.

Amira hadn't responded, but she had started to rub her thumb against Marisa's. It felt life-changing, potentially life-destroying.

"Because of the decathlon?"

"Yes. No." Amira bit her lip, glancing briefly out the window, the rain now coming down at a constant, if not all-too-heavy rate. "I'm mad at you about the decathlon because I'm not actually mad about it, and I should be."

Marisa wondered if she was just fuzzy-brained from the drugs or the pain or Amira's thumb. "What?"

"You took away this thing I cared about so much, this thing I wanted for myself. And I should be mad at you. I should hate you for doing it. But instead I'm just..." She stopped, reaching for words but only able to look down at their hands clasped together. God, what was she doing?

Marisa leaned in ever so slightly, her voice at a near whisper. Everyone in the foyer leaned in, too, hoping to catch Marisa's reply, though they hadn't caught a single word yet. "You're what?"

It seemed as if all the conversations inside the building stopped. Maybe all the ones outside, too, the yelling parents, the reporters, the kids who'd been locked out instead of in. Even the rain seemed to lighten up a little.

Amira shook her head, unable to find the words. Instead, she ran.

Eli watched the rain come down around him. Over the past few days, he'd become quite good at noticing the subtle changes in the glass dome. The rain today felt different than normal, harder and steadier, especially for the time of day. The way the drops streaked and scurried down the glass gave everything a cinematic sheen, and he couldn't put his finger on exactly what caused it.

Eli had watched so many movies in the last week—the computer that had been used for the marathon belonged to a teacher who'd been locked out, leaving Eli free to extend the marathon beyond his wildest dreams.

Except for breaks to do homework (brought up to him by bored teachers, eager to have something to grade), Eli hadn't given it a rest, didn't want to give it a rest. Until the internet shut off, of course. Now he sat and watched the rain and wondered about the film industry's environmental practices until Jordi Marcos appeared before him.

Was this really the first time Omar stood directly in front of Peejay, in full view of that face of his? He remembered scanning the crowds at the gym for just a glance. Remembered all the times throughout the year when he watched in awe of Peejay's charisma, his ease with himself. It was rather incredible, how you could think about someone all year, your feelings building like water in a tub, and then one day, right when they were about to spill over, there that person was.

Now here Peejay was, and Omar couldn't bring himself to look. Was he supposed to look? Supposed to say something? All these days and nights in the gym talking about Peejay with Joy suddenly erased themselves from his mind, the conversations meaningless in Peejay's presence. Lolo had told Omar about Hamish being in a coma, and he wondered if it was appropriate to say something to Peejay. To wish his brother well, or offer condolences, or what.

They stood just outside the door to the gymnasium, Peejay having led them there arbitrarily and stopping with just as little apparent reason. Omar heard someone dribbling a basketball inside. The rack from lock-in night had been left out this whole time, and at one point or another all the students inside save for those restrained or unable had come by to shoot around. The school's average free throw percentage had risen three points.

"Thanks for stepping in," Peejay said. "I'd like to say I

could have taken care of him myself, but I didn't see that punch coming at all."

"Oh, sure," Omar responded, feeling clumsy in his words, in his body. He didn't know where his eyes should land.

Peejay was confused by Omar's shyness, not sure whether to read it as embarrassment for having followed Peejay up the stairs or something else.

"You said you needed my help with something?"

Peejay bit his lip. "Yeah, I don't know why I said that. I don't. I just wanted you to follow me out. I'm an impulsive little weirdo, sorry."

In the pause after he spoke, he felt the familiar tug of darkness in his mind wanting to coax him back to thoughts of Hamish, gone now. His mind wanted him back under his pashmina. Maybe, impossible as it seemed, Omar sensed this, because otherwise, why would he say, "I actually have something to show you."

"Really?"

Omar looked at the gym doors, because Peejay's face was too much, especially now that he'd set in motion what he had. "It's not done yet," he added, and thought about saying more, adding more qualifiers, but decided it'd be better just to open the door and lead Peejay to the bleachers.

They walked toward Joy, whose heart fluttered on her brother's behalf when she saw who he was walking with. Then she realized they weren't heading toward her but the bleachers where Omar had been hauling all that plastic, and it occurred to her that Omar had only kept whatever was down there from her because it'd been meant for Peejay. She chuffed at her brother's sweetness, and hoped it did not approach creepiness.

Omar only realized it might come across as creepy when he stood by the bleachers and motioned Peejay into the dark space.

"I should warn you, it's weird," he said after Peejay had bravely and unquestioningly stooped down to enter. "I don't know why I made it," he lied.

At first Peejay couldn't tell what he was looking at, his eyes still adjusting to the dark. Then the outline emerged, something semispherical, and he glanced at Omar, who was so much stranger than Peejay ever would've guessed. Peejay knew Omar was smart and shy, but even those uncommon traits for an athlete didn't mean strangeness was present, too. Peejay liked strangeness, especially when he didn't expect it.

Omar looked at his feet, wondering what the hell he was thinking bringing Peejay in here. He had a brief flash of what he'd been like before lock-in night, how different things looked now, and he wondered if it was sad that he'd been so irrevocably changed. Then their eyes adjusted, and enough light filtered in through the slats in the bleachers for Peejay to make sense of the massive thing in front of him.

Hamish's face, sculpted from water bottles and candy wrappers, straws, coffee stirrers, plastic bags. Peejay thought it strange, of course, but that didn't matter much. What mattered was the realization, deep and sweeping, reaching all the way into the dark pits of his mind, that Omar had been paying attention. Omar had seen him all this time. He'd known about Hamish. Maybe not everything, but no one knew everything. Now it became clear why Omar had come by the foyer all those times.

He tried to resist because he knew it might hurt Omar's feelings, but Peejay couldn't help but laugh. All that time beneath the pashmina, hiding, and Omar had seen nonetheless.

Omar shrunk at the sound, stifled though it was, until Peejay put a hand on his shoulder and said, "I thought you were coming by to look at Marisa."

"What? No. I was…" Still, his words failed him.

"Yeah, I get it now. Me."

Omar ran a hand over his head. This had been a terrible idea. All that time picking up garbage had messed with his social skills, his reasoning. "I'm sorry. I should go."

Peejay kept his hand on his shoulder, though, squeezing firmly. "Don't." His voice was oddly tender, none of the usual affected pomp (which Omar rather enjoyed). And now Peejay felt himself start to cry, seeing this incredibly sweet, somewhat horrifying statue. Hamish, looking back at him, smiling. Omar had somehow captured his essence perfectly—he knew exactly which online picture Omar had used, one from the night when Hamish was Partyer in Chief—and despite the many circumstances which made the moment odd, Peejay felt as if it really was Hamish smiling down at him, as if in approval. Peejay pulled Omar into a hug, allowing himself to bury his head in Omar's shoulder and sob.

Lolo finished reading the letter and set it on her lap, where there was still a buttery stain on her pants from all those days ago. She'd had them laundered, of course, taken upstairs by one of the Protectors and handed off to her family's maid, who'd been sent over on public transit to collect Lolo's clothes and deliver some home cooking. But the fact that Lolo had waited cemented the stain in her pants, along with the memory of waking up to find the sticky mess and the ants crawling all over the keys.

It had been a solitary week for her, much more so than she'd been prepared for. Though the solitude was worthwhile because of how much it'd revealed itself to be a mere lack of physical companionship. Lolo wasn't actually alone. Joy kept her constant digital company; Malik, too. Omar, now, was a friend, and Peejay, despite what the others murmured about him in the group chat, still came around every day and sat with her for an hour. He refused to talk about Hamish, refused to talk much in general, really. But still he came and sat and kept her company.

Kids who'd before avoided her now found themselves wandering into the basement looking for a hidden escape, either from the building or from their boredom. They found Lolo, and rather than flee, they sat and talked to her.

As lonesome as the lock-in could be, at night especially, hours and hours of no one down there but her, it hadn't been all that lonely. Though it hadn't ended yet, she had to remind herself. It was hard to feel that opening the door wasn't ending it.

"Okay," she said to Amira, not exactly thinking of whether Amira was lying or whether Marisa's demands would really have a better chance of being met if Amira ran to somewhere with Wi-Fi. Lolo could only think of what would happen when she let Amira out, closed the door behind her, and would have to wrap the chains back around her body, would have to snap the padlocks shut again. Would she resist the urge to go run and hug Joy and the others? Would she resist the urge to just walk, to feel that simple freedom she'd denied herself all week?

She reached into the secret pocket at her hip and pulled out the key, marveling that she hadn't felt tempted to use it even once.

When Amira stepped out into the fresh air, she resisted the urge to close her eyes and hold her hands out, catch raindrops on her tongue, feel the wonder of being alive in the world, with its perfect mix of oxygen and nitrogen, its climate, the smell of trees breathing on her behalf, the mad rush of people within it doing the best they could to live, a lot of it without caring for how it changed others' lives. She didn't pause to appreciate the moment: being reborn into the world.

No, Amira just started running. She ran to the school gate, and before the security guard could ask for a pass, she reached for the door and sped out, leaving the guard to wonder how much trouble he would get into if he simply didn't report the incident.

Amira turned the corner and picked up speed, feeling at once freed and like she was being forced to flee her home. But there was also the unmistakable joy she'd somehow forgotten about. Her knees creaked and her legs burned much earlier than they had since she was very, very young, and she thought to herself, *Oh, right. I used to have this.*

She could go anywhere, run for miles and miles, do all the things she'd meant to on lock-in night, all the things she'd trained for. She could run home and tell her mom: *Look what*

I can do. Though she didn't, and she was sure that was another sin her mother would hold against her.

But every step carried her farther away from Marisa, too, from the lock-in, from the Amira that existed at CIS and toward the Amira that had to exist at home. Each time her feet hit the pavement, she felt a jolt of pain, of distance tearing through her. She tensed her jaw and ran harder, down a street she'd never been on before except on a car or bus.

People she passed by—the mechanic in his shop rubbing oil off his fingers with an already-soiled rag, the lady selling fruit on the corner—took in her appearance, identified her as one of the students from the rich school down the street and thought, *What now?*

In the distance, Amira could see the coffee shop chain's gawdy sign. There was nothing else to do, she thought, but to push her body to its limits, to run as fast as she could as if it would bring her closer to Marisa, not take her farther way.

The bell rang again, signifying the start of third period. No one paid it any mind, except the teachers, who wondered how it was still operational with the power out. What mechanism did it use to function, they wondered, and how did it know when to ring, since certainly the clock that kept its time was digital. They stood around in the halls and asked themselves the question, forgetting in the darkened building to herd the students into the classrooms. There'd be time enough for that, they thought.

All they had was time nowadays. They couldn't access their lesson plans and presentations, anyway, couldn't print out backup worksheets. The students were in no rush to get to class, so neither were they.

It was Ms. Duli alone whose suspicions were roused. All of this in succession—the fall, the lights, everyone standing around as if it'd been previously agreed upon, it was too much to be coincidental. Something was afoot. She put her phone, as useless as everyone else's, in her back pocket and took a lap around the building, trying to suss out if the kids knew why the power was out, and what, exactly, it had to do with Marisa.

It was strange for the Protectors now that Amira had gone. They couldn't even pretend she was simply in the gym. The air felt too different. A door had opened, Amira had stepped out and the door had closed again.

Kenji and Celeste hadn't seen this happen, but they knew it had, as deeply and unquestioningly as they knew their birthdays. Now it was clear: they would leave. This wasn't how the rest of their lives would go. They would return home.

"Do you get along with your parents?" Kenji asked. He and Celeste were closer to the library, sitting by some chargers under the guise of checking to see if the power had returned, though they were really just giving Marisa some space. Celeste was resting her chin on her knee, refreshing her phone. For a moment she was going to answer Kenji without much thought, just an "Of course" or a "Sure." But then, remembering his confession, and weighing it against the relationship she had with her parents, she decided to be more candid.

"I think they're actually my best friends." Even after all

this time with him, she expected Kenji to laugh at her. Hearts were so irrationally sensitive, so insecure.

"That would be so cool," Kenji said. "Friends with money and cars and access to booze."

Celeste snorted. "I mean, to be fair, they're kind of my only friends."

"Not anymore," Kenji said, so casually, as if he'd known all this time they'd end up here. He took his glasses off and cleaned them on the hem of his shirt, though they were still smudged when he put them back on. Celeste looked at the ground, hiding her smile.

"Even if that were the case—" now Kenji made a pointed effort to meet her eyes "—and it's not, I'd still prefer that to what I have with my parents."

"They're not good at improv, are they?"

Kenji instantly became animated, his eyebrows raised high above his glasses' frames. "Oh my God, they don't do it at all. They don't even improvise their coffee orders." He thought for a second and corrected himself. "Okay, that doesn't make them the worst—people have much harder situations than I do. But it's not exactly fulfilling to have parents that don't want me to be me. Which I get, to an extent. People have expectations, especially for their kids. I'm sure if you spend a good portion of your life dreaming your kid is going to turn out one way, it feels shitty when they end up being someone wholly different. But is that my fault?"

"It is absolutely your fault, Kenji. Stop being silly."

Kenji knew she was joking, but he sighed and hugged his knees to his chest, looking at the scene around him. A dozen or so people sat around the foyer, looking helplessly at their phones. A few others walked around aimlessly, leaving and entering rooms. In her chains, Marisa looked lost in thought again, every now and then twisting her body to try to find some sort of relief. Kenji couldn't help but feel time was ticking away too quickly, and he could do nothing to stop it, or even make it pass meaningfully. Even improv, if it came to him now of all times, could do nothing. The one thing he could have done to at least be a good friend to Marisa—call his father—he hadn't.

7

11:58AM

The parents were back, the media was outside and the world had heard Marisa's promise/threat. The students felt as if they were back at lock-in night.

The buzz in the air. The hands clasped together, the hope, the fear it would be taken away from them (not the night itself anymore, but Marisa's protest, which now felt just as much theirs as hers). Instead of itineraries and schedules, they looked at Marisa's demands and wondered if there was a way they could rearrange time and space and their previous efforts in order to accomplish every single one.

As the bell rang for fourth period, the parents arrived on

the lawn, terrified of what might happen inside. Dov's mom, whom he'd called after his fall, banged on the door, wailing as if she'd lost him for good. The reporters had a field day, no pun intended, recording interview after interview with people who had no information but made up for it with plenty of opinions.

Several factions sprung up outside the school: a) those who wanted to gawk, who watched the ambulances brought into campus with an illicit thrill, a sense of danger enjoyed only by those not actually faced with it; b) those, mostly students who'd been locked out, who made signs—some on the backs of cardboard paper they'd carried a week ago supporting Amira, and which they'd never been able to employ or get rid of—begging whoever was around to try to meet the demands; c) those carrying signs, made at home just an hour or so ago, or right there on the field with markers hastily grabbed on their way out the door, name-calling Marisa, disparaging her as a sadist, a murdererer (sic), a terrorist.

Armed with vans equipped with satellite antennae, the reporters relayed all this to the outside world. The rain had momentarily let up, but thunder still rolled and roiled overhead, threatening to drench the crowd—those who hadn't already been drenched by hours of standing in the worsening drizzle.

Then the police arrived. They were a menacing and ominous sight: three armored trucks rumbling in through the gates, blasting their sirens, like predators roaring just to show their dominance. As if from a clown car, dozens of riot-clad officers unloaded. The school hadn't wanted police involved, and the police had been happy to stay out of it. But now that the rumors had been buzzing about Marisa's threat, they felt compelled to go and get those children, particularly the children of diplomats, out.

They didn't bring guns with them—who would want guns around children? Even the commissioner who'd ordered them onto the campus was afraid of the blowback if there were a student harmed—but that meant little to the parents gathered on the lawn, to the cameras, the students pressing their faces against the window.

Mrs. Nudel wailed harder and banged on the door, pawed at the handles, jolting them back and forth.

On the other side of the doors, Marisa absorbed the jerks as best she could, trying to breathe through her instincts to slam her body back into the doors, which would only hurt her more.

It wasn't just Dov's parents who arrived on campus. All over town, the call had gone out. Parents left home, left work meetings, canceled flights, booked flights. They felt impelled to be there, suddenly presented with the possibility that their children might come in harm's way. They hadn't really believed all the things people had said about Marisa, and as much as they hated the situation, they knew their kids were safe. Now, though, seeing her message shared by coworkers, by friends living elsewhere in the world and checking in, knowing at least one kid was hurt (it'd been lost along the chain of communication, who, exactly, it was) and she hadn't been swayed, well, what kind of parents would they be if they didn't come to CIS?

Marisa's parents were there. They of course noticed the looks they were getting. The whispers. Marisa's dad shifted, stepping closer to his wife, whose presence always calmed him. Someone nearby muttered a comment about "the protestor's parents," at which point Mrs. Cuevas took two steps back to look at the mutterer and say, "You're goddamn right."

Diego, too, was there. He hadn't thought of lock-in night much since he'd left CIS that Friday morning, drunk off exhaustion and a pilfered pint or two of tiki drink he'd poured himself before heading home. He'd stopped attending school altogether, his talk with the DJ that night making him realize he was ready for a new chapter in life, regardless of how formally this one would end. His parents, knowing the road to a successful, happy life was not exclusively an academic one, had been okay with it. Unhappy, sure, but okay in the end. He'd find another road. This only led to further mutterings among the disapproving parents in the crowd once they got to talking.

Like with all things he didn't care about, Diego didn't pay much attention. He was there because he'd found he missed his sister's presence in his life. So when his parents left the house, he came along. A few CIS students noticed him standing by the bleachers on the soccer field and approached to say hi, maybe get some inside scoop. "What is she planning?" they asked. Reporters who'd done their homework and knew who Diego was cocked an ear, too. They'd all forgotten what he was like, though.

"Who?" he asked. His former classmates stared slack-jawed at him. How stupid could he be?

"Marisa. Your sister." They motioned toward the building, which ninety-five percent of people were currently looking at, despite the fact that almost nothing of interest happening inside would be visible.

"Oh, right. How would I know?"

"She never talked to you about this? Not even once? Texted you today with, like, what could be interpreted as a goodbye?"

Diego turned to look at the girl talking to him, whom he vaguely remembered from class. "I really like that necklace." He reached out to touch it, pausing a few inches away from the simple gold and cloth ornament, waiting for permission to take it in his hands.

"Oh, thanks," Diego's former classmate said, grabbing at her necklace and putting it in Diego's hands. "I got it in Laos." She suddenly remembered how much she had liked looking at Diego last semester when they'd had art together, how she'd glanced over the edge of her canvas at him, the focus in his eyes so rarely broken, unlike the rest of her classmates. Lost in this memory, all the questions about what he knew flitted from her mind.

Celeste's parents were out there, trying again and again to call her, even though their phones had lost signal an hour ago when they'd arrived. They'd taken turns all morning sneaking away from their work to call people they knew back home, working to get Marisa's demands met. When they hadn't heard back from Celeste after their latest check-in, they gathered their belongings and came down to the school.

They were glad to see other parents there, glad to see nothing was on fire or under fire. As oblivious now as anyone else on campus, they hoped their friends in Chicago were chipping away at the demands.

★ ★ ★

This time, Arthur Pierce had come armed with his own megaphone. He shuffled through the crowd toward the front of the building and waited for the wailing mother to calm herself before speaking, since it was unbecoming to shout over a mourning lady. Eventually, Dov's mom tired herself into silence, and Arthur saw his opening. He motioned for his assistant, Asher, to hand him the megaphone, and placed the umbrella he'd been holding into Asher's hand, angling Asher so he stood protecting Arthur from the blasted weather.

He raised the megaphone to his lips. "Kenji, son," he said. Many jumped at the sound. All over the field, other parents had been in the process of raising their own megaphones to their lips, meaning to call out to their children. But Mr. Pierce had beat them to it, and though they'd all brought the megaphones to avoid a repeat of lock-in night when they had to wait to shout, they figured it would be rude to interrupt, so they waited for him to finish. "This is your father."

Inside, Kenji made a face, as if a headache had just shot through his temples, coupled with a particularly unpleasant smell. "Oh, no."

"There are a lot of people gathered here who agree this has all gone on a little too long. I'd like you to come to the window and tell us what's going on."

"Why does he think I would know?" Kenji said to Celeste. They rose to their feet, making their way into a nearby classroom to look out the window. All they could see was the plethora of people gawking at them. "Shit, Marisa's going to find out."

"You should go tell her."

"That's a really good idea. But how about this other one: I don't."

"Kenji."

A whine worked its way through his chest. "I don't wanna."

"Yes, you do. I'll come with you. I'll be your moral support."

"Can we go back to when I was avoiding this with podcasts and you were too shy to give me good advice?"

Celeste laughed, blushing. "I'd rather not."

Kenji took his glasses off and cleaned them with the hem of his shirt. "Fine, let's go make Marisa hate me."

While they walked to the foyer, Arthur Pierce kept speaking into the megaphone, convinced his words were all it would take for the shenanigans to finally come to a halt. The calls to his office had been increasing all week, and that morning they'd risen so exponentially he hadn't had time for anything else.

Deep inside he was worried he couldn't solve this. That, even as an important man used to seeing his words turn into actions, this was a place where he was powerless, and that lack of power might mean his son would come to harm. He couldn't quite come out and say those words, not even to himself. So he went on speaking as if he held power here, like everywhere else.

"Ms. Cuevas, if you're listening, my name is Arthur Pierce, CEO of…"

Seeing Kenji approach, Marisa sighed. "Is he always like this?"

"Every second of the day, from what I gather," Celeste answered for him.

"How the hell did you turn out to be so laid-back?" Marisa asked Kenji.

There was a joke in here, surely. Some sarcastic response. He shrugged. "I, uh, have to tell you something," Kenji said. His father's muffled voice continued to ring out across the field and through the building. "My dad is in charge of Lokoloko." There was the occasional whine of feedback as other parents got antsy to have their turn and accidentally pressed the trigger on their megaphones.

Marisa laid her head back against the doors. "Why didn't you say anything?"

"I didn't think it would help. He doesn't listen to me. All he does is say no."

Right on cue, as if someone was turning up the volume on his megaphone, they could hear him continuing on his tirade. "...and if you think this tantrum will intimidate important men like myself, you are sorely mistaken. I've read your ridiculous demands..."

"Well, at least I was right when I guessed that a CIS parent was involved in the project," Marisa said, and it sounded like, for the first time since the whole fiasco began, her voice threatened to break. "You know, that was what led me to do this whole thing in the first place. That site." Just as she said it, she realized her mangled leg would keep her from the reefs for weeks or months to come. The next time she'd be able to snorkel or dive in the area, it might already be too late. The toxic runoff would've begun, the world would've inched however many days closer to the turning point, the oceans' acidification would've increased. She may have seen those greens, oranges and purples for the last time.

"God," Marisa said, closing her eyes. "Maybe I should just open up. Just take the wins I got and go home to take a normal freaking shower and sleep in my bed again."

"Hospital, Marisa," Kenji said. "I think you mean take a normal shower at the hospital."

"I know that's not our fearless leader I hear talking about giving up." Peejay approached from the staircase. Omar Ng was at his side. "Plus, don't pretend you were completely hating those sponge baths Amira was helping you with."

At Marisa's furious blushing and the others' scandalized looks, Peejay threw the pashmina over his head. "The depressed one sees all." Then he slid the pashmina back around his shoulders, followed with a defensive palm raised up. "Not all, mind you. I averted my eyes and let Amira ogle you on her own. A voyeur I may be, but I try not to toe the line into creepiness."

Marisa blushed on, wondering how much they'd all noticed, or if it was just Peejay. She blushed, too, with the memory of those baths, though they hadn't really been baths. Amira would bring her a bucket (not that one) filled with warm soap water and help her set up her curtain (a bedsheet procured from Marisa's duffel bag, brought in anticipation of the privacy she'd need). It hadn't ever been part of the plan: Marisa had prepared to suffer; she was definitely prepared to stink. But Amira had offered. It'd only been twice.

At first Amira had given her her privacy, left to go on a run or something. But she'd come back surprisingly early, staying just beyond the curtain, keeping Marisa company. Neither was sure how exactly that had happened, but neither had called attention to it, either, afraid to break the spell of normalcy it came with.

As uncomfortable as Marisa was in that moment, as defeated as she felt looking at those twenty-four uncrossed demands and the zero bars on her cell phone, Peejay was right, the baths at home wouldn't compare to the thrill of having Amira nearby, reaching timidly over the curtain with her eyes averted to offer the bucket of water. "Whatever," Marisa said. "So I'm feeling a little defeated, what of it."

"Well, my problem with your defeat lies mostly in the timing. We're in the final stretch here." He walked over to the nearby window, and if there were blinds to push apart with two fingers the way they did in movies, he would've done exactly that. Since there weren't, though, he just looked out. "It's going to end soon. At which point I'll be happy to make room for you beneath my pashmina and we can both tailspin into the darkest places our minds will go. We'll grieve together. But to do so now would be silly, and not in the way the esteemed Mr. Pierce says it, but a true waste of your herculean efforts to save the world." Peejay stepped toward Marisa.

All around, students who'd just been trying to glance outside or refresh their phones were tuning into Peejay's speech. *He's back*, they thought, feeling the old familiar stirrings of the spell he'd cast over them.

Peejay brushed Marisa's hair out of her eyes. "You and the others have fed me over the past week. You've given me reassuring touches that kept me tethered to my sanity and helped me avoid the worst of my grief." Grief? Those who'd heard shared looks, wondering what he was referring to. The few who knew about Hamish's accident felt a tightness clawing at their chest. "You kept me inside your circle. You've kept me from sinking." He looked at Omar again, so he'd know Peejay included him in this. "I'm not going to let you sink now."

Maya Klutzheisen and Michael Obonte gave each other a look. Shit, did they love Peejay now, too?

Then Peejay turned to Kenji. "Grab Marisa's megaphone out of that Mary Poppins bag. Let's talk to your father."

Again, Kenji reached to find a joke to distract Peejay, and the dozens of people whose attention had turned toward him. "Do I have to?" he said, but he was already shuffling over to Marisa.

"You don't have to do anything, party-saver. But if you'd rather sit here and chat, then I'll still go yell at him, and you'll have to spend the rest of your life knowing you didn't do all you could to slow the planet's death. You'll have to sleep every night knowing Marisa chained herself to a door and kept it shut while she slowly bled to death and you did nothing."

"I'm not bleeding," Marisa interjected.

"You'll have to explain to your children when they have food shortages and are living through extreme weather phenomenons—"

Kenji raised the megaphone to his lips, "Coming, Father!"

Peejay smiled and gave Marisa a wink. As he started to follow Kenji toward the nearest classroom, he looked at the other people standing near, by now at least half of those locked in. "Let's get to it, my darling Sea Cucumbers."

What exactly Peejay had meant was ambiguous. Some believed it was just one of those snappy remarks he was known for, that he was announcing in his patented style Kenji's talk with his father. Others believed he'd just bound the school in their common goal.

Sure, they'd been trying with the demands for a few hours before the power went out. Some longer than that. But, like Marisa, they'd been feeling useless, like doomsday was too close for them to do anything about it. In the end, what would it really matter? The doors would open, or the planet would die.

That throwaway phrase, though, that casual parting remark, struck much deeper than even Peejay had intended. *Let's get to it.* By which he'd meant: let's talk to our parents, let's shout out the windows at the reporters, do what we can to meet these demands. His classmates, though, felt the words crashing over them, big sweeping waves of emotion like few they'd felt before. The words were about the world itself, and that its saving was in their hands. And they could do something. Right now. They could raise their voices to their literal and figurative loudest.

Although that wasn't exactly right. The power was in *others'* hands, like Kenji's father's, like the board's, and they had to rip it from them. That, at least, was in their power. It wasn't just one or two who wanted to. It was all of them. Nearly all, anyway. If they'd been moved to action by Peejay's email earlier that morning, now they felt the urgency full-on. *Let's get to it.*

Jordi had shuffled off to the roof garden, though few had seen him go, and fewer had seen him arrive (just Eli, really, who'd tried to start a conversation with him, to no avail).

The rest of their group had fallen quiet, seeing what the rest of them were only now learning.

Those touched by Peejay's words had greater numbers. There was power in that. They all went to find windows, pushing chairs or desks right up to them so they could stand and speak into the slits, yelling out to their parents. Some begged and pleaded for their parents to help. To sign petitions, make phone calls, move investments away from fossil fuels and toward renewable energy sources. Others didn't beg, but demanded this of their parents, as if they were threatening to stay inside even if the doors opened, as if they had this whole time been on Marisa's side. Never mind whether they'd been before. They were now.

Arthur Pierce approached a window, Asher struggling to keep up and protect him with the umbrella. Beyond the glare in the window (in which he could see himself, looking put-together enough, and his assistant less so, the crowd shuffling about behind him, police lights, all those signs, at least one of them with the name of his company), he could just barely make out his son's face. He was standing next to another boy, older, darker-skinned, who held himself with the kind of presence Arthur often wished Kenji could hold.

There were others in the room, too, but Arthur couldn't see them and, either way, wouldn't have noticed their presence, struck as he was that he hadn't seen his son in person in a week. They'd of course chatted on the phone, but while his wife came down to pass clothes and other belongings through this very window slit, Arthur himself hadn't found the time. It hardly felt like seeing him through glass would be better than seeing him through a screen. "Son," he said now, some of the bluster gone from his voice. A whole week had gone by without him being in the same room as his child, and he hadn't quite noticed. He cleared his throat. "Kenji, I'm worried. What is this girl planning?"

Kenji turned to Peejay, knowing he had to speak, knowing he was going to, but needing the words, or at least the breath. Rather than telling him it was all just like improv or insisting he knew what to say, Peejay only gave him a little nod, as if he were granting him permission to speak what he already knew he was going to say. Kenji swallowed, then raised the megaphone. How was he supposed to do this?

His hand dropped again and he looked back, but instead of Peejay's gaze, he looked farther behind. As he'd guessed, Celeste was there, too. She smiled her shy smile and he thought about the way she could laugh on the phone with her parents.

"Dad," he said, comforted by the squint in his father's eyes, which meant he couldn't exactly see through the glass. "Have you heard about the demand to stop construction at your site on the coast?"

"Of course, it's my company. You know that. Don't be silly."

"If you knew it would help get me out, why haven't you scrapped it?"

Mr. Pierce scoffed, then tsked. Thoughts of the week gone by without Kenji faded. "Why are we talking about this? Answer my question. What is she planning?"

No acceptance of what Kenji was saying, no willingness to answer the question, to add to the conversation. Just rejection.

For the first time he could remember, Kenji turned the word he so hated hearing from his father back onto him. "No. You answer mine first. If you knew, why hasn't it been done yet?"

Arthur Pierce's hand, the one holding the megaphone, dropped to his side. Rain splashed off the umbrella onto his fingers, scurrying down the megaphone. Had that really been Kenji's voice?

Somewhere in the crowd, Rifta Wahid, who hadn't yet spotted her daughter skirting around the edges of the field, trying to stay hidden, shook her head. "A boy should not speak back to his father like this," she said to no one in particular.

Embarrassed by Kenji's question and how long he'd been silent, Arthur Pierce spoke again. "Because multi-million-dollar companies do not yield to the cries of a petulant child terrorist," he said, keeping his tone light and airy. "If she has some suggestions for us, we have a comment form on our website and a customer service hotline she can call."

A few chuckles in the crowd, mostly from adults. Mrs. Cuevas rolled her eyes. "How refreshing," she said, "an adult dismissive of a teenager." She didn't bother yelling. Publicly defending Marisa, standing up for what she'd done, could come at another time, and would, over and over throughout the upcoming months and years, but right now she'd let Marisa's actions speak for her, would let Marisa raise her voice if she felt the need to.

Now his father was joking? Kenji clenched his fists, the megaphone giving a whine. "That's a great answer for a press conference, Father, but I wonder how much comfort it would provide if you never saw me again."

Arthur Pierce staggered backward, nearly knocking into Asher, who had to step into some bushes to avoid the contact.

"Was that a little harsh?" Kenji said off-mic to Peejay. "It definitely makes it sound like she's going to murder me."

Peejay smiled. "Let him sit with that image for a second. Who cares if it's true or not."

Arthur didn't sit with it long. "None," he answered, trying to power through the shift in balance he'd felt. "Though surely there's a middle ground here." The project up the coast was the largest in the region for his company, and Kenji was right here in front of him, wasn't he, safe and sound. No need to be rash.

Again, Kenji lobbed his father's favorite word back up. "No. You've been telling me that word my whole life. Now listen to me say it. No. No middle ground. No talking it out. The project is canceled or you never see me again."

"There are plenty of other factors, though. Thirty demands, aren't there? Why would I commit to wasting millions of dollars and three years' worth of time if all the other demands don't get met?"

"Goddamn it, just pretend. Imagine, for one stupid moment." He'd yelled the first few words, but by the end, Kenji just sounded tired. Like he was ready for the scene to be over, since his partner wasn't cooperating at all. He pushed his glasses up the brim of his nose. "Listen to me, for once, will you? Just pretend."

Almost in spite of his son standing up to him—or maybe because of it—Arthur said, "Fine." He lowered the megaphone, at which point a bunch of other parents began yelling into theirs, most of them answering their children, who'd been yelling from other windows throughout this whole exchange.

So Arthur Pierce now allowed himself to sit with the image his son had put in his head. The project gets scrapped, or Kenji is gone. His brain, the wonderful, strange contraption that it was, was rather adept at creating new scenarios and treating them, at least for a moment, as real. He pictured an explosion at the school at 2:30 p.m. Or the girl pulling guns out from her duffel bag (that he pictured Marisa having a duffel bag was just a strange coincidence), the way things might happen at an American school. He pictured him and his wife on their knees by Kenji's body, imagined the terrible pain in his gut, in his throat, filling his entire body for the rest of his life. He pictured his marriage falling apart, pictured his board voting him out of his own company because he was no longer capable of running it adequately, no longer capable of doing anything adequately. He imagined—no, knew—this hypothetical version of himself wouldn't care about being voted out. He'd relinquish control of the company to have his son back. In an instant. God, even if Kenji lived but remained within this building, his days and months and years wasting away, what would Arthur's company mean to him? What good would it be without his son in his life? Was that really at stake here? He looked around at all the faces looking at him or at the building, hunching their shoulders forward to protect themselves from the drizzle and the wind, which were both picking up again. How had he not thought all this yet? He swallowed, amazed at how deeply he had fallen into that make-believe world.

Then the police started walking in formation, a moving wall of plastic shields and helmets. They guided the parents away from the building, though they couldn't help but add a bit of forcefulness to their voices. They may have come with batons and strict instructions to maintain control without force, but they'd be damned if they weren't going to show these rich people they had some power.

Arthur Pierce now was led away by an officer, a boy, really, not all that much older than Kenji. Asher followed with his umbrella, and the officer shoving him along allowed himself to act a little more forcefully with the assistant. The crowd got pushed back, grudgingly creating space for the police to do whatever it was that would free their children.

"But what is the girl planning!" Guillem Kim's mother shouted from the back. Others, like Arthur Pierce, had fallen into their own bouts of tragic daydreams. Granted, many of them had been living them constantly, ever since lock-in night. Celeste's parents and Marisa's and Omar's, everyone but Peejay's, who were too deep in a real tragedy to get lost imagining a new one.

To the rest, though, this latest bout of daydreams felt more immediate somehow, more likely. They couldn't help but ask themselves what could they do? How could they get their kids out? What demands could they meet?

8
12:45PM

Anais Duli stood at five feet two inches, which offered her few advantages in a crowd, save for the ability to remain out of sight. She was standing in the room where Kenji held the megaphone and was turning to Peejay to consult about what to do now that his father had fallen silent. The boy looked stricken by the silence, but that wasn't necessarily what stuck out to Ms. Duli.

She'd been flirting with the thought all week, and now it landed. Look at these kids coming together. Look at them shout for good. Marisa wanted to save the world, not harm it. Why was she doing anything but helping them?

Ms. Duli remembered her teenage self, remembered how quickly her soul could become inflamed with passion, how urgent her need to save the world could be, to fight for justice. She would see a video about some far-off unfathomable tragedy and look for flights to travel to the famine/disaster/violence-stricken region so she could lend a hand. For months when she was seventeen, she thought about how she would get home from school and lay out her plans to her parents about how they should take in a family of refugees in their spare bedroom. Hell, two whole families, one in her room, one in the spare bedroom. Anais herself would sleep on the floor if it could help ease some of the indefatigable, insurmountable pain in the world. She would let everyone use the bathroom before her, even.

But then she'd get home or hover over the "purchase ticket" button and the fire would sniff out, deprived of oxygen as soon as it tried to really flare up. Years of this. Of thinking she'd do something big for the world, and never doing it. It was a muscle that had lost its strength, weakened by apathy.

As an adult, she gave to charities and signed petitions. Hell, she was a teacher, shaping young minds. Her courses were designed to make sure her students thought about what it meant to have empathy, to instill some sense of civic duty and compassion in their young brains. She highlighted all the times in history when human beings had failed to keep these tenets in mind. Her students came away better, more aware people, many of them privileged in a way that meant their awareness, appropriately directed, could have a truly far-reaching impact.

But Ms. Duli, if she were being honest with herself, had always wanted to do something big, something dramatic. She'd looked at Marisa skeptically, because, as good as her cause was on paper, Ms. Duli hadn't quite been able to wrap her mind around the fact that Marisa had achieved what Ms. Duli herself had failed to: taking that bold step to realizing her aspirations. And perhaps that meant Marisa was impulsive, dangerous somehow. At least, that's what she'd thought in the days before.

Now, though, Ms. Duli realized she still had a chance to join in, to make her teenage self proud. She crossed the foyer toward Marisa. She'd done this so many times in the past week no one really paid much attention, busy as they were trying to find a window through which to shout at their parents.

Marisa, left alone while others acted out her desires, raised an eyebrow at Ms. Duli. "What does the board have for me now?" She groaned. "Some draft of a demand that's not actually giving me what I ask for?"

Marisa had some renewed energy and hope after Peejay's pep talk, though another dose of morphine or whatever it was Nurse Hae had gotten her hands on would do her good. She was glad to see her teacher, if only for the distraction from her pain, from her helplessness.

"What do you want me to do?" Ms. Duli asked.

At first, Marisa thought it was a rhetorical question, and she waited for her to go on. When she didn't, Marisa said, "What?"

"To help. For your demands. Your cause. I'm no longer mediating here, no longer taking your requests to the board. I'm on your side now." She took a symbolic step toward Marisa and put her back against the wall, facing the same direction as her student, one hand on the chains, as if that meant she were now just as locked up.

Marisa scoffed. "What, did they send you down as a mole or something? I'm not telling you what's gonna happen at 2:30, or how I sent the message." Only after she said it did Marisa realize Ms. Duli would have no way of knowing about Amira's post on her behalf.

But Ms. Duli didn't question the suspicion, simply rolled her eyes at it. She stopped herself short of a full roll, though. If she were still seventeen, if her soul was as impassioned as Marisa's, she wouldn't take well to an eye roll. "That's a fair question," she said instead. "But I know you're not planning anything. You're going to open the doors."

Marisa tried to open her mouth, but found her anger tensing her jaw shut.

"I told you," Ms. Duli continued, "I want to help. I want to see you succeed." A megaphone shriek made them both cringe. The wind howled as if in response. People on the field unconsciously huddled closer together, trying to shield themselves from the weather.

"Why now?"

"I feel time ticking away in which I can be helpful. I thought I could help from the middle, but I no longer believe that guiding the board to act is the right move. It's about time I chained myself to something, too."

Amira couldn't stop moving. At the coffee shop, she'd pushed the doors open and come to a halt, shocked at the other customers' lack of a response. She'd opened and closed the doors! As if unable to decide if she wanted to stay or go! As if it were a choice!

Now that she had run again, she wondered how she'd ever

stopped, how a girl chained to a door had supplanted all her previous drive to run, to jump, to do things others didn't believe her capable of. The more she thought about it, though (as she logged on to Marisa's social media accounts on her phone), the more it felt fitting. Marisa, after all, wanted to push the world to better itself in ways no one believed could be done.

No sooner had Amira posted the message than she felt the need to run again, but also to run to Marisa. To run home and tell her mother: *This is who I am.* That might have to wait, though.

She managed to sneak into school by crouching behind a car as it entered the parking garage. Then she snaked her way into the crowd, constantly moving because her body demanded it, because she could still control this part of herself, even if her tingles and cravings were dictated by Marisa. But also because she didn't want to be recognized. Luckily, plenty of people were wearing hijabs and most everyone was wearing head cover for the rain, anyway, their peripheral vision lessened by their raincoat hoods and umbrellas.

Now, as the wind howled and the temperature dropped, Amira's legs grew tired. It was amazing how quickly her body had fallen out of its old habits. An hour of running would have barely been a warmup a week ago. She stopped to stretch, by happenstance managing to choose a spot on the soccer field only a few feet away from her mom. Neither noticed the other.

Mrs. Wahid was tutting beneath her umbrella, muttering about this or that. Amira heard but didn't recognize the voice over the sound of the rain, and instead fixed her attention on the roof garden.

It was hard to tell exactly what was going on, but after a

minute or so of squinting, she felt like she could make out a figure standing at the edge of the roof, right by the glass.

Jordi Marcos hadn't said a single word in the twenty or so minutes since he'd arrived on the roof, and Eli was starting to wonder if maybe there was something wrong with him. He'd been standing still for a while, but now he shifted his weight from one foot to the other and Eli perked up, excited to have someone to talk to (other than Maizey Krokic and Anwar Gomez, who'd made the garden their lock-in home the past week and too often were grossly lovey-dovey or argumentative, and would only turn their attention to Eli to try to use him to win their arguments).

"Not feeling chatty?" Eli joked. Jordi turned, looking startled, as if he hadn't heard Eli the three other times he'd spoken, or had forgotten he was up there. "Everything okay, man?" Eli asked. "Do you want to watch a movie?" Nothing. "I was starting to think that…" He trailed off, not knowing what to say. It didn't seem to matter. Jordi had a far-off look in his eyes.

"I'm a bulldozer, not a speed bump," he said, so softly Eli barely heard him over the rain pounding on the glass.

He walked toward the exit, and Eli said, "What was that, mate? I missed it. The rain, you know." God, why had he said *mate*? He never said *mate*. But Jordi ignored him again. He crossed the entirety of the roof, down the little pathway that split the tennis courts from the picnic tables and led to the exit where Eli was chained.

Once he'd reached the door, though, Jordi didn't respond,

just turned around and faced the far glass wall where he'd been standing a moment before. "Speed bump this," Jordi said.

"Huh?" Eli said, just as Jordi started sprinting down the path toward the glass.

Jordi had no idea what would happen when he hit the glass. It would break, he figured, and he'd stand at the edge of the roof and finally have his moment. The police or firefighters or whatever would bring up the ladder, and Marisa and Pee-jay would lose. Jordi would end the lock-in.

Now, of course the glass was shatterproof, top-of-the-line stuff. Jordi knew this. Everyone knew this. His body didn't much care, though. Who knew how reliably the glass would resist shattering. Who knew how often a dud pane made it out into the marketplace, where its promise of remaining intact would likely go untested. Who knew how much the constant rain weakened it, the occasional hailstorm, the earthquakes not uncommon in the region, the wind, the slow way time undid everything. Maybe the school had tried to save money and gone for a cheaper model (this was what the future law-suit alleged).

Jordi ran, not knowing anything but that he had to throw his body at it. Marisa had done just that, thrown her body in the way, and apparently it was all going peachy fucking keen for her. People loved a protestor? This was his protest.

Eli was yelling for him to stop. Maizey Krokic and Anwar Gomez heard his pounding feet and ceased their make-out session as he passed the little bedroom they'd made for themselves beneath a picnic table.

Jordi turned his shoulder before he hit, angling his body

the way action movie heroes always did when they wanted to burst through doors. Unlike them, though, Jordi merely bounced back, falling on the floor. The pain he felt was nothing like Marisa's, though Jordi imagined it was the same. He took most of the impact in the spot where he'd gotten a tetanus booster a few days before lock-in night, perhaps adding to the pain (maybe?). He knew he was lucky to not have burst through the glass. But Jordi was mostly disappointed he hadn't gotten his way. He didn't care what was good for him. He just wanted to win.

He lay on the ground for a moment, in pain and on the verge of tears. Behind him, Eli yelled, "Dude, what the hell?" Then Jordi looked up at the glass that had defeated him. It seemed unaffected, but a little glimmer caught his eye.

He pulled himself slowly to his feet, wincing. Then he felt water on his cheek. Not a lot, just the finest drop, like the hint of a mist.

Jordi stared at the glass, his heartbeat already racing. It was hard to tell where the glimmer was, except if he moved his head a certain way it caught the light. Just to make sure he was seeing what he thought he was seeing, he ran a hand across the glass. It was almost imperceptible on the soft tiny ridges of his index finger. But it was there. A little drop of water squeezed through. A crack.

Below, Amira saw the figure sprinting back and forth, heaving himself over and over again at the glass. She didn't know who it was, but she had her guesses. "I have to get back inside," she said, the words leaving her mouth unintentionally, but leaving all the same. They carried on the wind just enough to cause the woman to her left to turn.

"I guess he's done talking, then?" Kenji said, looking out the window at his father staring blankly, his phone in his hand, the megaphone at his side.

"What would you do in improv if someone doesn't go along with the game like that?"

"You would just keep going until someone yells 'scene.'"

"So—" Peejay gestured "—keep going." Behind Peejay, Celeste gave what she hoped was a reassuring nod.

Kenji sighed. He wished he had a scene partner. No, he wished that, for once in his goddamn life, his dad would be that for him. Someone willing to go along with the world Kenji presented him with. He stood there for a moment, thinking they wouldn't be here—*they* being the Protectors, those locked in, the media, everyone—if his dad weren't so dead set against jokes. Laughter! As if it were the most terrible thing in the world. As if he couldn't imagine a worse fate for his son. He was just about to raise the megaphone to his lips when he saw his dad put the phone up to his ear to make a call, right as the cops were pulling him away.

Yes, the cell phone company had finally figured out the problem and fixed it, opening up the cell tower for the several hundred people gathered at CIS (more were accruing by the hour, drawn by social media, word of mouth, television and the irresistible human urge to join a crowd).

Word inside the building spread quickly, barely needing actual words, since the students' phones came alive with notifications again. They learned that while they'd been disconnected from the world, fear and hope had grown, almost in equal measures.

There were those certain Marisa was going to blow up the school, and they were on the internet and TV calling on the administrators and the government (they rarely specified which government, or how the one they'd named had anything to do with the CIS lock-in) to act to keep other children from fighting for causes.

People were holding preemptive candlelight vigils, prayer circles. Some for the students, others for the reefs, for the oceans, for the death of the world, which so many had witnessed and, even when it took center stage, had only discussed instead of acted.

The reef mourners worshipped Marisa and her Protectors (no one really knew how the term had made it out) but felt resigned. If children failed to cause change at their school, what hope was there?

Others said no: that's exactly where hope lies. Look at the children fighting. Look at the passion they could garner, the attention they drew. There were, as it turned out, many Ms. Dulis out there. People who'd always believed they had the necessary drive to do real good and had only been waiting for a strong enough push to give in to their better, albeit more passive, natures. They saw others acting and said, *Yes, I will join them.*

Marisa had no qualms with late adapters, bandwagon-jumpers. She cared little about intentions, only results. And in the last few power- and signal-less hours, these were the results, soon confirmed by a phone call Ms. Duli received from the board: the school was going to pay legal fees associated with breaking a contract with their fertilizer supplier, since they used it merely for pretty grass on their fields, and the run-off was further choking the reefs (demand number nineteen on the list). Similarly, they were breaking contract with the caterer that ran the school cafeteria after it'd refused to promise to get their fish from sustainable sources (demand number six). Alumni donations had poured in to help pay for all these fees, plus the new solar panels that would be installed on the middle school's rooftop (demand number twenty-three).

After a social media campaign went viral, a major detergent company had immediately halted production on any detergent they used containing phosphates, citing a responsibility to life over profits (not on the list of demands, but pretty cool, anyway). In all, ten more demands had been met during CIS's radio silence, and several more were in the works. It was clear the world wasn't done yet.

Marisa leaned over once again to grab her marker, tears welling in her eyes the way they had when the Protectors had first jumped in front of her to shield her from flying objects. No emotion wreaked more havoc on tear ducts than hope.

Ms. Duli watched Marisa breathe through the simple act of drawing lines through the newly met demands. Her heart soared. Over the past few days she'd seen Marisa cross a couple of items off and felt nothing other than the slight joy and relief she associated with completing an errand. This felt different.

A murmur broke out in the foyer. Maizey Krokic had just arrived breathless from the stairs. She was doubled over from the sprint, having, like Amira and so many others, not kept up with her conditioning over the past week. When she finally caught her breath, she sounded equal parts scared, excited and confused. "Jordi Marcos is going to break the glass upstairs."

It was Pok Tran, who immediately responded, as would be expected, with a mocking, "Yeah, yeah." They all knew about the shatterproof glass, and CIS's paranoia. Which of course Maizey had predicted. She pulled out her phone to show them the video she'd recorded, just as Marisa capped her marker again, wondering why she couldn't celebrate good news for one single second before someone barged in yelling about some fresh new hell.

There was a mad scramble up the stairs. Students wanted to see Jordi hurl himself at the glass. They wanted to be the one to stop him, tackle him and restrain him. Maya and Michael and all those who loved Marisa (and maybe Peejay a little) wanted to do it for her, for the reefs. Teachers rushed up, wanting to make sure no one else got hurt, curious as they hopped up the stairs two or three at a time whether the glass had really been so vulnerable this whole time.

Omar raced upstairs, too, sent by Peejay to check on whatever was happening and put those athletic, plastic-collecting muscles to good use. Of course, a bottleneck formed at the roof garden's entrance, caused both by the sheer number of people trying to squeeze in at once and the fact that the first who'd arrived froze a few feet from the door, watching the spectacle that was Jordi Marcos throwing himself full force at the same glass pane over and over.

In pain, he'd stopped sprinting the whole way, instead hauling himself to his feet and taking a few steps back before launching himself again. A few more cracks had appeared, oozing rainwater like a wound. Soon, he thought. It would all be over soon.

Amira watched the scene unfolding and felt an urgency to be there. She wished she'd never left. "Amira?" someone to her left said. She didn't want to turn toward the voice. She wanted to slink back into the crowd's anonymity and make her way to the basement door, where she would reenter the building and go take care of whatever was going on upstairs on Marisa's behalf.

Then a hand fell on her forearm, and she knew it was too late.

The bottleneck broke, mostly because Omar broke through. His love of basketball had waned over the past week, but not his muscles, or the way students revered his athleticism. Ms. Duli was making her way up the stairs, too, her diminutive stature ensuring she'd miss the day's second traumatic injury.

Omar, tall and near the front, could see it happening. Clearly before anyone else, or at least he saw more clearly that Jordi was about to need some help. He sprinted.

Jordi picked himself back up, aware now that he had a crowd, and the boy who'd stopped his punch was headed his way to try to stop him again. He wasn't going to let that happen. His shoulder was sore as hell now, but he was a god-damn bulldozer, not a speed bump.

Downstairs, the police, having cleared the crowd away, brought in the battering ram with which they intended to break the door down. Someone had to run toward them and explain that there was a child on the other side of the door. They shrugged and moved to the nearest window.

Marisa looked at her list of demands, and at the time, at the background image on her cell phone of the reefs in Fiji, at the messages of hope and fear and hate coming through.

Somewhere behind her, the cops grunted as they ran with their ramming rod into the window. There was a loud bang, which Marisa could feel in her bones (one in particular), but nothing else happened.

Jordi hit the glass again. His shoulder burned, but the sound of glass shattering masked the pain. What a wonderful sound. Joy filled him for a moment, relief so great it was like putting down a heavy bag after hours of lugging it around. Then he realized he wasn't bouncing back like he had all those other times. He tried to stop himself, as he'd imagined he'd be able to do. But his momentum carried him forward.

Rain soaked through his clothes, his hair. The city's sounds magnified at once, the colors—dimmed though they were by the day's gray cast—felt immediate and beautiful, almost impossibly so. It felt like he was moving in slow motion.

His perspective shifted as gravity tugged him forward. The ground. The hundreds of people below, who turned their attention to him, letting out yelps.

I did it, he thought. *There is a way in, a way out. The lock-in is over.* Just then he felt a tug on his legs, and he looked at the rain falling and the ground below and he thought, *What have I done?*

9
1:40PM

Wind flowed through the building, though the only person paying much attention to it was Marisa. The only wind she'd felt in the past week was the slightest breeze that managed to come in through the gap beneath the doors behind her. The little chill on her ankles had woken her up a few times, but this was something else. This was the beginning of the end. Probably well past that.

She didn't have to know what had happened upstairs to realize the experiment, her scrambling attempt to save the reefs, was over. Oh, maybe another demand or two could be met in the next hour, the next thirty minutes, however long it took for the building to empty out, for whatever had been broken upstairs to turn into an exit. She might as well reach for the key and get it over with. But something kept her from doing that just yet.

Lokoloko Island.

Instead, she looked out at the foyer, empty for the first time since she'd closed the locks. Only Nurse Hae remained, out of sight. And here came that same blond sophomore from lock-in night, emerging from the bathroom again. His fly was up this time, but he checked it, anyway, before hurrying up the stairs to catch up with everyone else.

The roof garden was in mayhem.

Most people had seen the glass break and Jordi disappear below their line of sight. There were screams and cries and people scrambling for their phones to capture what they could on video, or to let the world know what was happening, to call for ambulances.

The wind whipped around the shouts and clamored into a frenzy of sound, so that even those who could see Omar dangling halfway over the roof couldn't communicate it to the person standing next to them without someone's wailing muffling the words. Thankfully, those at the very front, rushing to pull Omar back in, could hear his shouts over the rain.

"Don't move me!" Those with their hands on his legs, gripping his waistband, froze as if they thought one wrong move might lead to an explosion. Still, they held on, feeling the incredible weight of two bodies succumbing to gravity.

"He's slipping," Omar shouted at them, not saying anything about the glass in his hip, how their first yank to save him before he'd started yelling had caused a hot flash of pain that weakened his hold on Jordi's legs. Another movement and he'd lose his grip.

The rain alone might do it soon, not to mention Jordi's dead weight swinging like a pendulum, shifting the pain in his side. Jordi's head had hit the side of the building when Omar had stopped his downward momentum and he was now dangling unconscious. If Jordi woke up and started freaking out, he'd pull them both down.

The students holding on to Omar all looked to Mr. Gigs, who was trying to help but had arrived late and at an awkward angle, so was now just holding on to the heel of Omar's left shoe.

"What do we do?" one of the students asked him.

Mr. Gigs, so used to joking around with students, so much more comfortable being real with them than he was with many of his colleagues, thought again of some faraway beach (not even; the nearest beach would do) and said, "Fuck if I know."

On the soccer field, a different kind of mayhem. Glass from above had rained down on the unsuspecting crowd before they'd even heard it smashing. The cops furrowed their brows and inspected the window they were attempting to break, wondering where the shards had come from, since this one was still holding strong. The paramedics who'd been stationed at the school all week suddenly found themselves having too many patients to deal with and radioed for backup. The injuries were mostly minor—only a couple of people required major stitches, the others were just panicked—but there was enough blood around to make the scene ghastly, like a disaster movie. Parents shrieked at the sight of a boy, two? dangling above.

Not far from where Amira stood with her mom's hand clasped around her forearm, a school board member watched the glass and the boy and the blood and thought, *We're really screwed now.*

Rifta Wahid was the only person not looking at Jordi, whose limp, dangling arms made him look like he was dead already (indeed, a few people believed he was, and a deep sorrow squeezed their guts at the thought. Their eyes welled with tears and they moved a hand up to their mouths to grip their chin as they stared at the swaying body).

"Amira, what…" Rifta didn't know how to finish the question, but it worked well enough on its own. She looked toward the building, then back at Amira, not understanding anything.

Amira, meanwhile, felt her mother's grip tighten around her forearm in direct proportion to how much she wanted to get away. She needed to be inside, needed to deal with the roof garden, needed to escape her mother. How was she this strong?

They might have stayed looking at each other like that for hours if it weren't for another shout from the crowd as Jordi slipped an inch from Omar's grip.

Just like that, Amira found whatever spell her mother still held her under had dissipated, at least for this moment, and she untangled herself from her mother's grip. "I have to go," she said, looking at the roof again. This time, her mother followed her gaze and gasped. Then she turned back and studied her daughter's face. How had this happened? Her little girl, now this strong-jawed woman, her muscles bulging as if her body was struggling to contain them. How had the years passed so quickly?

"You can't," Rifta said simply.

What Amira heard this time, though, was something that sounded like waves crashing on the shore. The sound of the padlock gently tinkling against Marisa's chains. The little snores that signaled Marisa had fallen asleep. She thought of that list behind Marisa's head, and what Marisa would do if someone told her she couldn't. She thought of Marisa being herself, loudly, unapologetically.

"Watch me," Amira said, and she tore away.

Amira maneuvered her way against the current of the crowd, toward where the shattered glass lay twinkling in the grass. She was close to the back staircase, which led up to the green room, more or less below Jordi and Omar and the occasional CISer who dared to lean over the edge of the shattered window to look below. The cops were still trying to break into the building, though a few of them were staring at the spectacle overhead and speaking into their radios. They didn't notice Amira, or Lindsay, who stepped toward her, feeling, by proxy, like one of the Protectors, too.

A beat passed, Amira half thinking of a plan but half in awe that she'd walked away from her mother like that. Something glinted in the sky, and Amira hopped back, grabbing Lindsay as she did to avoid a six-inch shard of glass that had come loose and crashed where they'd been standing.

"We could tell Malik to open up," Lindsay offered.

Amira looked at the time. It wasn't 2:30 yet. She knew how irrational it was, but it felt wrong to make the decision to open the door. That was Marisa's choice, and hers alone. Plus, the only thing opening the door would do in that moment was get more people inside. There were plenty on the roof, and if they hadn't been able to pull Omar and Jordi up from there already, a few more people wouldn't have helped. She had to buy Marisa more time, had to keep the boys from falling somehow.

She studied the side of the building, the nooks and crannies of its brick, its windowsills and attached pipes.

There was only one way. She looked back toward her mother, knowing she was about to give herself away, would have to explain years of hidden rebellion. This was going to unravel the version of herself that existed at home, and who knows what else would unravel with it. But, she supposed, it was better than the alternative. She began to scale the building.

Kenji was having lock-in night flashbacks. While Peejay had joined the others upstairs, Kenji stayed in the classroom with Celeste. He didn't want to see any carnage, didn't want to face another broken leg, another mob, another scenario which couldn't be "Yes, and…"-ed.

"Well, that didn't accomplish much."

Celeste watched the police officers coming at the glass a few classrooms over, somewhat halfheartedly, as if this was entirely a CIS issue and they weren't sure why they'd been called in. "You're wrong. You stood up to him, Kenji. That means something."

"Not for Marisa. And not even for me, either. I didn't want

to stand up to him. I wanted him to listen to me, you know. To care about what I had to say." He took his glasses off and rubbed his eyes. "This sucks."

The police hit the glass again, making them both flinch. They could hear the voices of the crowd clamor at whatever was happening upstairs. They'd caught a few words when everyone had scrambled out the classroom, but right now it was a bit of a mystery.

Celeste thought of her past self, the version that had existed back in Illinois, comfortable in her skin, filling all sorts of roles. Would that Celeste have any idea what to do in this situation? Would she be able to console an improv-loving boy while her parents ran around in the rain outside and police threatened to bring the walls in?

And even if she didn't really have her place at CIS, even if she only had a handful of people who weren't quite friends but had been friendly to her for a week, wasn't that something? Some proof she *could* fit in? Maybe not now, maybe not like she did in her previous home, maybe not among the other Americans, or the other black kids, but eventually?

"If it helps make you feel better at all, I'll play improv with you."

Kenji snapped out from his thoughts. "You will?"

"Yeah. Next meeting. If the school ever lets it happen."

He chuckled, shivering at the breeze now that the air could circulate from one end of the building to the other. He toyed with the megaphone in his hands, not wanting to look up at the soccer field, where his dad, last he saw, was still on the phone, even while people screamed in horror at whatever Jordi had done.

★ ★ ★

Ms. Duli and Peejay arrived on the roof around the same time and started working their way to the front. They both knew how to make a crowd part for them and soon enough they were at the front by the window, or what remained of it. They could feel the rain dampen their clothes.

Ms. Duli kicked aside shards near Omar, then got on her belly on the floor near him to peer over the edge. Peejay opted to stay away from the giant hole on the side of the building. Instead, he shooed away a stick-thin sophomore who had been trying to help but was one gust of wind away from getting sucked out of the roof, and took his place.

Peejay hooked his fingers into Omar's belt loop, and though he had no way of knowing who was holding on behind him, later Omar would swear he knew it'd been Peejay. ("No," Peejay would joke, "it was that terrifying, bodiless, plastic version of Hamish. It came to life and hooked you with its teeth, like something out of the horror movie it belonged in.")

"Help is coming," Ms. Duli told Omar, though it was only a guess. Good God, she hoped the boy didn't slip, hoped Omar had the strength everyone said he did.

"I know," Omar responded, trying not to choke on the rain. "I see her."

Zaira Jacobson muted the notifications on her phone. There were too many requests coming in from local affiliates, and she'd already told the BBC she'd grant them initial footage. She maneuvered her way to the front of the crowd, and though she was mostly preparing for a good, accurate report, part of her, while she waited for the video call to come in, marveled at a realization:

Before lock-in night, she'd had these visions of the story she'd been assigned to write about the evening, the fluff piece which in the end had never seen the light of day, propelling her into her journalistic career. A far-fetched fantasy, of course. But that was the lock-in night lore, after all. It made dreams come true. And now, as she positioned herself in front of the mayhem, framing Omar's half-present body over her left shoulder and prepared to go live on-air, she knew that, though she would still have many steps to go through, years of school, a lot to learn, even more to prove, lock-in night had delivered.

It wasn't lost on Amira that rock climbing was supposed to have been the final event in the decathlon. Not that this was quite like rock climbing. No harness, the side of a building, the rain. At least it had enough chipped pieces of brick and gaps for her fingers, enough window ledges and metal pipes to make it feasible. Her fingers were still strong, thank God, and she'd switched into her running shoes before leaving the building, and these had a decent enough grip on the wet exterior.

What would happen when she reached Jordi—if she reached him—she didn't know. For the moment it didn't matter. It only mattered that she could find somewhere higher to place her feet, her fingers. She reached the bottom of the second-floor window and had to kick her right leg halfway through her pull-up in order to rise up onto its ledge. Peering into the window, she noticed that it was the green room, and she could see Malik Harris reading without a care in the world. He didn't notice her.

Below, the crowd was breathless. A few parents, unable to just stand around and not *do* something, were going around the school looking for ladders. They came by after a few minutes with an almost comically small one, barely past where Amira had reached within ten seconds of climbing. The elementary kids wondered what these parents were doing running down the halls, knocking on doors. They knew it must have something to do with the high school, but the shades had been drawn hours ago to keep them from staring out the windows, even though the high school was barely visible with them up.

Other parents looked to the school gates constantly, wondering if a fire truck was going to make it through the goddamn traffic in time, what with it being a Friday and traffic in the city never letting up. The cops put up their shields to keep others from getting closer, but no one was willing to chase after Amira.

The kids who'd been around on lock-in night but had left the building for one reason or another—to play laser tag, to grab some food truck tacos, to hide a secret stash of vinegar-filled water balloons for the upperclassmen versus underclassmen war that would never come—who'd felt like something had been missing from them this whole time, looked at the broken window and knew it'd be over soon, and they wondered if they'd feel like themselves again.

No one wanted to believe Jordi might die.

Mrs. Nudel, who couldn't help but think that was Dov up

there swinging from the building, didn't even let herself think the word. The board members, four of them now in attendance, cursed themselves that it had taken so long to meet a teenager's demands.

Why had they fought so hard against her? Why had they fought so passively for the things she wanted? A cleaner world, with more reefs to explore, to keep their oceans alive and healthy. Was that so bad? A world without students hanging off their building. All of those who'd gone diving had loved it. Now a boy's life was in the balance, and what a precarious balance it was.

The only person who seemed to not be looking at the scene unfolding above was Arthur Pierce, who was yelling into his phone over the wind, not even noticing his assistant, distracted like everyone else, had shifted unconsciously toward the side of the building where Amira was climbing, taking the umbrella with him, leaving Mr. Pierce drenched.

Lindsay watched Amira shuffle across the window ledge to reach for a water pipe. It looked much too flimsy to hold Amira, but she seemed to know this, know exactly how much weight she could put on it. She saw another ledge jutting out, a shelf for an air conditioner made of concrete, not just one of those aluminum bits bolted onto other parts of the building. To get there, she'd have to use the water pipe running along the side of the building as a kind of video-game kicking-off point to give her the extra boost she needed to reach the ledge.

From there, she'd be able to reach Jordi, swing him onto the ledge with her. It was about ten feet away, off to her right.

A basketball hoop, essentially. But she didn't have any room to run, to build up to the momentum necessary for her to reach and not fall to her death.

She looked up, made eye contact with Omar. She saw blood on his shirt, his or Jordi's she couldn't be sure. She saw Jordi slipping a little at a time. The angle Omar had, there was no way he could hang on for long. Especially if he was hurt. So Amira jumped.

When she kicked the water pipe, it creaked before giving way with a boom, some bolts tearing free from the building. The crowd gasped, and her mother clutched at her chest, as if the sound had emanated from her heart. But Amira's foot had taken all it needed from the pipe. It tilted ominously over the people below, but Amira was safely on the ledge.

She's just as much of a badass as Kenji said she was, Lindsay thought. Dozens in the crowd had more or less thought the same.

It wasn't quite enough, though. Amira could reach Jordi's fingertips, but with him still knocked out and Omar unable to keep him from swaying, there was no way to bring him down. Even if Omar could drop him slowly, the ledge was only big enough for Amira to stand on.

It was at that moment the local fire department showed up with a truck that had one of those classic long, rescuing ladders. The crowd cheered, and in response the engine blared its horn, which scared the figurative shit out of everyone present, Omar included. His pained body gave a quick jerk, and though he almost instantly squeezed Jordi again, the body in his arms slipped at least six inches.

Amira took advantage and seized Jordi's wrists. More gasps

from the crowd, from the students who'd crowded into the green room to catch all the action from the window (poor Malik reached for his earphones to tune out their chatter, just thirty pages to go). The fire truck tried to drive into the school for the rescue, then stopped as a firefighter smacked his palm on the side of the truck. The ladder was too tall to fit through the gate.

In the foyer, Marisa watched all this on her phone. The cameras were rolling. Marisa found the feed with Zaira and was amazed to see what was happening outside, what she had put in motion. An email came in from the board. Re: Demand #23, on leading local initiatives… She clicked it open and scrolled past the part which read For God's sake open the door in order to scan the details. Another demand fallen. Still no Lokoloko.

It was 1:45. She switched back to the BBC feed, Zaira's face taking up most of the screen. Her classmates crowded around the broken window. That felt like a metaphor for something, but Marisa couldn't land on what. Something about lock-in night or the reefs or her opening the door early. She changed the feed to a channel that had outdoor cameras so she could watch Amira.

Peejay felt Omar's body quiver, the poor, brave soul. Whether it was fear alone, or fear coupled with exhaustion, with an inability to hold on much longer, it was hard to tell. With his demons gone for the moment, Peejay felt strong, and he held on to Omar a little harder, hooking his ankles around a nearby picnic table to anchor himself further. He noticed just how many people were holding on to Omar.

Not trying to pull, having heard his shouts, but just helping by holding on. Those who weren't were on their phones, and from the chatter he could make out amid the chaos, it seemed, improbably, they were all still working on the demands. Some were convincing their parents to withhold their tuition payments until every item was crossed off to Marisa's approval. These parents, watching two children dangle from the building, didn't have many objections.

More of Hamish in the world than he gave it credit for, maybe. Thinking of his brother, how much he wanted him to have stayed alive long enough to witness this, to see this, Peejay didn't cry. He felt his strength increase.

Ms. Duli watched Amira perform her wild maneuvers, her heart in her throat. Jordi stilled. The rain kept coming down indiscriminately, not caring about demands met or fire engines arriving or Jordi Marcos's father dropping to his knees in the muddy outskirts of the soccer field to pray.

"Now what?" Omar said as loudly as he could muster. The pain in his hip felt too intense to ever go away. "Can I drop him?"

Amira imagined the scenario, the forces at play and how well her body was prepared to counteract Jordi's weight. The bell rang. Sixth period. Jordi slipped another three inches and Omar slid with him, the glass in his side tearing through muscle and grinding against bone. Which bone, Omar couldn't tell.

A school board member threw up in the bushes.

Below Amira, she could hear someone pounding on the

glass. Students were throwing chairs, trying to get another window to shatter. The roof, it seemed, had been a fluke. Over her shoulder, the gray city stretched out. It was a nice view here, not marred by the glare or the tint of the roof garden's enclosure. She could see the whole campus, the fire truck trying to angle itself through the gate. She needed more time. For the ladder to arrive, for Omar to hang on, for Marisa to save the world.

She could see Omar's arms shaking. "I don't…" he started to say, the words draining his energy. "I can't hang on." Amira looked down at the space she stood on, just twelve inches wide, six inches across. They wouldn't both fit. If Omar let go, Jordi's full weight would come down on her, at an angle that was hard to predict. He'd likely knock her off the ledge.

Then Jordi slipped a little more and Amira got a better hold of his forearms, and she thought she could do it. She'd planned to be stronger than Omar all along. What other choice did she have now? She breathed in deep. "Okay," she said. "Swing him and let go when he's on your left. I'll carry the momentum and hang on. Just watch his head."

"Are you sure?" Ms. Duli shouted. She looked around for Jankowski, who taught physics and maybe could do an equation to figure it all out?

Omar said something Amira couldn't make out, but it must have been convincing to Ms. Duli, because she reached down and tried to help him shift his weight to control Jordi's movements. Amira felt the rhythm of Jordi's swaying, getting a sense of his weight, preparing her knees, her back, her core muscles. Then she nodded, and Omar let go.

She bent her knees to take on the weight, and felt her feet

slide on the wet surface below her. All over the world, but especially on the soccer field, especially in the foyer, breaths caught. Eyes closed in horror. Others widened. *How did we get here?* many thought.

In a judo move (decathlon event number seven), Amira swung Jordi's body around the A/C shelf she stood on, throwing herself down onto it so the brunt of her torso lay square on the only thing between her and the ground. Jordi's arms scraped the side of the building, and the brief sensation of falling made him come to. Thankfully, his first thought was that he was dead, and he remained still, trying to figure out where in the world he was. Amira was able to maintain his weight. She was curled on the A/C shelf, and Jordi still hung in the air, but her arms were fresh and strong and there was no glass in her hip.

The crowd whooped when they saw Omar pull himself back into the garden. Sure, there were still two children high above the ground, but they had a brief reason to cheer, and it felt worth celebrating. Even some police officers cheered a little, then cleared their throats and went back to holding their shields steady or ramming the window.

Watching this on Celeste's phone, Kenji thought, if only they had something soft below. Then he recalled a conversation with Lindsay from lock-in night about bouncy houses fashioned from gym mats. He texted her again.

Wait, the gym mats. Are those still outside?

Her response was almost instant. Yup. Been sleeping on one. Why...oh, never mind, I get it! Groupmind!

Within moments, Lindsay had pulled the gym mats she'd

been sleeping on from beneath the bleachers. Her parents, who'd waited so long for her to come home with them, saw what she was doing and helped drag the blue mats across the field. Others in the crowd, most of them students who had been out there all week, grabbed the remaining ones from inside tents and from the storage lockers by the bleachers. They made a wide pile beneath Jordi. When they had stacked them high enough, Amira let go.

The cameras didn't capture this, but as soon as Omar had been pulled safely in, Peejay swatted away everyone else to come face-to-face with Omar. Dazed though Omar was at the pain and the experience of dangling off the side of a building, he couldn't help but smile at the sight of Peejay's magnificent face.

Peejay had a hand on Omar's cheek, just like that. He was looking into his eyes. Hamish was gone and everything was mayhem, but somehow he'd found this boy who looked at him like this. Who had tried to bring the one person into the building who had missed out on the party.

"I'm sorry about the statue thing," Omar moaned. "It was really weird."

"Shut up," Peejay said, and leaned in and kissed him.

Now that Amira was safe, and yes, Jordi, too, Marisa put her phone down. She looked out at the empty foyer, with its scattered backpacks and blankets, the garbage that had accumulated over the past week (minus the plastic). How strange, to feel an affinity for this temporary home she'd forced herself and others into. But that was what goodbyes did, she supposed.

They made you look back fondly at the things you were saying goodbye to. Even if they'd broken your leg in the process.

With no one inside watching, Marisa reached for the key hidden beneath her waistband. She shifted on her stool, cringing with the pain, nearly screaming with it. But she managed to stand on her good leg, the other one held awkwardly out, throbbing with the effort. As she slipped the key into the lock, Marisa eyed the poster she'd taped up a week earlier, when she'd had no idea how this would all turn out.

Jordi landed with a rib-cracking thud, right as the fire truck made it through the gate. He was swept up by paramedics onto a stretcher who checked for spinal injury, then carted him away. In the frenzy of those moments, he couldn't quite tell why the crowd had gone from cheers to silence and back to top-of-their-lungs yelling. He couldn't understand the shift in the air. The ambulance drove away, and he missed it all.

At 2:05 p.m, with ten demands left to go, and the Lokoloko project still running as scheduled, Marisa Cuevas had unlocked herself, unraveled her chains and opened the front doors to CIS.

10

2:06PM

One by one, the rest of the doors opened. Eli on the rooftop first, as soon as he got the word from Marisa. There were already paramedics waiting by each door, and upstairs they rushed toward Omar, the crowd parting way reverently.

Barely anyone noticed Lolo emerging. After Amira left she'd looped the chains through the handles, but hadn't been able to bring herself to wrap them around herself again, and no one had been the wiser. Joy peed first, then came out, and Malik was last, waiting until he'd turned the last page of his novel before procuring his key.

For the past week, whenever anyone pictured the doors

opening, they'd imagined people running. They pictured the doors bursting open, just as many people coming in as those yearning to break free. A mad rush for freedom.

But it was more of a trickle. Marisa faced the crowd for a moment, her leg screaming for a painkiller.

After their initial shock and relief, and the joy that had caused them to shout, the crowd didn't know what to do. Rush the building? Did the kids need rescuing? Was Marisa to be arrested? They didn't know, so they did nothing, just stood in the rain as Marisa, met by Kenji and Celeste, wobbled forward on unsteady leg(s).

God, it felt so good to stand again.

Terrible, actually, uncomfortable and so painful it was as if Marisa was learning how to do it all over again, even with Kenji and Celeste holding her up. But good, too. When it became clear no one was going to apprehend her or throw anything, the three of them hobbled over to the gym mats by the side of the building. Amira had waited a minute for the fire truck to come and raise the ladder to make her descent easy, but had tired of waiting for them and thrown herself down on the mats.

The reporters snapped from their trance and chased after her, shouting questions, trying to get the crowd to make way for their cameramen. The paramedics, too, tried to make their way to Marisa, but the reporters were a little more strong-headed, and anyway, Marisa wasn't ready to get pulled away.

Kenji and Celeste eased her down onto the mattress by Amira, right as their parents rushed in their direction.

The Rollinses embraced their daughter, putting a week's worth of lost embraces into their arms. It wasn't lost on them that she'd walked out in someone else's company. "You smell," her mom said into her hair.

"Shut up, I showered every day." Celeste laughed.

"I just meant in general," she shot back, thinking she wasn't ever going to let go of her daughter again.

Arthur Pierce, too, to the surprise of everyone who'd heard him speak—and especially to Kenji—wrapped up his son in a hug. "It's done," Mr. Pierce said softly, like he was letting out a breath. Kenji thought he was talking about the lock-in, the whole ordeal. Mr. Pierce meant the construction project. They wouldn't figure out the misunderstanding until the next day, when Kenji would wake up from a sixteen-hour sleep and the story was on the news. He'd learn of his father's change of heart, piece together why he'd been on his phone. "You did it?" he'd ask.

"Yes," his father would respond. "And I'm sorry I didn't do it earlier."

Now he let himself be held, feeling something was different between them, though not yet sure what. The hug itself, maybe, which Mr. Pierce was not wont to give.

Rifta Wahid approached her daughter on the mat, not sure what to say. There was too much, not enough. Amira met her eyes, and they looked at each other for a long while. Amira did not feel any one emotion more than the other. They all swirled around, anger and guilt and shame and relief. There was going to be a reckoning, and Amira wasn't sure what would happen, how her relationship with her mother would change, just that it would. Somehow, she felt ready for it.

"Are you okay?" her mother asked, her eyes flitting to

Marisa, and back to Amira. Amira could only nod her head, and then the crowd surrounded the mat, engulfing Rifta.

Celeste wanted to keep holding on to her parents forever. She wanted to go home with them and change into pajamas and eat her dad's mac and cheese and play board games with them as if it were a Christmas morning back in Illinois. Instead, she pulled away from them and said, "Mom, Dad, I want you to meet my friend Kenji."

Amira and Marisa sat on the mat, surrounded by shouting and bodies. Marisa kept her leg floating above the wet grass, and somehow no one bumped into it, despite the frenzy on the lawn. It may have been noteworthy that the paramedics and the reporters were kept at bay if it weren't for the fact that, at the moment, it felt like no one else was near them.

"I'm sorry," Marisa said.

"What for?"

"I'm not sure, really. Ruining the decathlon for you. Not telling you how much it's helped having you there with me. You can tell me anything else I need to apologize for, but before that, can I, like, hold you for a second?"

Amira laughed, happy that the rain might obscure the welling in her eyes (though Marisa knew that was no raindrop). She looked around the crowd for her mother, wondering if she was ready for that to be a part of the reckoning, too. But she couldn't spot her, and anyway, there was nothing she wanted more right now, reckoning or not. She nodded. "Shouldn't you be going to a hospital?"

But Marisa was already holding her tightly, thunk thunk.

★ ★ ★

Next out of the building was Omar, on a stretcher. Paramedics were working on him as they walked. He was lucid, watching interestedly as they applied pressure to the wound. When one of the paramedics opened a syringe and was about to toss away its plastic wrapper, Omar reached to grab it from her hands, and shoved it into his pocket. Joy trailed behind him, trying to keep up as well as her legs would carry her.

A few seconds later, Peejay emerged. His pashmina was dotted with some of Omar's blood, and he splashed some rainwater onto it and tried to dab it away. "That boy's gonna have to learn some boundaries," he said, not really directing the comment at anyone, though Kenji and Celeste were near enough to hear and chuckled in response.

They stood apart from their parents and the other kids who'd come out after gathering their belongings and taking a moment to stare at the foyer, or the roof garden, or the photo lab where they'd spent the majority of their lock-in. They bid adieu, surprised by their emotions, sadness or gratitude or amusement. The reporters, who'd had no luck interviewing Marisa or Omar, now turned their attention to these other students. They didn't know about the Protectors' closeness to Marisa, and so they didn't focus their efforts on them.

Master Declan came out, looking terrified of having to answer questions. Thankfully, Ms. Duli stepped to his side. "I'll handle the media," she said, doing so less out of a favor to the feckless headmaster and more so she could frame the story the way she and Marisa had discussed.

Ludovico Rigo was practically chased out of the building by his ever-adoring gaggle of giggling freshmen, who'd finally decided to stop their giggling and just try to talk to him for once. Unfortunately, they all tried at the same time, and Ludo sought refuge amid some reporters, who'd recognized him from his composting video.

Mrs. Wu, Mr. Sanchez, Mr. Jankowski, Mr. Gigs and all the other teachers who hadn't already rushed to the exit to hail cabs or take the metro back to their significant others or families now took the long way around the school's perimeters. The last thing they wanted to do right now was face parents. They wanted to find the nearest bar.

Zaira Jacobson, her phone's miraculous battery life petering out, stood outside the building, signing off for the first time.

The ambulances left. The fire truck was trying to maneuver out. The cops were high-fiving each other over getting into the building. The crowd had started to dissipate, all those happy, tearful reunions giving way to an anxious desire to beat the rush out of the parking garage. And shoot, there was the 2:30 bell going off now. If they didn't beat the buses out they'd be stuck in a line of cars for forty minutes. Parents pulled at their children's sleeves while the kids exchanged parting words with those they'd spent the past week with. Those friendships that had been forged, improved, mended on lock-in night, the loves which had been professed, discovered, cemented throughout the course of Marisa's lock-in... they all had to be properly seen off. It felt like saying goodbye at the end of summer camp, mixed, perhaps, with the feelings inmates had on the last day of their sentence. It felt like some of them might never see each other again.

The middle schoolers and elementary kids circumvented the

soccer field in quiet, reverent awe, heading toward the school buses in the garage or to their parents and drivers waiting in the long queue of SUVs outside the main gate. The rain hadn't stopped on account of the open doors. Rain didn't care about such things, so now that it was all over, people scurried for cover, scurried to leave, no longer indifferent to getting drenched.

On everyone's minds or tongues or social media accounts: after all this time, Marisa had lost. Her list of demands, still taped to the doors, right now a corner curling as the tape lost its strength in the rain, hadn't all been crossed out.

The reporters were jostling to ask her about it. They wanted their headlines, their sound clips. Or at least their bosses did, the viewers did. But Marisa's Protectors had wordlessly gathered one more time to form a circle around her. It wasn't just the original crew, it was a group of thirty or so students and teachers, arms locked, deflecting reporter questions by answering them. At the center of the circle: Marisa, Amira, Kenji, Celeste, Peejay.

They stood (or, in one case, leaned) in their own little concentric circle, looking at each other and not looking at each other.

"We should turn this into a pizza party," Kenji said.

Peejay balled up his now-soaked pashmina and threw it at Kenji while the others laughed. When the laughter stopped they went back to looking around. The crowd kept thinning. Some maintenance workers were coming out of the high school, looking confused at the general lack of trash. Instead, they hauled out forgotten backpacks and phone chargers toward the lost and found, and a strange number of socks, too.

Ms. Florgen was going to be late to the happy hour gathering because the damn gym mats were going to get mildewy in the rain. She barked at the remaining crowd to move and made some cameramen help her carry the mats back to the storage room at the far end of the field.

"You okay?" Celeste asked. They all turned toward Marisa.

Marisa grimaced a little, but she was already nodding. She didn't say anything.

"How many were we short?" Amira asked.

"Five? I think. Got hard to keep track at the end there."

"Damn." Kenji got that look on his face, and everyone knew what he was about to say, but they let him say it, anyway, laughed afterward, too. "Should we go back inside, then?"

"Sure, you go ahead. We'll catch up," Celeste said.

"Someone else's turn to get chained," Marisa added, rubbing her ribs. "I think I'm going to have a chafe here for the rest of my life."

Beyond the circles, their parents looked on, as they had this whole week. They were trying to be patient and understanding when the truth was none of them understood a single thing that was happening. The past week, however, had taught them to resign themselves to that, and so they small talked with each other, granted interviews to reporters for whom the story hadn't ended, since people reacting to a story was almost as important as the story itself.

"You don't seem sad," Kenji said, looking back at the building with awe and a sense of wonder. "I'm a little sad. I really thought we would get them all."

Peejay reached over to Kenji and ruffled his head. "What beacons of hopeful innocence these freshmen are."

"The way I see it, I won twenty-something battles. There's a lot more to win. A lot," Marisa emphasized. "And I don't want to lose sight of that. But the world watched. You guys joined me. The school got behind me. When this started I just wanted that one project scrapped. Just to save one little corner of the world, you know? I didn't. But I saved something, I think." They sat with this for a while.

The rain had soaked through their clothes by now, but it felt so nice just being out there in the world.

"I have an announcement," Peejay declared, his arms up so people in the larger protector circle knew to tune in, too. "In keeping with lock-in traditions as Partyer in Chief, it is now time to pick my successor."

"You don't have to say it, we all know Jordi earned that title tonight," Kenji said.

Peejay reached over and smacked him on the back of the head. "No jokes for a week and suddenly you're flowing with them during my speech?"

"The dam broke," Kenji said, adjusting his glasses, which Peejay's smack had pushed down his nose. "Prepare to be flooded."

"For God's sake, don't say 'prepare to be flooded.'" Peejay winced. Then, after looking around to make sure no teachers or staff were around, he turned to face Celeste. "Celeste Rollins, I hereby pass the torch to you."

"Wait, what?" about ten people in the vicinity said, including Celeste. "How am I qualified?"

Peejay shook his head. "The host has spoken."

★ ★ ★

Though they didn't say anything about it, they all recalled lock-in night then, those waning hours of the party, right before the sun rose, when all that was to be accomplished momentarily felt not daunting but colored by hope, by energy. Exhaustion, sure, but a steadfast belief that it would all be okay.

Beyond their circle, CIS continued dealing with the mayhem. Police ran through the building. Parents weepingly hauled away their kids. School board members answered phone call after phone call, like they had all week, the doors' opening changing nothing for them. Inside, it was almost quiet, as if under some protective spell.

The only thing that eventually broke this peace was Marisa getting hit by another cramp. She held on to Amira's hand through it, even when her mom broke through the circle of Protectors and put an arm around her daughter, peeling her away from Amira and Kenji. "Let's get you to a hospital," she said.

Marisa didn't protest. It was time. She held her gaze just a moment longer, before turning her attention to the rest of the group. They thought maybe a speech was coming, but Marisa just smiled at them, and let her mother lead her hopping away toward the car. Her father followed behind, carrying the surprisingly light duffel bag over his shoulder.

Once Marisa was gone, the others felt the call of their beds, the comfort of their homes. They found their parents and followed them to their cars.

The school slowly emptied out, falling quiet save for the relentless patter of rain.

★ ★ ★ ★ ★

ACKNOWLEDGMENTS

Each book I've been lucky enough to publish has required the work of many more people than I can remember to thank. Here's another attempt at trying to name them all.

Everyone at Inkyard Press from acquisition through publication. T. S. Ferguson, Lauren Smulski, Tashya Wilson, Laura Gianino, Linette Kim, Brittany Mitchell, Bess Braswell and all the others who are surely working to my benefit without my awareness, from sales teams to marketing and beyond. Thanks to Gigi Lau and Dave Homer for a wonderful cover.

My agent, Pete Knapp, for his guidance, wisdom and knowledge of the bookish world, which still evades me after all these years.

To early readers Ally Condie and Jen E. Smith for their enthusiasm and incredibly helpful feedback while I was still figuring out how to shape this story. Thanks to Eric Smith for sending a draft back with a bunch of hearts all over it right when I needed that most.

My deep gratitude to sensitivity readers Kiana Nguyen and A'Ishah Amatullah for their time and insight, and for helping improve the book with their comments. I'm constantly attempting to do better in my portrayals of characters outside of my own experience, and their work helps me do just that. This is a better book because of them. Any failings or issues of misrepresentation are mine alone. Thanks, too, to Mark O'Brien for his line-edit pass.

Thanks to Hannah Locke and Ben Marcy-Quay for their time and efforts regarding ecological fact-checking. Thanks to Professor Elisabeth Holland at the University of the South Pacific for answering questions while I was still drafting, as well as for providing hope, and a place to stay in Suva without a second thought. Thanks to the Aja-Hajj family for the unmatched paradisiacal hospitality, the family lunches, the snorkeling outings.

Thanks to my family. I don't know if they did anything specific to help this book in particular, but I'm thankful nonetheless.

Thanks to The Ploips for a helpful title brainstorming session in beautiful environs. I want to thank the Patagonian jug wine, but Mook probably deserves the bulk of the credit for the title.

Thanks above all to my first reader and best friend, Laura Fairbank, for not only helping me talk this book into existence, but for taking me all over the world to do it. There's no one I'd rather share hundreds of meals, overnight flights, overnight buses, hostel stays, bike rides, wine tours, city walks, mountain hikes or scooter rides with. Sorry again about the scooter ride. I love you.

Lastly, I'm extremely thankful to the kids fighting for change in a way that we adults have failed to. You didn't ask for this fight, but it was handed down to you, and you are responding admirably (and, dare I say, inspirationally). Keep fighting.